Readers love the
SEX IN SEATTLE
series by Eli Easton

The Trouble with Tony

"With a light, slightly sweet and definitely interesting story, Ms. Easton has managed to make me a fan of not only her characters but her storylines and I'm definitely looking forward to reading more from her!"

—The Blogger Girls

"This story was warm, funny, entertaining, and made me feel all sunny inside. I will definitely be reading more by this author."

—Hearts on Fire

"I have enjoyed both of the books that I have read by Eli Easton. Both made me laugh and left me feeling good. I am definitely looking forward to her next publication."

—Live Your Life, Buy the Book

"The writing was very solid. I give this book 4.5 stars because I wanted it to be longer! And I'm hoping for a sequel!"

—The Novel Approach

The Enlightenment of Daniel

"A love story between friends with true complications in their lives that was both touching and beautifully written."

—The Romance Reviews

"I can honestly say that it is a book that won't leave you emotionally uninvolved, since it is quite a turbulent read, but it is worth all the drama!"

—Pants Off Reviews

"If you like your friends-to-lovers romance realistic, sensual and poignant, you'll love this. Recommended."

—Top 2 Bottom Reviews

By ELI EASTON

Closet Capers (DSP Anthology)
A Prairie Dog's Love Song
Puzzle Me This
Steamed Up (DSP Anthology)
Stitch (with Sue Brown, Jamie Fessenden, and Kim Fielding)

SEX IN SEATTLE
The Trouble with Tony
The Enlightenment of Daniel
The Mating of Michael

Published by DREAMSPINNER PRESS
http://www.dreamspinnerpress.com

the Mating
OF MICHAEL

eli easton

Dreamspinner Press

Published by
DREAMSPINNER PRESS

Where Dreams Come True...
International publishers of quality gay romantic fiction since 2007

5032 Capital Circle SW
Suite 2, PMB# 279
Tallahassee, FL 32305-7886
USA
http://www.dreamspinnerpress.com/

The Mating of Michael
© 2014 Eli Easton.

Cover Art
© 2014 AngstyG, www.angstyg.com.
Cover content is for illustrative purposes only
and any person depicted on the cover is a model.

ISBN: 978-1-63216-015-7
Digital ISBN: 978-1-63216-016-4

Printed in the United States of America
First Edition
June 2014

This paper meets the requirements of
ANSI/NISO Z39.48-1992 (Permanence of Paper).

To beautiful, brave, talented, loving, extraordinary Raleigh. Fight on.

ACKNOWLEDGMENTS

It's a challenge to tackle characters with very specific jobs or disabilities. I'd like to thank my beta readers for helping me gain confidence in what I was portraying and in helping me see the rough spots. Thanks to Stacia Hess, Mandy Lebron, Kim Fielding, and Kate Rothwell.

I also found some excellent resources and would recommend them to those looking for more information.

On Polio:

7 Wheelchairs: A Life Beyond Polio—by Gary Presley

Small Steps: The Year I Got Polio—Peg Kehret

Broken Wings—documentary directed by Rainer Loeser (on Amazon Instant Video)

A Paralyzing Fear: The Story of Polio in America—documentary directed by Nina Gilden Seavey (on Amazon Instant Video)

On Sex Therapy:

Sessions of a Sex Surrogate—by Joanne Ferro

Private Practices—documentary directed by Kirby Dick about surrogate Maureen Sullivan (on Amazon Instant Video)

~1~

Seattle, February, 2014

"GIN! DUDE, you're history!"

Tommy laid down a set of fours and a run in hearts and laughed in triumph. The words and the laugh sounded garbled, thanks to the damage to his throat and palate, but Michael understood him just fine.

"Damn, man! You are wicked lucky today." Michael Lamont shook his head, trying to look disappointed. But he didn't really mind. Making Tommy laugh was more than worth losing a few card games.

"Well, Monday *is* my lucky day," Tommy said with a wink. He pushed his chair away from the table.

"Are you flirting with me?"

"Yup."

"I see how you are. First, you trounce me, then you try to butter me up. Do you wanna play again?"

Michael asked because he always asked. It was part of their routine. Three rounds of gin, which Tommy won more often than not. After cards came the massage. But Michael asked anyway, even when, like now, Tommy had pushed back from the table and already had the start of an erection in his shorts. The look in his eyes said he'd forgotten all about gin rummy.

"No more cards," Tommy said quietly.

"Okay, champ."

Michael stacked the cards neatly while Tommy went over to the bed. A large photo of the Seattle Mariners, inscribed with "To Tommy, best wishes," and signed by all the players, was framed and hung over Tommy's bed. He'd gotten that, Tommy had once told Michael, when he was in the hospital after the fire, and they didn't know if he would live. It was one of Tommy's most prized possessions.

Tommy dropped his shorts, leaving on his oversized T-shirt and briefs and sat on the edge of the mattress. He watched while Michael put his gym bag on the table and unzipped it. Michael carried everything he needed in there—a large bottle of Eucerin lotion, massage oil, wipes, condoms, a few styles of vibrators, and a few simple toys. He rarely used the toys, but he carried them all the same. He removed his shirt and folded it neatly on the bag before picking up the bottle of Eucerin.

He stood at the side of the bed while Tommy looked at him. Tommy liked to start by gazing at Michael's chest for a while, and then touching it lightly with his damaged fingers, getting himself aroused. When he was ready, he laid down on his stomach. As always, there were no blankets on the bed, only sheets, so clean they smelled of fabric softener. A few small towels were stacked on the bedside table. Tommy himself had been freshly bathed, and even his ever-present baseball cap looked new. Michael appreciated the effort. He knew Tommy's mother was very particular about his care. The house was on Lake Washington in the Madrona district and was easily worth several million. But he had a feeling it was Tommy himself who insisted on everything being perfect on Mondays. The thought caused a small ache in Michael's chest as he gently tugged up the hem of Tommy's T-shirt and rolled it tight near his shoulders.

Tommy didn't like to have his shirt removed. Michael thought it gave him a sense of modesty to be able to pull it down over his scars quickly, even if he never did. Michael squeezed a line of lotion up his ravaged back.

Tommy's life had been devastated one terrible night six years ago. He'd been sleeping over with a friend when the house caught fire. Michael had never been told what had caused the fire or the details of what'd happened, only that Tommy had been severely burned over 70 percent of his body. Despite years of what must have been painful surgeries, including extensive cosmetic reconstruction, no one would ever look at Tommy and not see a burn victim. No one, that is, except Michael.

His fingertips soothed the lotion into the scar tissue, rubbing in circles. Tommy gave off a little moan.

Michael took his time. He massaged Tommy's back, then pulled his briefs down and off and worked his arms and legs. The scar tissue had been well cared for. It required daily massage to avoid getting painfully tight. Tommy's mother or his PT routinely massaged him, but Michael's massage was different. He kept it sensual rather than functional. He placed both hands on the backs of Tommy's thighs and massaged firmly up to the cheeks of his ass, repeating the move a dozen times before massaging Tommy's buttocks. They were only mildly scarred, and Tommy liked to have them handled.

"Wanna turn over," Tommy said in a rough voice.

"Go ahead, champ." Michael removed his hands and let Tommy turn.

Tommy's penis was mercifully undamaged, thanks to the way he'd protected his core by curling up into a ball. He was fully erect and red. Michael squeezed some lotion on it and stroked for just a minute before moving on to Tommy's chest and the front of his arms and legs. He knew what Tommy liked, and Tommy liked to take it slow. He liked to make it last, like a favorite dessert he only got once a week. His moans of pleasure were loud, but there was no one to hear. Only Tommy's mother was in the house on Monday mornings, and she stayed out of the way, tucked away downstairs in the kitchen.

Michael drew his fingertips lightly over Tommy's belly, causing him to shiver and groan, before finally taking him in hand. Michael was erect too. He always got that way when working with clients. If Tommy had wanted to see or feel Michael, he would have been happy to oblige. But that had never been what Tommy wanted. Nor was this about relieving Tommy of sperm. His hands were damaged, but he could hold his cards and a pen, type on the computer—he could get himself off. No, what Tommy needed from Michael was human touch, loving touch, to feel that he was not alone, that he could have sexual contact with a cute guy his own age, someone who would not look at him with horror. That was a privilege his twenty-one-year-old peers took for granted, gay or straight.

Michael touched Tommy lightly until he indicated with a panted *"Go"* that he was ready to come. Then Michael stroked him firmly until he climaxed hard.

Michael cleaned Tommy up and pulled his briefs back on. He always wanted to sleep afterward, no talking, no fuss. So Michael leaned over and kissed his cheek, smiling.

"See ya next week, champ. I'll remember to bring that Stephen King book I've been promising. And I swear I'm going to beat you at rummy one of these days, at least two out of three."

Tommy laughed, opening his eyes only long enough for one last fond look. "In your dreams. Excellent work today, Maestro. Laters."

"Laters."

MRS. CHELSEY was waiting for Michael in the kitchen as usual. But this week, when he popped in his head, she looked up at him anxiously.

"Would you like a cup of tea? I made us a pot."

She'd set the table in the kitchen with two cups and a china pot, like some sort of fancy B&B. Michael hesitated.

"Unless you have to be somewhere?" Mrs. Chelsey's worried tone said she shouldn't have presumed.

Michael glanced at his watch. "No, I'm good. I'd love to try that tea." He smiled and joined her at the table.

Mrs. Chelsey was an attractive brunette in her late forties, her body slender and her face drawn with perpetual worry. Still, she was always very pleasant to Michael.

"How did he seem to you today?" she asked as she poured the tea. "There's cream and sugar."

"Black is good, thanks. I got the impression he was a little down when I first got here. But he creamed me at three rounds of gin, and that cheered him up considerably."

Mrs. Chelsey seemed relieved. "He's been depressed lately. His friends are all graduating from college, getting married, moving on with their own lives... I'm worried about him." She eyed Michael's face with a searching gaze as if somehow he could provide the understanding she needed. "He's always better on Mondays, though. I can't tell you how much your visits mean to him."

Michael was glad Mrs. Chelsey and Tommy were happy with him, but it was never easy for him to accept compliments. "Just doing my job."

"You don't have to play cards with him, though, hang out, and treat him like a friend. That means a lot."

"Tommy *is* a friend. He's a client but... I'm happy to call him a friend."

Mrs. Chelsey smiled sadly. "*My* friends would never understand about you. I don't even... not even Tommy's father knows that I hired a sex surrogate."

Michael wanted to argue with her, to say something like "It's not a big deal," or "It's not that unusual." Because he truly felt that way. But he knew other people—most people—saw sex surrogacy as a very big deal.

Michael loved being a sex surrogate. It felt entirely natural to him. He'd graduated from nursing school at twenty-one and did an internship with a VA hospital in Seattle. A few of the patients there were young, just recovering from injury or PTSD. One in particular, a sweet boy named Wayne, had lost a leg and was severely depressed. Michael was fairly certain Wayne was gay, and he was so devastated by his injury. Sometimes, Wayne would look at Michael, then look away. There was pure need in that look, a need so deep it ran red with blood. Michael had a strong urge to hold Wayne, to comfort him, to, yes, give him relief in any way that he could. Instinctively, he sensed that Wayne needed physical contact, needed someone to make him feel like a man, to remind him that being alive meant the possibility of great pleasure, not just pain.

Of course, as a young nurse, such a thing would have been entirely inappropriate. Michael had never acted on it, but it started him thinking. He researched online for types of therapy that involved touch. That's when he discovered sex surrogacy. He fell in love with the idea literally at first sight. He applied to the IPSA, the International Professional Surrogates Association, and took their 100-hour course via mail part-time while he worked. A year later, he was licensed.

He believed so strongly that love and intimacy were key components of healing and mental health. But he'd learned that very few people were capable of understanding what he did.

So instead of arguing with Mrs. Chelsey, he just said, "Well... you're a very cool mom. Tommy is lucky."

Mrs. Chelsey laughed. "A cool mom would give her son a little weed, not sex. I've done the weed too, on occasion."

Michael looked at her in surprise. He'd never smelled it in Tommy's room.

"A few years ago when there was more pain," she explained. "We got it prescribed. Thank God for the Medical Cannabis law. But Tommy doesn't want it much anymore. Says it makes him fuzzy. Anyway, I just... I feel he's missing so much in life. Anything I can give him, I *will* give him."

She said this last fiercely. Michael's heart ached for her. He reached over and stroked her hand. "Hey, Tommy is lucky to have you, to have this beautiful home, and to be so well-cared for. You're doing a great job."

She clutched desperately at the hand Michael offered and, with the other, took a casual sip of tea as if she hadn't a care in the world. It reminded Michael of that saying about one hand not knowing what the other was doing.

"I just wish our lives weren't about me taking care of Tommy. I wish he was out there being a normal twenty-one-year-old, having fun, even getting into a little bit of trouble."

Michael wasn't sure what got into him, but he stage-whispered, "Well, he did just have sex upstairs." He waggled his eyebrows at her.

She barked out a laugh. "You don't say."

"I have it on good authority." Michael tried to release her hand, but she clung on. He let her.

Mrs. Chelsey looked down into her cup, took a couple of deep breaths. "It's my fault, you see. His father and I were newly divorced, and I... I got a little crazy. That night, Tommy didn't want to go to Samuel's house. He wanted to stay home, play his video games, and chat with his pal in Norway. But I insisted he go. I had a date."

Michael swallowed down a painful wave of empathy and rubbed his thumb over the top of her hand.

"I'll never forgive myself for that." She looked up at him, her eyes bright.

Michael got up and went over to Tommy's mother. He hugged her, leaning down and holding her tight. She took the comfort, placing her arms around his back and tilting her face against his shoulder.

"It's not your fault. A million other times that same scenario would have gone fine. Tommy would have come home the next morning like always. You couldn't have known."

She nodded, but she didn't say anything. She hugged him back for a long moment, the tension of grief thick in her body, until at last, she relaxed. Michael's mother had worked as an intensive care nurse for a while, and she always said her job was as much about helping the relatives deal with what was happening as it was about the actual patient care. Michael's job wasn't often like that, but now he understood what his mother meant. That fire had devastated Tommy's mom as much as it had Tommy.

Mrs. Chelsey pulled back. "Thank you."

"Any time. You know, you have needs too, not just Tommy."

He said it sincerely, but when Mrs. Chelsey quirked an *oh really* eyebrow, he laughed. "Oh. Um... I didn't mean those kinds of needs."

"Good. Because, no offense, Michael, but that would be really weird."

"Right." Michael laughed, embarrassed. "Well, on that graceful note, I should probably get going. Thanks for the tea."

Mrs. Chelsey stood up to show him out. He headed for the kitchen doorway and his gym bag.

"Oh! Just remembered. I saw something in Sunday's newspaper, and I clipped it for you." She took a newspaper page off the refrigerator and brought it over. "Tommy said you like science fiction?"

"Love it."

"Well, maybe you already know about this, but when I saw it, I thought of you."

It was an ad for "Science Fiction week" at Elliott Bay Book Company. "Excellent," Michael said politely. His eyes scanned down the list of events and his heart stopped. "Oh, my God. No way!"

"What is it?"

"J.C. Guise? Seriously?"

Mrs. Chelsey shrugged, obviously not getting it.

"I don't believe it! J.C. Guise is doing a book signing at Elliott Bay on Friday night. He's like… my favorite author *in the world*, and he never does book signings. He's a legendary recluse. He doesn't go to conventions, he doesn't do Twitter or Facebook, he's a ghost. He has a one-page website that lists his books, and that's it. I can't believe this!"

"That does sound exciting." Mrs. Chelsey looked pleased that her small offering had been so well received.

"Exciting?" Michael laughed. "Don't take this the wrong way, Mrs. Chelsey, but right now? I freaking *love you*."

~2~

"I CAN'T believe I let you talk me into this. Forget everything I've ever said about you being my fucking fairy godmother. At this moment? I freaking hate you."

James rolled out of his bedroom, uncomfortable as hell in too-new jeans, an Oxford shirt, and a rust-colored cable sweater he'd express ordered from J.Crew. He'd tried for an hour in his bedroom mirror to get the casually hip look that had appealed to him in the online image—the sleeves of the sweater bunched up and the blue Oxford cuffs folded back just so. He'd failed, and now the cuffs were a limp mess.

Damn it. He'd hoped the new clothes would give him confidence, but he felt like a hedgehog in a tuxedo.

"Oh, James." Amanda adjusted her skirt casually, not taking him seriously for a moment. "Grouse all you want. You look great, you're going to *do* great today, and maybe afterward you'll even decide I can have my tiara back."

"Oh, you can have it back after. The question is where you should stick it."

James was teasing, mostly. He knew he was being a pill, but if he had to do this, then Amanda damn well had to put up with him bitching about it. Arguing with her kept his mind off the incipient terror that lurked in his bowels like some slavering, ugly beast in a cave.

God, he had to use that. His fingers itched for his notebook.

"The store did lots of advertising, and it was in the publisher's newsletter. People *want* to meet you, James. I promise you won't be sitting there twiddling your thumbs at the signing table."

James wasn't sure what terrified him more—the idea that no one would show up for his book signing or that dozens of people would.

No, that was wrong. It might spell the end of his career, but right now, he'd give anything for a completely empty store—like swine flu epidemic empty.

"Not really helping," James muttered. He drove his chair over to the desk, picked up his old briefcase, and put it on his lap. He'd packed it earlier with pens and markers, aspirin, tissues, hand lotion, sanitary wipes, and breath mints. He even had a single Valium in there in a little baggie, in case he decided he really couldn't deal. The prescription was so old he wasn't sure it would work even if he did take it. But it felt good to have a mental escape route on his lap, like his own personal poison gas tooth.

He steered his chair to the front door and waited, but Amanda made no move to leave. She just studied him.

Amanda Barnsworth had been James's literary agent for ten years, ever since he was an eighteen-year-old with a one-pound manuscript and big, big dreams. His books had gotten a lot shorter since then and his dreams smaller, too. But Amanda hadn't changed. Except that now, all her pushing about his public persona had gone from modest suggestions to life or death lines in the sand.

"James…." She seemed to consider her words.

"I get it," James said, hoping to head off the lecture. "If I don't start doing self-promotion, Egret will dump me. I understand. I do. I just… hate it. You know how I feel. A writer should be known for his words, not for how well he can dance a dog-and-pony show."

Amanda sat down on the couch, indicating that she was gearing up for a serious talk. She looked very concerned. Now James wished he could take the words back. It was an old argument between them, and he wasn't really in the mood right now to pummel that dead horse.

The publishing world had changed so much in the past ten years, it was crazy. It used to be you didn't get published without an agent. It used to be the big publishing houses controlled the market and you had to be really, really good to get started as a new author. You got started because your agent believed in you and they took some editor from one of the big five to lunch and chatted you up, got them to actually look at your manuscript. When James had sold his first novel to Egret, the future seemed so bright.

Now there were hundreds of small digital publishers and indie authors flooding the market. The big publishers, and their stable of midlist authors like James, were finding it more and more difficult to grab their piece of the pie. And these days, authors were expected to be on social media constantly and out in public too. James had resisted as long as he could, but he'd finally had to cave.

Amanda spoke carefully. "I understand you don't like people to know about your disability, James, but... you're wrong. No one's going to think any less of you as an author because you're in a wheelchair. In fact," she took a deep breath, "Egret wants to do some new author photos with the chair, and they want you to update your bio to be a lot more explicit. They want you out there, as you are. Readers like to feel they know authors these days, and your story has a great human-interest angle. And there's the Millennial Award to consider."

The Millennial Award, given out annually by the SFFA, the Science Fiction Fans and Authors Association, was the sci-fi equivalent of the Hall of Fame. Only the most influential and classic of works were considered. There were rumors that *Troubadour Turncoat* was under consideration this year. And if James won, the status would help his career tremendously.

But even if he had a snowball's chance in hell, it wouldn't be for that reason. "You think they're going to give me a Millennial Award because I can't fucking walk?" James asked in disbelief.

Amanda frowned. "No. But what they *won't* do is give the award to a man whom no one has ever seen and who clearly won't show up at the awards dinner. Maybe that's not right, but that's just how it is. My point, and I'm sorry to have to bring it up, is that no one cares if you're in a wheelchair." Her voice softened. "I'm not suggesting you try to take advantage of your situation, James, but you don't need to let it hold you back. Honestly, you don't."

James knew Amanda believed what she was saying, but she had no idea what she was talking about. People *did* care that your legs were useless. James knew that all too well. They left you behind, and they went on to live their own, unfettered lives. And why wouldn't they? If he could leave his own body behind, he would. Isn't that why he wrote? To escape?

But the writing itself, his work, he'd wanted it to be free of all that, to let it be pure imagination, not weighed down or defined by this damaged human form, by who he was physically. He fucking *loved* that no one knew him, that he could be anyone at all. Isn't that what science fiction was about, pure imagination? Was it really so much to ask to remain anonymous?

Apparently, it was. Today, everyone would see J.C. Guise for what he really was. His stomach clenched tight, and he opened the front door.

"I'm here, aren't I?" He cocked an eyebrow. "I even bought a new goddamn sweater. So… yeah. *Yo comprendo.* The sleeping giant awakes, the worm turns, the virgin sacrifice is ready for the altar, etc., etc. Now unless you have a pill that will render me charming, chatty, and unconscious for the next three hours, let's just get it over with."

Amanda gave him a quirky smile as she joined him. "If I had a pill that would make *you* chatty and charming, James, I wouldn't have to work for a living."

"So no change, then."

She barked a laugh. "You're lucky I have a thing for acerbic writers. Flail at me all you want. I can take it."

"And that's why you're no fun at all," James groused.

He steered his electric wheelchair out to Amanda's car. She paused before opening the door. "Seriously, I know this is hard for you, but it's going to be fine. Who knows, you might even enjoy the attention."

"I might. Or I might projectile vomit on a fan. Remember, I did warn you."

"No worries. I have vomit bags in my purse."

James set his brake and swung himself into the passenger seat. He helped Amanda figure out how to collapse the chair so she could put it in the back.

When she climbed into the driver's seat, he said. "Do you seriously have vomit bags in your purse?"

"No. But I would have bought some if I'd thought of it."

James tsked. "Falling down on the job. Didn't they teach you anything in agenting school?"

"They taught me to not get emotionally invested in my clients. You can see how well I learned *that* lesson."

James felt himself, stupidly, blushing. He had no easy quip for that one.

MICHAEL SPENT a ridiculous amount of time getting dressed for the book signing. He first tried on a gold sweater and black pants, but the gold was too sparkly and a bit too over-the-top. After going through everything in his closet multiple times, he ended up in a body-hugging deep royal blue V-neck sweater that was soft around the revealed skin at his chest, and his best jeans, which sat low on his hipbones and were tight in all the right places. The deep blue sweater emphasized the contrast between his dark hair and pale skin and made his small, tight body look even thinner.

He put his shiniest silver gauges in his ears along with a few tiny faux diamond chips, added some clear lip balm and a trace of charcoal eyeliner to make his eyes pop, and brushed his hair forward on his face with a little more edge than usual. No need to overdo the fem thing, but it was a statement. *I'm gay, so if you're interested, here it is.*

God, even the thought was enough to make him tingle with nerves and heady anticipation.

Michael lived on Capitol Hill, so he decided to walk over to Elliott Bay. He was worried about sweating since it was a warm day for February and he had a bag full of books to be signed, but parking would be atrocious. No way could he deal with the endless circling and trying to snag a spot today.

In the name of all that is holy, I'm about to meet J.C. Guise.

It was hard to explain to anyone what J.C. Guise meant to him. Michael was sixteen when he'd read *Troubadour Turncoat*, a novel in which a young medic on a Federation starship discovered that the Federation was using biological weapons against civilians. The medic single-handedly brought them to their knees through sheer determination, a fierce sense of right, compassion, and moral honor. It was a book that changed Michael's life, cementing his decision to follow his mother's footsteps into medicine and become an R.N. The way J.C. wrote Acton Halliway, with his deep sense of empathy and his absolute core of right and wrong, had shifted something inside Michael. Maybe it was silly to say you were who you were thanks to a science fiction novel, but it was true. It wasn't that the book created Michael's personality, but it had *plucked* certain attributes he already had, making them resonate at the precise time in his life when he was trying to figure out who he was.

And then there was the small matter of his crush. When Michael got the hardback of *Troubadour Turncoat* from the library, the back inside flap had an author photo. To Michael's knowledge, it was the only photo ever acknowledged to be of J.C. Guise. It wasn't a very good photo, being about an inch square and one of those artsy black-and-whites where the focus was a little fuzzy. It was a candid shot of J.C.'s face as he looked off to the left, smiling. But the photo was big enough—big enough to see that his hair was long and dark and his face was young, square, strongly featured, and mysteriously attractive. The brief bio beneath the photo said that J.C. Guise wrote the bestseller *Troubadour Turncoat* at the age of eighteen and was considered a science fiction prodigy.

Michael had looked at the book's publishing date and figured out that J.C. Guise was only a few years older than Michael himself— nearly his own age, cute, and so fucking brilliant. A serious fanboy crush had begun right then, aimed at that little one inch square of a face. Interestingly, although Michael read every book J.C. published since *Troubadour Turncoat* and had googled him many times, he'd never learned any more about him. In fact, the lack of information on Guise was noted loudly in the online community. Some said J.C. Guise was a pseudonym for a celebrity or a prisoner. One guy swore J.C. Guise was a sixty-six-year-old grandmother living in Georgia who wouldn't acknowledge the books because there were sex scenes in them. Then again, that same guy thought Mars had pyramids and sphinxes.

Michael turned the corner and saw Elliott Bay. There was a line out the door. He stopped abruptly, his stomach flipping hard enough to threaten him with a second breakfast. *Shit.* J.C. Guise was in *that building right there.* He was about to meet J.C. Guise.

God, he was such a dork. Even if J.C. *had* been that cute eighteen-year-old in the photo, he was likely overweight, married by now, and not even a little bit gay. So there was no reason for Michael to be freaking out. Yes, he loved the guy's writing and was going to adore getting his autograph—but that was all. Right? *Do not press the panic button.*

Michael took a deep breath and got in line.

HE ENDED up in a conversation with the girl in front of him—about J.C.'s books among other favorites. It was a good way to self-medicate his nervousness, and so he went with it. He was so caught up that he barely registered when they moved inside and he had to hand over his ticket for the signing. He looked up and suddenly realized that he was only about twenty feet or so from the signing table and *there he was.*

Michael shouldn't have been able to recognize J.C. based on that one small, ten-year-old photo. And yet he so totally did. J.C.'s head was turned three-quarters to the side as the older woman sitting next to him said something, and the angle was quite close to the one in that old photo. He was more mature, more fleshed out, but his strong features were the same. J.C. had high cheekbones, heavy dark brows, a good-sized Roman nose, wide lips, and a rather full jaw. His hair was long enough in the back to curl up a bit, and he had bangs slanted over his forehead. It was a lighter brown than it had looked in the old photo, more of a light chestnut. His long, thin neck with its strong Adam's apple gave him a geeky, professorial look that was exaggerated by a dark orange crew neck sweater over a blue Oxford shirt.

In those first few seconds, Michael couldn't tear his eyes away. At some level, he knew he was staring and being way too obvious. But most of him was too amazed that he was actually looking at J.C. Guise, the guy who had penned almost all of his favorite books, to care. And then two things happened. First, J.C. looked forward to talk to the next person in line. He smiled at them, and then his gaze moved down the line and *his eyes met Michael's.* The second thing was this—Michael noticed the handles on J.C.'s wheelchair.

Michael stopped breathing. For what might have been a few seconds or might equally have been several lifetimes, J.C.'s eyes were locked on his. And then J.C. looked away, took a book from the person in front of him, and started to sign it.

The girl Michael had been talking to hit him on the back, hard. "Breathe," she said, sounding a little bemused.

Michael gasped in air. "Oh my God."

The girl laughed. "Gee-yah. And I thought I was a fan."

"He... he...."

"Yeah, I saw it. He looked right the fuck at you. I'll be your eyewitness in case you ever wanna tell the story."

She was teasing him, but Michael was too distracted to react. Because J.C. *had* looked at him, with scarily intelligent brown eyes, and he'd looked for several seconds too, like Michael's face was a sticky pad and it had grabbed that sliding gaze and held it tight, and... *gah*.

But also, *J.C. was in a wheelchair.*

Michael had to know. He squatted down and fiddled with the buckle on his boot, trying to get a look under the table. Someone moved, and he got a glimpse, just a glimpse, of jeans that were baggy around very thin legs. Michael straightened and stared at J.C., his throat suddenly dry.

Withered legs: it was a long-term disability. Michael watched the man sign a book with strong, steady hands, his upper body broad, healthy-looking, and tremor free. So it wasn't a recent accident nor was it a nerve disorder that affected his whole body. It was something like a long-standing spinal injury or birth defect.

So many things fell into place for Michael in that moment—why J.C. Guise had avoided the public eye, how an eighteen-year-old boy had managed to know enough about medicine and pain to write *Troubadour Turncoat*, and the many characters in J.C.'s stories who were damaged in one way or another. Hell, in *Gorsham's End*, the main character was a BAMF warrior who wore a cyber-suit and had paralyzed legs when he took it off. It also explained, in a strange way, the deep connection Michael felt to J.C. through his work that had never completely made sense before. It was suddenly so *obvious*.

Of course, J.C. Guise was disabled.

And Michael knew something else too in that moment. As weird and sort of awful as it was, he was glad J.C. was in that chair. Not only because a whole man could not have written what J.C. wrote—Michael could see that now—but also because it meant that Michael had a shot with him. That assumed a lot of things he had no reason to assume—that J.C. was available, that he was gay, that he would have any interest in Michael. Yet none of that fazed Michael's immediate gut reaction. *I'm for you.*

If only it were true.

By the time the girl in front of Michael was done talking nervously with J.C. and had walked away—shooting Michael a *go-get-'em* look as she went—Michael's palms were damp and he was feeling light-headed. He suddenly found himself standing in front of the author's table at the head of the line, and he had, what, twenty seconds to make an impression?

So, naturally, he lifted his fabric bag full of books onto the table, landed it with a painfully loud thunk, and said, "Hi."

Up close, J.C. had medium brown eyes that seemed determined to skitter away from Michael's. His mouth twitched nervously. "Hi."

"I'm Michael. I'm really…. God. I can't believe I'm meeting you." Great. His voice sounded higher than usual, he was so nervous.

J.C. finally looked up into Michael's eyes, almost, *sort of,* holding his gaze, if you didn't count the nervous flickers here and there. J.C. didn't say anything. He tapped a pen on the table.

"I read *Troubadour Turncoat* when I was sixteen," Michael continued to gush uncontrollably. "You have no idea what it meant to me. I went into nursing because of you. I've read every book you've written since, like the day it comes out."

Michael could hear his mouth running like a bad infomercial. He tried desperately to think of something to say that wasn't more repetitive praise. He'd prepared up all sorts of insightful points to make about J.C.'s plots and themes last night in bed, but seeing the man in person had fried his short-term memory. It was as if J.C.'s magnetism were the pulse of a dirty bomb.

"Thank you. I appreciate that. Do you want me to sign your book?" J.C. asked flatly.

"Oh! Oh, my God. Sorry." Flustered, Michael battled with the fabric bag and pulled out the copy of J.C.'s latest book that he'd bought at Elliott Bay in advance. He had a baker's dozen books left in the bag.

"You don't have to sign all these. I don't know why I brought them. But I would love it if you would sign *Turncoat* for me and...." He meant to ask J.C. to sign the latest one as well, but now that he knew about the wheelchair, he dug out *Gorsham's End* instead. "And... and this one. It's my second favorite."

Michael hoped J.C. would get the message. But he pulled the bag toward him, apparently intent on signing them all. "M-i-c-h-a-e-l?" he asked, peering up at Michael again. His eyes seemed darker, and there was a high spot of burning color on his cheeks that Michael was positive hadn't been there before. And, *man*, it might be silly, but it was totally hot that J.C. was saying his name. Well, spelling it really.

Michael held J.C.'s gaze for a moment, and he smiled, big and slow. "Yes."

The color on J.C.'s cheeks deepened as he looked down to write, and he licked his lips. Michael was very attuned to sexuality, and his body reacted to the unconscious signal at once, the heat of his nervousness sliding into a different kind of warmth. He paid no attention to what J.C. was writing as he took book after book from the pile and quickly did them all. Michael was too busy studying those high cheekbones and the little blush on them. He was too busy floating on air. There'd been a spark when they'd looked at each other, Michael was sure of it—a serious-ass, *I-think-you're-cute-and-you-think-I'm-cute* spark. He could not stop smiling, and his heart was going a mile a minute.

He noticed J.C. wasn't wearing a ring, not on any finger. Michael had never been so in love with bare fingers in his life.

J.C. stacked the books and pushed them back toward Michael. "Thanks for supporting my work like this. I appreciate it." God, his voice was so rich and deep. It felt like a caress on Michael's eardrums. J.C. looked Michael in the eye, smiled nervously, and then looked past him.

At the next person in line. Shit.

Damn it. Michael had had precious seconds while J.C. signed his books when he could have said something, shown how much they had in common, demonstrated his intelligence as a man, the species higher in cognition than, say, a chimp or a barnacle. But instead, he'd just stood there *grinning* like a love-struck mime. And now he was holding up the line.

"Thank you," Michael whispered. He stuffed the books in the bag and moved out of the way.

MICHAEL STOOD browsing a nearby shelf in the bookstore while J.C. signed. The signing was supposed to be an hour, but when the hour was up, there were still a few people in line and J.C. stayed. After the line ended, Michael watched several lingering fans talk to the author for a good ten minutes while J.C. tried, with varying degrees of success, to appear rapt with interest. Michael kicked himself for not sticking around the table longer and actually talking to the man.

He had to do something.

The trouble was, Michael Lamont was not a bold person. He wasn't a big guy—five seven, weighing one hundred thirty pounds in good periods and one twenty-five in bad. He'd always been shy, though he was able to overcome it with his patients. But he was not the sort of person who would walk right up to a stranger and ask them out, much less a famous author.

He should just go home with his little bag of signed books because he really didn't need to have his guts trampled on the floor of Elliott Bay Book Company. Then again, given the fact that this was the first time in ten years J.C. Guise had done a book signing, the odds were high that if Michael walked out the door now, he'd never see J.C. again.

He kept glancing at the author's table as he pretended to browse the bookshelves, hoping for some sort of sign. J.C. didn't look at him, but the woman who was at the table with him—his mother? Friend? Manager?—did. She looked over at Michael curiously several times. And she smiled. That smile felt like encouragement and helped him make up his mind.

He waited until J.C. and the woman went to leave. J.C. rolled himself away from the table and, after shaking hands and chatting with the store manager for a minute, headed for the front door, the store manager on one side of his chair and the woman on the other.

Oh God. Witnesses. Michael was so anxious he felt sick. He couldn't do it. He really, really wasn't going to be able to put himself out there.

Go for it right this minute, or you'll always regret it.

He stepped forward and got between the small entourage and the door. J.C. stopped the chair and looked at him. Michael took a deep breath.

"I'm sorry for bothering you. I was wondering... maybe you'd like to get a bite to eat or some coffee. I know the neighborhood. There're a few places close by."

Michael's voice sounded far away and tinny in his own ears. He could hear his heart galumping in his chest, and he thought it was very possible he might faint in the next minute or so from sheer embarrassment, and wouldn't that be special. J.C. met Michael's gaze, blinked a few times, and turned a rather awkward shade of red.

He opened his mouth, said nothing, swallowed, and then mumbled in a very deep voice, "Sorry, I have other plans." He looked down at his lap where a briefcase was perched askew.

Even through his own mortification, Michael realized at once that he was blocking the path and preventing J.C. from making a much-desired escape. He stepped aside, and J.C. rolled by without another glance.

Michael stood there, looking at his shoes and feeling numb. He couldn't bear to look up to see who might have noticed the exchange. He was sure half the store must be looking at him in pity or suspicion he was some loser stalker. Which was, in fact, accurate.

Shit, he had totally misread that. Of course, J.C. hadn't flirted with him or given him any real indication that he was interested. But the way his gaze had held Michael's several times, the way he'd blushed.... Michael had thought for sure....

He felt a touch on his arm. He looked up to see the woman who'd been with J.C. Guise looking at him with a sad smile.

"You look like a kicked puppy."

"I'm sorry," Michael said instinctively. "I didn't mean to—"

"It's fine. Don't apologize." She pressed her lips together and looked conflicted. Michael glanced around, but he didn't see J.C.

"I took him out to the car. Listen, I really shouldn't do this...."

Michael had no clue what she was going to say, but suddenly, a little ray of hope pieced his misery. "Yeah?"

"You said you were a nurse? You look very young."

"I'm twenty-six. And yes, I work for an in-home nursing care company here in Seattle." It was true enough, though it wasn't all he did. He knew better than to bring up his other job.

The woman studied his face. "You seem like a nice guy. Please, *please* don't turn out to be insane."

Michael laughed nervously. "I was hoping to avoid it."

The woman closed her eyes briefly as if still arguing with herself internally, and then stared directly into his eyes. She spoke firmly. "Okay. He's local. He swims at Medgar Evers pool most mornings."

Something warm blossomed in Michael's chest. Oh, God. J.C. lived in Seattle, and Michael would be able to see him again. He was so damn *grateful. Go, life!* He blinked rapidly. "That's... Thank you so much."

She sighed and shook her head. "God, I shouldn't do this, but he's...." She sighed and bit back whatever she'd been about to say. "Just, please don't make me regret it." Still shaking her head, she left before Michael could assure her, with every grateful cell in his body, that he wouldn't.

~3~

EXCERPT FROM Sentimental Cyanide *by J.C. Guise*

"I'm Winston," the man said in a low voice, his eyes darting nervously. "I'm not supposed to be here with you, but...." He stroked Lamb's chest with his fingers. Lamb registered the fact that his chest was bare. Being touched while nude was a sexual advance. Lamb tried flirt program #101, parting his lips and tracing the inside with his tongue. Winston stared at Lamb's mouth with interest, and Lamb made a mental note on the move's effectiveness.

"The Lamb series is my favorite. You're so b-beautiful. I've been working out some special AI so you can love me as much as I'm gonna love you. I'm gonna get you out of here. I'll take you home with me, and you'll be all mine. Wouldn't you like that?"

It took a second for Lamb to find a similar question in his database so he could gauge the right response. Do you want me? Does this feel good?

"Yes," Lamb said. It was the first time he ever heard his voice, and he was delighted by it. It sounded very smooth and soft.

"My name is Winston, and you'll be only mine. But don't tell anyone. It's our secret. Okay?"

"Yes," Lamb said. He tried a wink.

Winston's lips twitched in an almost-smile. "I need to shut you down now so I can work on you. Remember me."

~4~

THE VAN picked James up Monday through Friday at 6:30 a.m. He didn't like getting up early, but he did love swimming at the pool before the crowds and the kids filled the place. Mornings at Medgar Evers public pool were low key, mostly regulars who came before work, some seniors, and a small contingent of disabled swimmers. There was a handicap lift in the shallow end that made getting in and out of the pool much less awkward for those in wheelchairs.

This particular Monday morning, James was really looking forward to a long swim. The book signing on Friday had been super stressful and had left him tied in knots. On the one hand, he grudgingly had to admit Amanda was right. He'd enjoyed it more than he thought he would. It was the first time he'd allowed himself to meet readers, and the positive comments and, in some cases, weird adoration, were ego stroking and inspiring. It was amazing and humbling to hear in person how much his work had affected others. And the turnout had been excellent. But part of that was because J.C. Guise was such a long-standing mystery. He'd drawn the curious. Unfortunately, that interest didn't seem to translate to his recent book sales.

But on the other hand, there'd been the pitying looks and awkward attempts to ignore the chair, which made James very uncomfortable. And then there were the cell phone photos that had shown up on the sci-fi forums almost at once. Everyone had an opinion about the revelation that he was disabled. Most were supportive, but a few were fucking rude. One guy even pontificated about how the problem must be degenerative and affect his mind because J.C. Guise's work had been going steadily downhill since *Turncoat*. James had shut the forums off after reading that.

But the thing that tied his stomach up the most was *Michael*. It was bizarre. Probably fifty people had told James their names on

Friday, and he'd written them all out by hand, yet he couldn't have told you a single one of them now.

But he remembered Michael.

James had been caught by beautiful brown eyes and striking looks the first time he'd laid eyes on the guy in line. Michael was… ethereal. James had looked up to see a lithe body, a thick mass of lovely brown-black hair combed forward in an Emo style, beautiful, delicate features, a mouth so full and sexy it ought to be illegal, and heart-stopping warm dark eyes.

God, those eyes. Especially when Michael had been standing at the signing table, those pretty brown eyes had been so full of life and luscious, sweet, inviting warmth and, *shit*, something like understanding, connection. But that was total crap because Michael looked like he'd be at home in a fashion magazine or possibly in some off-world bar that specialized in the most beautiful boys in the universe. He made every nerve in James's body wake up and sing.

And then the guy had the audacity to ask James out for coffee and reality crashed around him. Because James was not J.C. Guise, some sophisticated writing god to be worshiped, and he wasn't any of his on-page heroes either. He was plain old James Gallway, a struggling writer with two useless legs and severe limitations, a tiny house in south Seattle, a pathetically modest income, few friends, and zero experience at sex. He was, in short, no one a guy who looked like that would want.

And the bitterness that evoked was the foulest-tasting remnant of that book signing. That was why it was so much easier not to put himself out there. That way, he never had to see what he was missing. For now, he needed to burn off that frustration by pushing his body as far as it could go.

He changed in the locker room and rolled into the pool area. He exchanged smiles and nods with a few regulars he knew by first name—Louise, a grandmother who had been partially paralyzed in a car accident, and Dustin, a paraplegic vet. James wheeled over to the lift. The lifeguard, Emile, came to give him a hand.

"How are you today, James?" Emile asked with a smile.

"Desperately seeking exercise," James answered dryly.

"I hear ya."

James pulled up alongside the lift and locked his brakes. Emile knew James didn't need or want help getting onto the lift, but he stood close by in case there was a problem. James lowered the arm on his wheelchair and swung himself onto the lift seat. Emile pulled his wheelchair out of the way while James buckled the lift's seat belt. The belt was ridiculous for the enormously risky trip of two feet, but it was one of those lawyer-appeasing rules that was easier to obey than argue over. Emile operated the lift, and James swung out over the water. The seat slowly lowered. The water was too warm to be shocking, and the sense of buoyancy as his body settled always made James smile. He unhooked the belt and pushed off into the water.

"Thanks, Emile."

"No problem. I'll be here when you're ready to get out."

James treaded water to an empty lane and began to swim. For a time, he forgot about all the things that were worrying him. He forgot about the negative advance reviews for his upcoming release, *Tears From The Dragon's Eye*. He forgot about his dwindling sales figures and royalty checks. He forgot about the Millennial Award and even the book signing. He cut through the water with his strong arms, and for the time being, all was right with the world. The water was the one place where he could forget that he was not whole.

At some point, he realized that someone was swimming in the neighboring lane and then, that the person was a young, hot guy. James focused on his strokes—alternating the butterfly and the crawl, then rolling over for some backstroke to work his chest. He shot surreptitious glances at the guy in the next lane—the guy had dark hair and a nice looking face the few times James caught a glimpse of it.

Feeling self-conscious, James decided to get out as soon as he'd finished his laps instead of lingering around in the free area like he usually did. A few times, women had started to chat him up in the pool, and there was always that awkward moment when he got out and they realized the bottom half of the jack-in-the-box was broken. He didn't need to see that look today, even if the chances of the hot guy in the next lane giving a shit were remote. He'd park off to the side for a while and air dry until he felt like getting dressed.

He swam to the lift. Emile saw him and came over. It was a matter of moments before James was seated off to the side of the pool in his chair. He always put a thick towel over the chair seat and back when he came to the pool, and he carried another beach towel on his lap for drying off and covering his unsightly legs.

He had just settled when he noticed the guy in the lane next to his pull himself out of the pool on strong, wiry arms. Damn, he was small, but he had a killer body—narrow shoulders and hips, a lean but toned chest, tight little bubble butt, the most gorgeous pale olive skin James had ever seen, and dusky mauve nipples.

James watched blatantly from the sidelines as the guy dried off, confident in his status as an ignored wallflower. But then, to his utter chagrin, the guy looked right at him and started walking over.

James, panicking, contemplated how fast he could safely maneuver into the locker room, but it was too late. The guy walked directly to him—form-fitting, wet swim trunks, bare legs, smooth chest, and all. His towel was draped casually around his neck. James dropped his eyes, hoping to send a clear "unapproachable" signal, but it didn't work. Those tight hips stopped in front of James's chair, and he had no choice but to look up.

Oh shit. In a chemical rush, all the hair on his body tried valiantly to stand up despite being damp. He felt goose bumps break out everywhere as he recognized the beautiful face looking down at him.

"Hi," Michael said. He smiled nervously, but his eyes held that same, inviting warmth James remembered. A man could drown in those eyes and never been heard from again. Could long for it, even.

"Hi." James's reply was a conditioned response. He anxiously worked his hands at the towel over his lap, tugging and arranging to make sure his legs were fully covered. He couldn't bear for Michael to see them, not so much as an inch. Even the outline of the towel over his wasted legs was humiliating as hell.

When he looked up again, Michael had a soft, sad smile and his eyes were so damn sympathetic James wanted to scream. He was about to invite Michael to go fuck himself, but then he saw something else in those eyes too—a flare of heat. It made the words dry up on James's tongue. In fact, his entire mouth went arid even as lower parts of him became distinctly flooded. He folded his shaking hands strategically in his lap and looked away at the pool.

"Mind if I sit down?" Michael asked.

James, not trusting his voice, shrugged.

Michael pulled over one of the white poolside chairs and placed it near James. He sat down and went all casual, leaning his head back and stretching out his *perfectly formed* legs. For a long moment, Michael didn't say anything. And James, trying to deflate his inappropriate erection, ignored Michael and watched a trio of old ladies doing water aerobics instead. But when his pulse slowed enough for his brain to kick back online, his curiosity, and a nagging suspicion that was downright annoying, made James speak.

"How did you know where to find me?"

Michael laughed nervously. "Just lucky, I guess."

James practically growled. "Amanda. She said she forgot a pen and went back inside. I'm going to kill her."

Michael was quiet for a minute, then he said, "I'm sorry. I was hoping you wouldn't mind. I just wanted a chance to maybe say something more meaningful than 'gah' or 'hrumph' or 'nghng'."

James couldn't stop a smile. Despite his extreme self-consciousness at being caught in a bathing suit *by this guy*, of all people, and his annoyance at Amanda—the pool? Really? Why not invite the guy into my shower?—the remark was funny.

"Nghgn? How do you spell that?"

"No idea. You're the writer."

"Don't think I've ever used that word before."

"Yeah, but your characters have the advantage of editing. I have to make an impression in real time."

Another silence enveloped them. James felt slightly less awkward, but only slightly. He was painfully aware of the beautiful boy in the chair next to him and had no idea what to do with that except feel even more unbeautiful and uncomfortable by comparison.

He felt something tickling his stomach and looked down. A drop of water was making its way down his torso from his hair. He caught it as it reached his stomach and wiped it off. At least his upper body was in shape from swimming and was not something he had to cover up in shame.

Michael made a small noise, and James glanced at him. He was looking at James's bare stomach, and when he raised his eyes, the spark in them was hotter than ever and his lips were slightly parted.

Fuck. No one had *ever* looked at James like that—warm and sweet, needy and surrendered. He might be a virgin, but he knew damn well what that look meant. The heat of it hit him in the gut like a wrecking ball. His erection, which had faded once already, came back with sirens blaring. James dropped his hands into his lap and stared at the pool. In his peripheral vision, he could see Michael shifting about and messing with his towel. *Oh, God.* Was he having the same problem? The mere idea of Michael becoming erect caused James to grow dangerously hard.

He was going to embarrass himself publicly in about ten seconds.

"I should go," James started to say, just as Michael said, "Would you like to go out to breakfast?"

They stared at each other for a second. James looked away, his heart pounding.

"Look," he said tightly, still staring at the pool, "I don't mean to be rude, but I don't know you and we have nothing in common."

"I think we have a lot in common," Michael said softly.

"Really? Please enlighten me."

"We both love science fiction. I love all of it—movies, games, books, blogs…. We both think you're a brilliant writer—"

James snorted.

"We're both relatively young and devastatingly handsome."

James pursed his lips as his bullshit meter jumped to the right. He couldn't help feeling warmed by the compliment, though.

"We both live in Seattle. And you probably have to deal a lot with doctors and hospitals and I'm a registered nurse, so we have the whole healthcare thing in common."

The warmth vanished in an instant as the world fell away from under James's feet, plummeting him into a very dark place. He felt a flush of hurt, hurt and anger. He remembered now that Michael had mentioned at the book signing that he was a nurse, but it hadn't really sunk in. Now it felt like a slap in the face. So much for being chatted up at the pool by a cute guy as if he were *normal*. He was such a buffoon.

"Is that supposed to make me fall at your feet?" James said in a blistering voice. "That you're a 'registered nurse'? Are you trolling for work? Well, I don't need a fucking nurse! Not professionally or privately. And, by the way, you might want to research how much midlist authors make before going to all this trouble." James felt hot acid in his mouth and a prickling heat behind his eyes. He released his brakes, desperate to get away.

"That's not... I didn't mean...!"

James had one last glimpse of Michael's stricken face before he was gone, heading for the locker room.

James dressed as quickly as he could manage between his limited mobility and his shaking hands. He was sure Michael would follow him into the locker room, but Michael didn't. James safely made it out of the pool only to have to sit and wait outside for the van. It wasn't due 'til nine. This was one of the things he loathed about being in a wheelchair. He couldn't just take off like a normal person. He had to wait for people to take him places. And right then, that made him vulnerable to someone badgering him like he expected Michael to do at any moment. James wouldn't be able to get away.

But Michael never did come after him. By the time James was in the van and safely on his way home, he actually regretted that. But then he reminded himself—it would never work.

He didn't like to think about Chris. Chris was the only boyfriend James had ever had. James's writing friend, Lance, had introduced them. Chris was a hair stylist and, James realized much too late, a celebrity groupie. He loved the *idea* of James—or rather, of dating a "famous author." It was the reality of him that Chris had trouble with. Chris avoided looking at his legs or at the chair. He would kiss James, but only as he was leaving. As soon as James would start to respond to the warm tongue work and reach out for more, Chris would pull away with some cheerful excuse or another. James was not stupid. It didn't take him long to figure out that the idea of sex with a man with James's deformity was more than Chris could handle—however he tried to hide it. It disgusted him.

James should have called a stop to it much sooner than he did. But when you got a ticket on the only ship leaving the port, you didn't bitch that it was in steerage. The truth was, James enjoyed the company. Chris came over to James's house a few times a week, and he was funny and flirty and told outrageous stories about his clients. James kept alive the hope that Chris would get over his aversion with time. He wanted… yes, he really wanted to go to bed with Chris.

But that never happened. Eventually, Chris broke up with him. He'd been pushing, more and more, for James to write something "commercial," a big YA like *The Hunger Games* or Harry Potter. James had refused. He had no interest in writing YA or in chasing the latest hit with a "me too." The last time he'd seen Chris, they'd had a huge fight. Chris told James he was "never going to be anyone important." Those words were as damning as they came in Chris's eyes.

The stupid thing was, even though James knew—he damn well *knew*—that Chris was shallow and not incredibly bright and they were a terrible match, it had still really hurt.

Fool me once, shame on you. Fool me twice, shame on me.

He wouldn't fall for that again.

~5~

Varanasi, India, 1991

THE LAST day of James's normal life, he and his mother spent hours roaming around the market in Varanas and looking at all the strange and wonderful things. There were funny-looking animals, delicious things to eat, and even some toys, but James knew better than to ask for any of them. He knew what his mother would say—that they didn't have the money, and anyway, it was better to look at nice things than to own them. James didn't think that made any sense at all, especially not when that thing was a lovely bit of pastry, but he knew it didn't do any good to throw a fit. Besides, his mother was being wonderful, making jokes, tickling him, and kissing his cheek.

They shared a bowl of rice and curry on the steps at Kedar Gate. James was fascinated watching the people bathing in the Ganges River. From very young to very old, naked or fully dressed, they waded into the brown water.

James, being five years old, wanted to go in the water too. And his mother, being an unrepentant adventurer, let him. James adored his mother. She was always up for something fun. She helped him remove his clothes, even his underwear because the other little boys in the water had nothing on. She took off her own sandals and tucked up the long hem of her skirt so she could wade in with him while James splashed around.

He played with two little Indian boys for a while. At first, they examined him and touched his pale skin with curiosity, and then, deciding it wasn't that interesting, the three of them tossed a little plastic top around. But the two boys swam like fishes and James could not, so after a while, they got bored with him and swam off. The area near the steps got crowded with adults, including some scary-looking old people. He decided it wasn't fun anymore and got out. His mother rubbed his arms and legs with her hands and then finished drying him off with his T-shirt. They went back to the hostel where they had a small room to themselves with two cots. James thought about trying to find some of the neighborhood children he'd played with before, but he felt very tired. That night, his mother made him canned tomato soup in the hostel's kitchen. It was James's favorite.

The next morning he awoke to agonizing pain. His head felt like someone was hitting it with a huge hammer, like in the roadrunner cartoons. His mother gave him aspirin and rocked him on the bed while James screamed and screamed. He got so hot he was burning up, and then he would get cold and shake all over. He ached everywhere, but especially his legs. It felt like they were being twisted and squeezed by an invisible giant. And his lower back was on fire. His mother kissed him, whispered soothing things in his hair, and gave him more pills. She bathed him with a cool rag. She talked worriedly with someone at the foot of his bed, but he didn't know who it was and he was too sick to care. He cried and cried.

On the third day, James woke up in the morning and found his mother deeply asleep on the cot next to him. He felt terribly weak, but he had to go to the bathroom so bad! He swung his legs out of the bed, stood—and fell to the floor. He cried out in fear and surprise. His mother sat up.

"James? What is it?"

"Momma, my legs don't work!"

~6~

Seattle, February, 2014

"WATCH OUT today," Jasmine said under her breath as she let Michael in. "The queen is in a nasty old mood."

"Is she feeling bad?" Michael asked worriedly as he set down his bag. Jasmine was a five-foot nurse of Hawaiian descent who was round as a nested doll. She was a nice person and, Michael assumed, a good nurse, but she and Marnie never got along.

"No change," Jasmine said with exasperation. "Her blood pressure's been fine today, and she had a bowl of chicken noodle soup and some toast for lunch. Just feeling her ever-lovin' oats. She's been asking for you. I swear, if I hear 'When is Michael coming?' in that petulant tone one more time—"

"I got it," Michael assured Jasmine with a smile. "Go on home and relax."

"It'll take me a big-ass margarita to relax after *this* day," Jasmine muttered as she left the house.

Michael went in to check on Marnie. She looked like she was sleeping, lying on her side in bed. But he stood there for a moment, and sure enough, she peeked with one eye. "Michael!" she said, coming vibrantly to life.

"Hey, Miss Thing." He went over and kissed her cheek. "I hear you've been giving Jasmine a world of grief."

"She's boring!" Marnie struggled to sit up. "She wants to yammer on about her grandchildren and never lets me do anything fun."

Michael helped her to sit, being careful not to hold her fragile upper arms too tightly. She bruised so easily.

"Take this thing off me," Marnie demanded, pushing weakly at the afghan that had been covering her up.

Michael did and whistled at her ensemble. "Aren't you looking fierce today?"

As usual, Marnie was *dressed*. She'd been a burlesque dancer in the forties, and she had the pictures to prove it. She still had an unusual sense of style. Today she wore tight lime green leggings and a leopard print slinky top with a low "V" neckline. Her hair was a bouffant bleached blonde that she had done every Monday. Her makeup was thick and obviously applied by a shaky hand—dark outlining around the eyes, mascara, white face powder, and heavy rouge. Her freshly applied red lipstick showed she'd been waiting for Michael to arrive. He'd never been on morning duty with Marnie, but he'd heard the nurses tell horror stories about how difficult she was to get bathed and dressed. Michael admired her enormously for making the effort. At eighty-nine, Marnie needed in-home nursing care from sunup to sundown, but she refused to give up on fashion.

"I'm tired of being in bed. Let's go out to the living room and pretend we're sophisticated society folks," she said brightly, giving Michael a crooked red smile.

"Marnie, you'll always be sophisticated society." Michael helped Marnie to her walker, and then helped her settle on the couch, propping pillows on either side so she didn't have to hold herself up.

"Perfect," Marnie said with a sigh. "Now get us both a big old glass of wine and let's dish."

Marnie couldn't have wine, but they pretended she could. Michael got them both a little apple juice spritzer in a wine glass and settled down on the couch with her.

"Let's talk about sex," Marnie said, as soon as Michael sat down. "I need some entertainment. At my age, talking is all I have left."

Michael smiled, but he wasn't really feeling his usual chipper self today. "Sure, Marnie. What about sex?"

"Oh, you've heard all my stories a dozen times. Tell me what you did this week. Come on, lemme live vicariously."

"It was a slow week in the sex department," Michael sighed. "I had my usual session with my one and only surrogacy client at the moment."

"Massage and hand job?" Marnie said knowingly.

"Marnie! You know I can't tell you about my clients!"

"How long did it take him to come?" she asked curiously.

Michael snorted a laugh. "I didn't time it. You are too funny."

"How can I live through you without all the nitty gritty details?"

Michael thought about it. "Details, let's see... he beat me at three rounds of gin. *Again*."

Marnie humphed. "Oh, cards! Cards are boring. What about the rest of your week?"

"Hmm. I masturbated in the shower Wednesday. Friday night...." He felt a heavy ache in his chest. *Friday night, after meeting J.C., I lay in bed and thought about him while I touched myself.*

"What happened?" Marnie asked, immediately cooing with concern. "Did you go out? Did someone hurt you?"

Michael shook his head. "No, no one hurt me. Well, not exactly. I met someone I really liked and got whole-heartedly rejected. Twice in a row."

"Oh, honey! What is he, blind? Who could not want such a cute young thing! Tell Marnie all about it."

So Michael told her about J.C. Guise—how he'd been crushing on that one small picture of him for years, his immediate attraction when they met, the wheelchair, and how J.C. had shut him down at the signing and then again at the pool and the disastrous way that had ended. Marnie listened to it all, digging for more details at every turn.

"Are you sure he's gay?" she asked.

"Not *sure*. But based on his writing, it makes sense. He's written some pretty hot male-male scenes. And I'm sure I saw a look in his eyes a few times.... You know that *I-want-you-bad* look."

Marnie sighed fondly and put one ring-bedecked hand on her chest. "Oh, Lord! Do I remember that look. Can't recall the last time I got it, but I know how it feels. Heaven!"

"And there was this moment by the pool. I got sort of turned on, and I'm pretty sure he did too. He has a really sexy upper body and a strong face and… I dunno. There's just something about him, that mysterious quantity X, ya know?"

"Sounds like you two have some serious chemistry. I think this Mr. Intellect is just shy. He's probably not used to boys who are as open-minded as you are about the wheelchair. He must have thought you were implying that you wanted to take care of him. A man likes to feel like a man. Big and tough." She tsked and made a face. "Never, *ever* underestimate a man's ego."

Michael sighed. "I know. I should never have mentioned the nursing. But it's ruined now. I can't stalk him anymore. Poor guy would probably get a restraining order, and I wouldn't blame him one bit."

Marnie snorted. "Fuck that. It's your pride that's the problem. Well, take it from me—your pride and a nickel will get you a nickel's worth of dime candy. Haven't you heard all the grand stories about true love? My Winnie wouldn't take no for an answer, even though I was married. She pursued me for months, and she won in the end. She was right, too. We had thirty wonderful years."

Michael gave her a sad smile and rubbed her shoulder. "I know. She sounds amazing. I wish I'd known her."

"She was. I did miss cock, though," Marnie said wistfully. "I loved that woman to death, and she could make me scream in bed, but once in a while, a hard cock would not have gone amiss. Being bisexual is like spending your life choosing between meat and potatoes." Marnie suddenly guffawed. "Make that bananas and mangos!"

Michael giggled. "You are too much!"

"So here's what you do," Marnie said in her no-nonsense voice. "You go back to that pool, daily, and swim at the same time as Mr. Important Writer."

"Marnie, I can't—"

"Don't interrupt your elders," Marnie said sternly. "Don't approach the man. Just swim, show yourself off, look delectable," Marnie touched her hair with one frail hand, giving a little pout. "Maybe start giving him a wistful smile here and there." She demonstrated wistfully. "Then, when he's gagging for it, give in and let him approach you. You need to turn from the hunter to the huntee, my dear. You're a bottom boy if I ever saw one."

"Marnie!" Michael gasped. "I am not!"

"Oh, I know you're good at being in charge when you need to be. But you need to work with what nature gave you. And your looks are pure, sweet Georgia honey, 'fuck me now'. You should go with that."

Michael covered up his face with his hands, laughing. "You're evil, woman!"

"Um-hum. I've never worried about people calling me evil when I was young enough to be worthy of the name, and I'm not going to start now. Take my advice, and you'll have that man eating out of your hand. Or lower. That's even better."

Michael's laughter died off, and he sighed. "I dunno, Marnie. Why would J.C. Guise like me? I'm just a nurse. And a sex surrogate. Once he finds out about that, he won't want me anyway. No guy does."

Marnie slapped at his arm. "What's the matter with you? You're gorgeous and fun, you have a big heart, and you're sexy to boot. He should be so lucky."

"Thanks, Miss Thing."

"Besides, one of us needs to get laid so we can chat about it, and the odds of it being me aren't great. It's hard to run after a potential sex partner with a walker. Now! How 'bout we watch some porn?"

Michael looked at his watch. "It's almost time for your pills. I need to make you a snack to go with it, and I need to check your vitals."

"Okay, nursey nurse. After that, can we watch porn?" She gave him her patented big-eyed pleading look.

Michael felt guilty. "You know your daughter would have me fired in a heartbeat if she knew I let you do that."

Marnie glowered. "Fuck Susan. I'm still an adult in my own home. God knows, if you can't be an adult at eighty-nine, what's it all for?"

Michael hesitated, chewing his lip. "Is Susan due over?"

"No, she's at work, thank God. Come on. Let's watch *Misty Beethoven*. Please?" She batted her false lashes at him playfully.

Michael rolled his eyes. "All right. After pills and vitals, I'll let you watch some of *Misty* while I put on fresh sheets and tidy your room. Okay?"

Michael started to get up, but Marnie gripped his hand and looked at him seriously. "Thank you for letting me be myself. You're the only one who does, you know."

Her eyes were a little damp, and Michael felt a catch in his chest. She was so sweet—in her uniquely raunchy way. He brought her hand to his lips and kissed it. "Well, from one eccentric to another, I wouldn't want you any other way."

"Oh, Michael. I love you too."

~7~

"SO, WHAT'S new and exciting, James?"

Over Skype, Felicia looked just as she had when James was growing up. She was a wiry, unadorned woman who wore little makeup and favored easy to wash polo shirts and khakis. Her super curly hair, worn pulled back into a braid, was now more snow than slate, and her face grew lines like they were wild daisies in a field. It was really good to see her.

James blew out a breath. "New—I bought a toothbrush the other day. Supposedly, it's the latest technology in angled bristles. Exciting—I had a book signing and survived it. That also falls under the categories 'miraculous' and 'terrifying'."

Felicia bounced a little dark-haired girl on her lap. The child had a recently repaired cleft palate and what might be a mild case of microcephaly. "Rachel, James had a book signing! Isn't that exciting?" Felicia told the little girl. Then she smiled at her computer camera. "I'm so proud of you, James. Were there lots of lovely fans there?"

"It was a good turnout. Best they've had in a few years, the store manager said."

"Wonderful! You deserve every success. You're so talented. You know how proud we are of you, and how much we appreciate your support."

"It's nothing." James didn't want to discuss that. He sent Children of God, the home where he'd grown up, a check for four hundred dollars every month. He figured he didn't have a car like most people his age, so it wasn't a big sacrifice. But with the way his royalties had been dwindling lately, he didn't know how long he'd be able to keep it up. He didn't want to worry Felicia, though. Not until he had to.

"Tell me how everyone's doing," he said.

Felicia filled him in. James had left the home ten years ago, when he was nineteen. He was lucky. A lot of the kids he'd grown up with weren't capable of living on their own. Because of Children of God's nonprofit status as a home for children, anyone over twenty-one had to be transferred to an adult care facility. But Felicia kept up with them all. And there were still some kids at the home that had been young when James was there. It took her a while to give him an update on everyone.

And then there were the new kids James had never met, kids like Rachel, who appeared to be around five years old. She never said a word while they were on Skype, just sat and clung to Felicia with one strong hand. James had a feeling Rachel wouldn't be one of the lucky ones.

"Are you dating anyone?" Felicia asked, as she always did.

"No. My harem wouldn't put up with it."

Felicia smiled. "What about Chris? Do you ever see him?"

James's hands clenched at the wave of bad memories. He shook his head. "I told you that ship sailed, was bombed in the harbor, and is now fish condos."

Felicia looked at him warmly. "You'll meet someone else. You're an amazing person, James."

James didn't know what to say to that. There was no point trying to explain to Felicia why he would never have a romantic life. She was the most ardently "can do" person on the planet. She and the reality of limitations had never gotten along.

"Well, I should let you get back to your minions," James said at last. "I'll talk to you in a couple of weeks."

"James, wait." Felicia looked like she didn't want to tell him the thing that she obviously had to tell him. He steeled himself. Was the home in trouble? Had someone died?

"What is it?"

"I got a call two days ago from someone looking for you. James, it was your mother."

The pain that lanced his chest at those words took his breath away. He swallowed a gasp.

Felicia frowned in sympathy. "I'm sorry. But she really wants to speak to you. I told her I'd ask you if it was okay to give her your contact info."

"*No*," James said firmly, finding his voice.

Felicia hesitated, searching his face over the camera. "Are you sure? It might be good for you to talk to her, get some closure. And she sounded very... sincere."

"Felicia, I *do* not give you fu—" James remembered there were little ears listening. "I do not, in any way, shape, or form, give you permission to relay my contact info. I will not see her." His voice sounded barely controlled. "Please," he added out of desperation.

Felicia gave in without another word. "All right, James. I won't. A big hug and kiss. I need to go. I can hear screaming in the hall. Never a good thing." She smiled. "Bye, James."

"Bye, Felicia."

JAMES HAD a deep sense of unease after hanging up. *His mother had called the home.* Why now? What the hell did she want?

He told himself it didn't matter. He wasn't going to see her, and he didn't give a shit why she'd tried to get in contact with him. But it was still upsetting, and he couldn't get back to work. He tried to find something else to think about, anything to get the idea of her out of his head.

He thought about Michael Lamont.

James hadn't been back to the pool since the day he'd fled from Michael. He knew he was being a coward, but he decided to give himself a few weeks off. Hopefully, by the time he returned, Michael would have given up.

He wasn't sure what bothered him the most. There was, of course, the fact that a hot-looking guy like Michael could not possibly want anything from him that wasn't either delusional or mercenary. There was his fear of stupidly getting his hopes up and revealing himself as pathetic. There was the fact that he felt like a total douchebag for the way he'd overreacted last time. *You're a nurse? Damn your eyes!* It was so embarrassing. And then there was the fact that he didn't want to go back there hoping Michael would show up and then be disappointed when he didn't. For all those reasons, he didn't go back to the pool, even though his muscles were beginning to ache from want of exercise.

He tried to get back to work on his latest novel, but he just couldn't get himself into the headspace to write it. He didn't want to be working on it in the first place. It was book number three of a trilogy, so he had to finish it. It was promised to his publisher. But the reviews and sales had been disappointing on the first two books. Even his most ardent fans had been less than enthusiastic in online reviews. Which made writing book number three almost torture, like giving birth to a baby you knew was already dead.

He had a few other book ideas he was more anxious to work on, stories he thought would do better, but what if they didn't? Amanda had made it clear that if his sales didn't pick up, his publisher would drop him. If only he had a real shot at winning the Millennial Award. That would so goose his career.

He gave up on the day's work, tired and more than a little depressed. He swung himself into bed with his idea notebook and sketched out some story ideas until he feel asleep. He dreamt of warm brown eyes, soft olive skin, a tight body, and the prettiest lips he'd ever seen.

~8~

Varanas, India, 1991

FOR THE first few weeks in the hospital in India, James was so weak that he had little strength and he couldn't move his legs at all. The pain continued, burning his legs until he shivered and cried. Worse than the pain was the sense of frustration and a child's rage at being moved around like a doll. The nurses rolled him in the bed, coldly and quickly, and paid no attention to his protests, *I'm sleeping*, or his desires, *I don't like lying on this side*. They washed him, slapped his back over and over to clear his lungs, stuck him with needles and put a tube up his wee, and he couldn't do anything about it. When they did something he didn't like, shoved him around or propped him up in a position that hurt, he could only cry and try to think about other things. He had to wait for them to come back and move him again or for his mother to show up to visit. There were no books, no games, and no TV. He started making up stories in his head to escape when he couldn't stand it anymore.

Every morning, they would wake him from sleep by pulling down his pajamas, lifting his hips, and shoving a cold, hard metal pan under his bum. It hurt his back so much to lay on it. They'd leave it there for a long time, usually with nothing to show for it in the end. He knew they wanted him to go number two, but his stomach hurt and he couldn't go.

Finally, after many days, he started feeling better. He could sit up by himself and hold a cup. As soon as he was able, he would pull himself off the hated bedpan the minute the nurse left. Many of his ward mates weren't as fortunate. The little boy next to him would cry on the bedpan every morning—silently, ashamed of the tears rolling down his cheeks.

"Can't you move your arms?" James had asked the little boy.

The boy just stared at him with big, dark eyes, not understanding James's English. So James held up his arms and wiggled his fingers. The boy tried to mimic him. He was able to move the fingers on one hand a little, but he couldn't raise his arms. James understood then— the little boy's arms were like his own legs. He thought about all the things he wouldn't be able to do if his arms didn't work. He felt sorry for the little boy, but he was also very glad it wasn't him.

Even though James was more fortunate than many in his ward, even though he was soon allowed the privilege of having the bedpan on the table next to his bed for him to use when he wanted to, he was deeply ashamed of having to poop in his bed in front of the other children. Worse was being left with the stink of it—no hiding that— until someone wandered by to take the bedpan away.

He hated it all. He hated going to the bathroom in the bed like a baby. He hated not being able to get out of bed, go to the window to look out for his mother, or follow a boy he saw limping down the hall. He couldn't get out of bed until someone came to put him in a wheelchair. And when he was in the chair, he hated not being able to crawl back into his bed on his own when he was tired. James's mind was bright and quick. His legs had always taken him wherever his interest landed. Now he was trapped with two legs that couldn't take him anywhere.

As James got stronger, his mom would take him on trips around the hospital in the wheelchair. Through the doorway of the room next to his, he could see two big machines with the heads of children stuck out of the ends like lollipops. Other beds in the room had smaller machines next to the bed that made pumping sounds, *shhht, shhht, shhht*. One bed went up and down like a seesaw. It looked like fun, but the little dark girl on the bed was as thin as a skeleton and she was always sleeping.

"What's wrong with those kids?" James asked his mother loudly.

She hushed him and talked about taking him out to the courtyard. But later, when he was back in his bed, she said, "You know those children in the next room?"

James nodded.

She put her hand on his chest and pressed a little. "They have polio just like you, only instead of it just hurting the muscles in their legs, like it did to you, it hurt their muscles *here*, the muscles you use to breathe. The machines help them get air because they can't breathe by themselves anymore."

It was the first time James had heard the word *polio*. He tried to imagine what it would be like if he couldn't breathe. He could feel his mom's hand, as his chest rose and fell with his breath, and it made him aware of the movement his body made when air went in and out. He tried holding his breath, puffing out his cheeks, but it hurt and he couldn't do it for very long. He let it out.

"That's scary. I feel bad for those kids."

His mom gave him a shaky smile. "Me too. But you don't have to worry about that, Sweetpea. We're very lucky."

Very lucky.

Those words would haunt him forever, along with the look on his pretty mother's face, a frozen sorrow that made him understand they weren't lucky at all, that something very, very bad had happened and things would never be the same again.

~9~

MICHAEL WALKED into the Expanded Horizons clinic, put on a smile, and tried to pull himself into a more positive mood. They had their Wednesday staff meeting today, and he was hoping for a new client. He was still upset about what'd happened with J.C. Guise, even two weeks later. He needed a distraction, and he needed to feel good about himself. Making progress with a patient always made him feel so much better.

As soon as he walked into the waiting room, Loretta, the buxom, red-haired receptionist, flew around from her cubbyhole of an office and body slammed him. Michael hugged her back, alarmed.

"What's the matter? What happened?" Michael asked, sure some calamity had fallen. Had something happened to Trudy or Jack?

But Loretta only pressed him tighter for a moment, her breasts like conical pillows—not quite memory foam, more like down-filled—before pulling back and looking him in the face. "Nothing. I just wanted to hug you." She tweaked his cheek with one hand and made the sort of face one would make at a baby. "You are sooooo cute, Michael Lamont."

Michael blinked at her in surprise. "Uh... thank you?"

His arms were still loosely around her, and she snuggled closer as if she meant to stay there. Thankfully, there were no patients in the waiting room to observe this little scene, but it was still... weird.

"Want to get some coffee later?" Loretta sighed against his neck.

As gently as he could, Michael put his hands on her arms and pulled away. "Loretta," he said in the nicest possible voice, "you do remember that I'm the clinic's gay surrogate?"

She smoothed down her sweater and arched an eyebrow. "I *know*. Sexuality is not as rigid as people think. I have learned a thing or two working here. Remember that cute Mr. Derenzo? He thought he was straight for years."

"That can be true," Michael said slowly. "But personally? I'm really, seriously gay."

Loretta rolled her eyes and went back to her chair.

In the staff meeting, the clinic's two doctors, Dr. Trudy Kaplan and Dr. Jack Halloran, went over their cases. Andrea and Philip, the clinic's two other surrogates, sat in at the weekly meetings, as did Michael. Andrea worked with straight men. She was in her midthirties, slim and attractive but not glamorous. She had an earthy, no-nonsense sensuality that Michael admired. He also envied the fact that she worked for the clinic full-time—straight men were the bulk of their clientele.

If Michael could do surrogacy full-time, he would. He probably could manage it if he took freelance too, but he liked working with a reputable sex clinic. That way he could be sure his clients had been screened through a sex therapist like Dr. Halloran, and that they legitimately needed him. He didn't want to run the risk of getting curiosity seekers or those looking for, essentially, a prostitute. Besides, he'd worked hard to become a nurse and he'd become very attached to Marnie. She'd insisted Happy At Home assign him to her second shift Monday through Friday, which gave him steady work for the foreseeable future.

Phillip, the other surrogate, was also part-time. He worked with straight women. He was not a fan of Michael's and vice versa. Michael found him a little too good-looking and a lot too cocky. He had a slight air of being god's gift to women instead of being a healer. But Michael supposed he was biased. He had a lot of baggage about big, buff, straight guys like Phillip giving him a hard time in school. And Phillip always ignored Michael, as if he didn't exist, and that was just annoying.

Dr. Jack Halloran, on the other hand, was a lovely, lovely man. He'd been a combat surgeon and he was tough, with a core of steel under a boy-next-door exterior. Jack looked Michael right in the eye when they talked, gave him respect. He treated Michael as though they were a team. Of course, Jack Halloran was also gay. That might have something to do with it.

Michael had had a mild crush on Jack way back when. When Jack had first come to the clinic, he'd been depressed and suffering from PTSD. There'd been a depth of sorrow in him that drew Michael like a moth to a flame. He'd just wanted to wrap up the good doctor and love on him and make him feel better. But Jack had made it clear that was not going to happen. And really, Jack had been right. It was smart not to do the dirty with anyone at work. Now Jack was in a relationship and was way, *way* off the market.

Trudy turned to look at him. "Michael? How are things going with Tommy Chelsey?"

Michael sat up straighter. "Good. I saw him Monday for touch therapy, as usual. His mother's worried that he's been depressed lately, but I didn't see that when I was with him."

Jack looked concerned. "Did she give you any indication of why she thinks he's depressed? How he'd been acting?"

"Nothing specific. She just said his friends were graduating from college and getting married and she was worried about how he was taking it."

Jack nodded. "Please remind her that if she'd like to bring him in to see me again, I can make room for him on my calendar. Or I can recommend another therapist if she wants him to see someone who specializes in depression."

"Sure, Jack."

"So you're continuing with Tommy for the time being?" Trudy asked.

"Yeah. His mother said he really looks forward to my visits. She thinks they're helping."

Phillip made a very unprofessional noise. Michael frowned at him.

Trudy tapped her pen on the table thoughtfully. "This is getting to be fairly long-term. Is there any chance Tommy could get overly attached to you?"

Michael thought about it. "We seem to be well-established as a friendship with the, uh, professional benefit. I don't think there's any danger of him getting hurt."

Trudy smiled. "All right, Michael. Thanks for the update." She turned to Jack.

"New patients.… Jack, tell us about Lem Peterson." Trudy put up a client bio. Her laptop hooked into a projector that showed the patient bio form on the wall. It included a photo of a heavyset man in his forties, balding and with a beard. He had a shy, quiet look about him.

Jack nodded, looking grim. "This is Lem Peterson, forty-three-year-old tax accountant. I've had two sessions with him so far. His mother recently passed away, and he's finally seeking treatment for long-standing emotional issues. He lived with her all his life, does his tax business out of a small office in the front of their home, and he's never had a relationship of any kind. He has moderate social anxiety disorder, which he's able to temper enough to meet with his accounting clients. But when he gets around a man he finds attractive, it can get severe. His mother was very religious and extremely derogatory about any form of sexuality at all. As a result, he has emotional issues around sex. He masturbates rarely, and when he does, he finds he can only do it in the closet of his bedroom, in the dark, even now that his mother is no longer in the house. The good news is, he realizes he has a problem and he's seeking help."

"So he identifies as homosexual, but he's a virgin?" Trudy asked, getting to the heart of it.

"Yes. He's known he was interested in men instead of women since he was eight years old, but his mother was very controlling. She drilled into him the idea that any sex was dirty. She lectured him frequently about girls, which worked, as it happens, but he ended up never dating anyone at all. He's morbidly shy." Jack paused and looked at Michael. "I've talked to Mr. Peterson about surrogacy. I'm meeting with him twice a week to deal with his emotional issues, but he has a lot of anxiety about the mere idea of physical contact. I think he'd benefit from some very gentle touch therapy soon, try to get him past his fear of even being in the same room with an available sexual partner."

"I'd love to work with him." Michael sat forward eagerly. It didn't take a lot to tug on his heartstrings, and right then, they were playing Beethoven's Ninth. The idea of someone reaching the age of forty-three without any human contact was so, so sad. Poor Mr. Peterson.

"Thanks," Jack said with a smile. "You're going to have to go extremely slowly. We can meet after this to go over a therapy plan."

"I can go slow," Michael said, looking at the picture of shy Lem Peterson. "Don't worry, Jack. I'll take good care of him."

AFTER THE meeting, Michael and Jack got a cup of coffee in the clinic's staff kitchen and went into Jack's office.

Michael perched on Jack's desk. He started to spread his thighs and caught himself. Jack was definitely taken, and he was no dummy either. He'd called Michael on flirting more than once. Jack was happy and well now, and he didn't stir Michael the way he had when he'd been alone and hurting. Still, Michael liked Jack a lot and old habits died hard.

"How's Tony?" Michael asked.

Jack's serious doctor face transformed into a warm, shy blush of a smile that took ten years off the man and would not have been amiss on, say, an old Dutch painting of a milkmaid and her beau.

"Aw! True love. You're so cute," Michael cooed.

"Shut it. I am never 'cute'. Tony is great. He's been doing a lot of insurance work lately, which he finds boring, but we've been, um, enjoying the low workload. Went camping last weekend."

"Yeah?"

Jack bit back a smile and tried to get his love-struck face under control. "Yeah. We went over to the Olympics. It was a perfect weekend for it. What about you? Been having any non-work fun lately?"

Michael shrugged. "You know me. I'm all about my patients."

Jack tapped Michael lightly on the forehead. "There's part of you in there that's not a nurse, you know."

Michael huffed a laugh. "Yeah, and that guy reads Heinlein in bed in his underwear. Not a compelling picture, I can tell you."

"Oh, I don't know." Jack's eyes twinkled. "Could be quite compelling—for the right guy."

Michael felt a twist of disappointment in his gut. *Yeah, I thought I'd found that guy, but I was wrong.* He gave a dismissive shrug. "Anyway, let's talk about Mr. Peterson."

Jack gave him a look that said *I know you're just trying to change the subject*, but he went with it anyway. "Lem agreed to meet you after I showed him your profile, but he's extremely anxious about it. In fact, he told me flat out he didn't think it would work, but he wants to try. He really does want to get better. Some part of him does, anyway."

"I'll take it slow with him," Michael assured Jack. "Does he have an injury or performance issues I need to be aware of? E.D.?"

"No, I managed to coax him through a physical, which was extremely uncomfortable for him. He has no physical impairment, but his emotional issues are acute. I think just getting comfortable being around you at all would be a win. I've outlined some suggestions for your sessions, but of course, when you meet with him, you should follow your gut, as usual."

"Don't worry, Jack. I'll be the prince of sensitivity. I won't scare him."

Jack put a hand on Michael's shoulder. "I trust you, Michael. Believe me, if I didn't, I wouldn't send Lem Peterson to you."

That touched Michael down deep in the core of who he was as a person. Jack didn't give his approval lightly, and his validation of Michael as a surrogate meant more than just about anything in the world. Michael's throat got a little lumpy with pride, but he swallowed it.

"Thanks, Jack. I really needed to hear that today."

Jack studied his face. "Oh, yeah? Is everything okay? You know you can talk to me anytime."

"Sure," Michael said, though he had no intention of talking to Jack about his love life or lack thereof. At this point, all he could do would be to whine about not being able to meet the right guy, and given the people with *real* problems that they both dealt with day to day, that was just pathetic. "So. Do you want to go over your outline?"

WHEN MICHAEL opened the door of his apartment, Lem Peterson looked as if he was on the verge of expiring from mortification. His milky blue eyes dropped immediately to stare at his shoes, and his round face went an alarming shade of tomato pink. He looked seconds away from fleeing, and Michael steeled himself to prevent that at any cost. He'd just have to be the sweetest, most innocuous little damn ray of sunshine Lem Peterson had ever seen.

"Mr. Peterson? It's so lovely to meet you. Please come in. It's drafty in the hall, isn't it?"

Michael's apartment was on Capitol Hill, Seattle's gay neighborhood, and it was in a converted old house. Michael loved the high ceilings and 1900s moldings, but it was a bit cold. Nevertheless, the nudge was meant more to give Mr. Peterson a good reason to step inside. Thankfully, he did.

"I…," Mr. Peterson said, before his throat apparently closed up. He was still looking at his shoes.

"Do you like hot tea? I made a nice pot of chamomile. But I can also make you a cup of coffee if you prefer."

Choices. Give the man something to agree to.

"Tea is fine. I like tea. Thank you," Mr. Peterson said in a very soft voice. He dared a glance at Michael's face before blushing harder and looking down again.

Well, that was progress.

"Good. I'll go get the tea. You can toss your coat on that chair and take a seat on the sofa in the living room. I'll be right there."

Michael stepped into his little kitchen, giving Mr. Peterson a chance to decide to take off his coat and sit down without any pressure. Michael's living room was cozy and warm, with deep orange and red Oriental prints, an electric space heater, low lighting, and a few lit candles and incense. He hadn't gone all out with the candles, didn't want to scare Mr. Peterson off, but a few were always nice to create a relaxed ambience. Soft instrumental Hindu music played in the background.

When Michael brought out a tray with a pot of tea and two Japanese cups, Mr. Peterson was sitting at the far end of the couch, pressed up against the side. He'd removed his coat but not his scarf. Michael put the tray down on the coffee table and took a seat in the middle of the couch. He poured tea into both cups.

"Cream or sugar?"

"No, thank you."

Michael held one of the cups out to Mr. Peterson. The man hesitated, then took it quickly, as if afraid to get too close to Michael's hand. Michael made no comment.

"So you've been working with Dr. Halloran. What do you think of him?" he asked, sitting back casually.

Mr. Peterson sat with his thighs close together, leaning forward with both elbows on his knees. He was not a small man, at least two hundred pounds, and the position looked uncomfortable, poor guy. He held the small teacup with two beefy hands.

"I like Dr. Halloran," he said quietly. He darted a glance at Michael. "I'm very nervous. I'm s-sorry."

"Don't be sorry," Michael said softly. "You can be whatever you want with me. You're safe here."

"But, I mean, you're so…."

Mr. Peterson chugged his tea in a single gulp, then turned redder. Damn, the tea was hot. That probably hurt.

Michael spoke lightly. "I'm just me, and you're just you. I hope we can be friends."

Peterson darted a look at him and nodded once. "That would be nice." He shifted his shoulders uncomfortably. "I'm really sweating. I'm sorry."

"Are you hot? Sorry about that. I get chilled." Michael got up and shut off the floor heater.

"It's okay, I—"

"Can I take your scarf or would you like to keep it on?" Michael stood in front of Mr. Peterson, smiling.

Mr. Peterson's eyes got stuck at Michael's waist, darting back and forth as if fascinated by his sweater.

"Okay." He swallowed loudly, took off the scarf, and handed it to Michael. Michael put it on the chair with Peterson's coat and sat back down where he'd been before.

"What exactly makes you nervous about being here? Would you like to talk about that, Mr. Peterson?"

"Please call me Lem."

"Thank you, Lem. You can call me Michael."

"Okay. Michael." Lem reached out and poured himself more tea, which Michael counted as a win. "You're very... handsome. It makes me nervous to be around... men. I mean any man who.... you know, isn't really old or a child or something. My mother... she was a wonderful person, but she didn't approve of s-s-sexual feelings of any kind." Lem blushed again. "Not that I have sexual feelings for you," he said hurriedly. "I just get nervous around anyone when it's even a possibility."

Michael could tell Lem had been working with Jack. He seemed to have a handle on what the issue was, at least.

"I understand. But I think that's sad, that your mom felt that way about sex. Sex is a part of love, and love is the nicest part of being a human being."

"That's what Dr. Halloran says." Lem looked down at his cup. "I'd like to get better. I'd like to be able to maybe... m-meet someone. Or maybe be with someone I've already met."

Michael perked up. "Oh? Do you like someone now?"

Lem tittered nervously. "Not exactly but... I have a client named John. I do his taxes. He... he seems to like me. I think. But I have no idea how to... I mean, I get like this when he comes to my office, and it's...." He shrugged, unable to find the words to go on.

"That's good, though," Michael smiled. "It's so much easier to work at therapy when you have a specific goal in mind, don't you think? Have you talked to Dr. Halloran about John?"

Lem nodded. "He thinks it would be a good goal for me to be able to go out on a d-date with John. But I have a lot of work to do before I would feel comfortable doing that. I mean, look at me. I'm a mess." He chuckled nervously.

He was, poor thing. His voice shook, his face was still red, and he had sweat gleaming on his temple. He couldn't meet Michael's gaze for more than a second at a time, and he looked about as uncomfortable as a Lutheran in a flophouse. But he was still there, bless him, and he was talking. That took heart.

"Well, I think you're doing great. Tell me what kind of guys you find attractive."

"I don't know. I don't really care about that. Just someone nice, I guess."

Lem seemed put off by the question. Well, that topic was a no go. Michael made himself take a breath and try to get a read on the situation. He wanted to make Lem feel less anxious, and Michael sensed he was scared to death about what might be coming, about the possibility of contact. It was like being worried about a first kiss on a date. Maybe it would be better to just get it over with and make sure Lem knew the game plan.

"We'll take this slow, Lem, don't worry. For today, I'd love to just talk to you and get to know you better. And maybe we could try having you touch my hand. Would that be okay?"

Lem sort of shuddered and studied the cup in his paws. "I... how would that...."

"Do you have a pet?"

Lem smiled and glanced at Michael. "I have a Pekinese. Her name is Margaret. She's a really sweet dog."

"I love dogs! Do you pet Margaret?"

"Oh, yeah. We watch TV together at night, and she sits on my lap. I pet her a lot. That doesn't bother me," Lem said in a rush.

Michael's heart ached for Lem, but at least he was getting some affection in his life. Thank God for animals.

"Then maybe you could try touching my hand the way you pet Margaret. See what you think of it." Michael carefully placed his hand, palm up, on the sofa between them.

Lem glanced at it and then away. "You have a n-nice hand."

"Thank you." Michael left it there.

Lem put the cup down and rubbed his eyes. He turned his body, which was stiff with tension, slightly on the couch toward Michael. With his eyes fixed on Michael's hand, he licked his lips and then reached out and touched Michael's palm. He kept his fingers tightly together and petted Michael's palm three times before putting his hand back in his own lap.

"That was nice," Michael said gently. "It felt good. You doin' all right?"

"I'm okay," Lem whispered.

"Good. Would you like to try it again? And this time, I'm going to give you an assignment, all right? I want you to describe for me how it feels—the texture, the way it looks, anything that comes into your mind."

Lem took a deep breath and licked his lips nervously. He reached out and stoked Michael's palm again, this time with his index and middle finger taking a more active role.

"Your... your skin is cooler than mine," he said. "But then, I'm, uh, I'm really w-warm right now."

"Your fingers do feel warm. What else can you tell me about how it feels?"

"It's softer than I thought it would be. Softer than my hand. Maybe you use lotion?"

"I do use lotion. What else?"

"You have a lot of lines in your palm." Lem stroked them lightly. "Is that supposed to mean you're an old soul or something?"

Michael smiled. "I've heard that. I don't know if I believe it. Do you?"

"I don't have much of an imagination, I'm afraid," Lem said regretfully.

"Being practical is good. Sometimes, I wish I were more practical. Is there anything else you notice about my hand?"

"You have very l-long fingers. Long and thin."

"Do they feel bony to you?" He elevated his index finger so Lem could get around it.

"Um...." Lem felt it cautiously.

"It's okay. You can say whatever comes into your head. I won't be insulted."

"Maybe a little bony. But not in a bad way. More like, I dunno, a bird or something."

Michael smiled. "That's a lovely image. And the back of my hand?" He turned it over.

Lem took a deep breath of a sigh, but he seemed to be a little less nervous. He stroked it repeatedly. "Softer than your palm. I can see your veins. That means you're in good shape. I mean, I can tell that just by looking at you but... veins are good. You have wide nails."

"I do have wide nails. How do you feel inside when you touch my hand?"

"All right." Lem kept petting the top of Michael's hand as if it was, indeed, a Pekinese. "But I'm not really thinking about it like... like... you know." He couldn't get the words out, and just thinking them made him blush scarlet again and pull away his hand as if he'd been caught doing something wrong.

"Like something sexual? That's okay. It would be awesome for you just to get used to touching someone. You don't have to think about it in a sexual way right now." Michael turned his palm back over and left his hand on the couch.

There was a tentative pause before Lem reached out and touched Michael's palm again. By his elevated breathing, and the blotchy affect appearing on the back of his own hand, Michael would put money on the fact that Lem was thinking about sex this time. Michael felt a little touch of arousal as Lem stroked his palm. He could go with it and get hard if he wanted to, not because he found Lem physically attractive, but because the man was sweet and he tugged hard at Michael's empathy. But Lem was far from needing an erection from Michael, and if he sensed there was one, it would probably scare the poor guy to death. Michael took a deep breath and willed it away.

"That feels really nice," Michael said gently. "Would you like to talk about how it makes you feel when you think about sex?"

Lem huffed. "Bad."

"Bad how?"

"G-guilty. Like it's wrong to think about it. To want it. Like I'm a bad person."

"When you pet Margaret, do you feel guilty about that?"

Lem looked insulted. "No. But I don't feel that way about her. I mean, she's a dog."

Michael smiled. "I know. But it's affection. You give Margaret affection, and she gives you affection in return."

"I guess so."

"Do you think she likes it when you show her affection?"

"She loves to be petted."

"And you feel happy when she licks your face and shows you she loves you?"

"Sure. She's my best friend." Lem smiled at the words. He really did love that dog.

Lem was petting Michael's palm, calmer now, and Michael let his fingers curl up just a little so they brushed against Lem's hand as it moved.

"That's not something to feel guilty about, is it? Giving affection to your dog and getting it in return."

"No. But that's different."

"It is different. But when you really like a person, and they really like you, then it's natural to want to show each other affection. And sex is a great way for two people who really like each other to show affection and make each other feel good, feel happy. You don't need to feel guilty about making someone happy, or even making yourself happy."

"That's what Dr. Halloran says. He says my body was made for it, or I wouldn't have those feelings. I wouldn't be able to... you know, if my body wasn't made to do that. It's just like it was made to breathe or eat and digest food and eliminate waste. That means it is by definition natural and being natural means it's not wrong."

Michael could tell Lem was a logical thinker, and this reasoning brought him some comfort.

"Well, Dr. Halloran is a hell of a smart guy."

Lem frowned, looking conflicted. "I know that's all true in my head. That is, I know it *now*, but it's hard to change your thinking. My mom.... She always told me I shouldn't... t-touch myself and stuff because it was a sin and God found it disgusting. She found it disgusting."

Lem's voice shook a little, and Michael knew there was a tidal wave behind those words, years of rants, years of belittling. God, some people should never be parents.

"What about your father, Lem?"

"He died when I was ten," Lem said calmly, not looking up.

"I'm sorry to hear that. It is hard to change your way of thinking, but you're your own person, not your parents, and you said you'd like to have a relationship someday?"

Lem swallowed. "Yes. I really do. I don't want to be alone."

"Then you can do it. I have faith in you. Dr. Halloran is a really good doctor. And I'd like to help."

"Thank you," Lem said to Michael's hand. "You seem like a very nice person. This is...." He expelled a heavy sigh. "This is the first time I've ever touched anyone like this. I'm still nervous but... it's not bad."

"Yeah?" Michael felt a swell of pride and pleasure. God, he was such a basket case. It meant more to him to hear someone like Lem say holding his hand was "not bad" than having some good-looking leather daddy plow him in a club's bathroom. By a million miles.

He tried very hard not to sound as moved as he was. "Well, I think you're doing great, Lem. Would you like to hold my hand now? We can just sit here and chat while we do that. I'd like to hear more about what you like to do for fun."

Lem froze, his hand hovering over Michael's. "I guess that would be all right."

It was clear he wasn't sure how to go about it, so Michael interlaced his fingers with Lem's and placed their paired hands on the couch.

"There. Okay?"

Lem gulped. "Okay."

"So tell me what TV shows you like to watch...."

LEM PETERSON stayed for another half hour of talking and holding hands. After he left, Michael typed up some quick notes for Jack on their progress and e-mailed them off. Then he flopped down on the couch and stared up at the ceiling. He ran the fringe from the shawl on the back of his couch through his fingers. Mr. Peterson was a very sweet man. He'd make someone very happy someday if he could get past the number his mom did on his head. Michael sincerely hoped he could.

Even Lem, as shy as he was, wanted to find love. And considering Michael's track record, he'd probably find it before Michael did. He felt sorry for himself for about five minutes before he made himself put a stop to it. Shit, this thing with J.C. Guise had really gotten under his skin, and it didn't seem to be fading.

The thing was, he couldn't shake the idea that J.C. needed him too, that he was used to pushing people away and getting away with it, but that it wasn't what he wanted at all. Michael could be wrong, but what if he wasn't?

Marnie was right. He needed to give it one more try.

~10~

AT TEN o'clock on a Monday morning, someone pounded on James's front door. It wasn't a tentative knock, either. It was a "get your ass out here now" kind of knock. James couldn't imagine who would be knocking on his door like that unless it was a neighbor with an emergency or possibly his friend Lance, who had the world's stupidest sense of humor.

He was shocked when he opened the door to find Michael Lamont standing on his doorstep. "Um...."

"What am I doing invading the sanctity of your home? I know!" Michael said in frustrated anger, gesturing widely with his arms.

"Excuse me?"

"You stopped going to the pool!" Michael said in the sort of tone one might use to say *"You killed my dog!"* or *"You cheated on me!"*

James was momentarily too surprised to react. Then it sank in that Michael Lamont was standing on his front doorstep—the guy he hadn't been able to stop thinking about, the guy he'd blown off so rudely and had since regretted. He wasn't sure if he should be thrilled or freaked out, but thrilled seemed to be winning by a wide margin.

James drove his wheelchair back a foot. "Please. You have me on tenterhooks. Do come in." He stuffed down any trace of interest, using his droll voice.

"I...." Michael hesitated. "No, I really don't want to invade your private space. I just came to say—"

"*Come in.* It's cold with the door open."

"Oh. Sorry." Michael looked abashed. He stepped inside and closed the door. "Look, I didn't come here to throw myself at you again. I came because *you stopped going to the pool!* That is so wrong. And I'm so upset that you did that. And that I did that. It's really good for you to go to the pool!"

James's mouth was hanging open. He snapped it shut, feeling inexplicable mirth bubbling up inside him at the absolute absurdity of the situation.

He swallowed it down and glowered. "How is that any of your business?"

"Because it's my fault!" Michael said in frustration. "I stalked you at the pool, and now you stopped going! I just came here to tell you that I won't go there again. I promise. But I can't stand that I took that away from you. The guy at the desk said you'd been going there daily for years. If I swear that I won't go there again, will you go back? Please?" Michael looked at him beseechingly.

It was James's turn to talk, but he was busy drinking in Michael's appearance. Geez, he looked better than James's very active and overexercised imagination had remembered. He was wearing a light jacket over a rust-colored embroidered tunic shirt that looked like J.Crew and India had had a 60s love child. Very skinny jeans hugged his slender thighs. His dark hair fell swoopingly over one brow as he regarded James, apparently waiting anxiously for a verdict.

It was sort of sweet that he cared so much, really. In a strange, stalkerish way. "I'll go back," James said at last.

Michael looked relieved. He shut his eyes and took a deep breath. "Good. Because I know you probably just think I'm weird, but I really admire you, and if I screwed things up for you, I'd never forgive myself."

James cocked an eyebrow and waited with an expectant expression.

Michael looked guilty. "Bet you want to know how I found your address."

"I had wondered, yes."

"Right. Well, I went back to the pool this morning. I wanted to apologize. No—sorry. That's a lie. I wanted to see you again. This friend of mine… never mind. Anyway, you weren't there so I asked the lifeguard, and he said you hadn't been back in a few weeks! And then I felt so awful thinking I'd ruined the pool for you. So I found out from the guy at the front desk that your real name is James Gallway—sorry. Is that creepy? And then the online white pages gave me this address."

James nodded calmly. He knew he should be pissed, he did. But his body did not seem to be getting the memo. A feeling of happiness constricted his chest. It was so foreign he didn't quite know what to do with it. *Michael had cared enough to look for him. He hadn't been scared off.*

"Good to know," James said with faux calm. "Guess I should look into that online white pages thing."

"Maybe you should," Michael agreed. "Because, you know, you wouldn't want some fan just showing up."

"No, that would be bad," James quipped. But he could not for the life of him stop the smile that hijacked his mouth. He told his lips to knock it the fuck off, but they wouldn't cooperate.

Michael was watching him closely, and his brown eyes just sort of... melted. He tentatively smiled back. "You know, I'm not usually this forward. But then, it isn't normally this difficult either. You meet a guy you like, you mutually agree to lunch or a movie. You go on a date."

James swallowed hard, the smile fading as his emotions shifted into something far more desperate and wanting and a little unnerved. He wasn't sure quite how to respond, but he could feel his cheeks heat.

"Oh. You're suggesting that you're... gay?"

Michael barked a laugh. "I am decidedly gay, yes."

"Well, that's... lovely for you, but what makes you think that *I'm* gay?" He was trying to buy himself some time while his brain caught up. He was used to guarding himself, always. He didn't like the idea of a total stranger, a fan, knowing he was gay. The wheelchair was disadvantage enough.

Michael cocked an eyebrow. "You know that scene in *Hellion for Hellfire* where Sabatini is thrown into prison with that gladiator? That's the sexiest homoerotic scene I've ever read."

James shrugged. "I'm a writer. It's called imagination. I'm not a seven foot tall Draconian female either."

Michael gave a bitter huff of a laugh.

"What?"

"Oh my God. You don't make it easy on a guy, do you? You've told me to go away twice. Now you're telling me you aren't even interested in men. I guess I should take a hint, huh?" Despite the teasing tone, there was a look of defeat and embarrassment in Michael's eyes.

And suddenly, James knew that if he agreed with that sentiment, Michael would walk out the door and that would be that. And he didn't *want* Michael to stop trying. The very fact that Michael was making the effort, wanted to get to know him, was… flattering. Amazing in the most literal sense of the word. It was a gift he didn't want to refuse. Not this time.

Michael turned for the door. "I'm sorry, James. I promise I won't go to the pool, and I won't—"

"Wait." James shut his eyes and took a deep breath. "Look, I'm not good at this sort of thing. And for that, I win the 'understatement of the year' award. I'm… sorry if I've been a dick. Could we, I don't know, just get to know each other—as friends? See how that goes? Would that be acceptable to you, Mr. Lamont?"

Michael's face got a frown, but it was the sort of frown that was good, the way tears could sometimes mean joy. "Yeah," he said quietly. He took a step closer and squatted down, put his hand on the arm of the chair, not touching James, but very close. "I would love that."

It was meant as a friendly gesture, or at least James supposed it was. But as he looked down into those big brown eyes, a current went through him that seemed to wake up every longing he tried so hard to bury—for sex, yes, but also just to be with someone, to not be alone.

Fuck it. I'm in trouble, he thought, and it was frightening but weirdly exhilarating too. And his second thought was that this "let's be friends" thing was going to last about five seconds if he wasn't careful. Michael's eyes were growing heavy-lidded, and he was eying James's mouth. Jesus Christ, the guy was sex on legs. James had always appreciated attractive men, but he'd never met anyone who was capable of stirring such a strong sexual response in him before.

He used the button to wheel back a few inches, out of harm's way. "Any interest in getting breakfast?" he asked roughly.

"Yeah." Michael smiled, standing. "I'm starving."

THEY WENT to the local shopping plaza. It was one of the key attractions when James bought the house six years ago. The tiny single-level fixer-upper had been nothing exciting. It was in a neighborhood with boring suburban homes. But the house had wide doorways and was cheap enough that he'd been able to afford a handicap-accessible remodel on the kitchen and bath. And it was located three blocks from a shopping plaza with sidewalks good enough to drive his chair. The plaza had a grocery store with a pharmacy, a barbershop, a Chinese place, and a diner that served a good breakfast and burgers. James liked being able to get to those things without needing a ride. He was desperately committed to his independence.

Michael walked beside him as they made their way there. It felt weird, but only because James was so hyperaware of Michael and they were virtual strangers. Michael didn't seem at all fazed by the wheelchair.

Once seated, Michael ordered a lone egg and a cup of oatmeal and James ordered his usual ham and eggs.

"I thought you were starved?" James asked as the waitress left.

Michael shrugged. "I'm not a big eater."

James supposed he shouldn't be surprised, given how lithe Michael was. He forced his gaze away from that delicately slender torso and waistline.

"Tell me about your job," James said. "Do you work at a hospital?"

Michael picked up his coffee cup and sipped at it slowly, his eyes drifting around at the other diners. "No, I work for an in-home nursing care company called Happy At Home."

"Oh? And are you happy at Happy At Home?"

Michael's lips twitched in a smile. "I'm happy. I work with a patient named Marnie Monday through Friday. And sometimes, I fill in elsewhere when someone's out sick, so I can end up all over the Seattle area." Michael's smile grew to something so fondly sweet James decided against putting sugar in his tea. "Marnie is eighty-nine, and she's a hoot. She used to be a Burlesque dancer in New York. She has all these old postcards and photos and stuff from back in the day. She can be testy at times, but I love her to death."

"A Burlesque dancer. It must be really entertaining watching her get dressed for bed."

Michael laughed. "Well, she's not quite up to her old tricks, but yeah, she's a character." Michael told James about Marnie's outfits and how she loved to watch porn and wanted to hear about his sex life. And then he changed the subject, for which James was grateful. He really didn't want to hear about Michael's sex life. It was no doubt robust, and James didn't think he could deal with the details.

"So what's your next book?" Michael asked.

James looked around, hoping the waitress would choose that auspicious moment to arrive with their food, but she was nowhere in sight.

"*Tears From the Dragon's Eye*. It comes out next month."

Michael's face lit up. "Hey, yeah. I saw the cover for that one on Amazon. I can't wait."

James rubbed his lip with his thumb.

Michael was studying him with those big, brown eyes that seemed to see way too much. "You aren't happy with how it turned out?"

James shrugged. "The early reviews aren't exactly gushing. Well, unless your definition of 'gushing' includes getting pissed on." James tried to sound droll, like it was no big deal. But it was. It was a very big deal.

"I'm sorry." Michael frowned. "That must be so hard, getting reviewed and critiqued all the time. I'm so sensitive. I'd never be able to handle it."

"A lot of writers are sensitive. But there's not much you can do about a bad review—at least nothing that doesn't lead to addiction or arrest."

"Well, I'm looking forward to it," Michael said decisively. "I've enjoyed every single one of your books. I'll be the guy waving the five stars around on every book review site out there."

The waitress brought their plates, and they started eating. It was a great chance to let the subject go. And wow, that was a brilliant fucking idea. But James couldn't. It nagged at his mind.

"The reviewers are right, as it happens. The book isn't all that. One reviewer said my recent work was 'like a faded image of my first few books.' A malicious little dig, but not, I fear, entirely inaccurate."

He expected Michael to do the fan thing and protest or offer him placating words, but he didn't. He took a bite of his oatmeal, and he put the spoon down with finality. "No author has a hit every time. But... why do you think your recent books aren't as good as your early ones?" Michael's face was serious and really interested.

James shrugged. "Lack of inspiration? It gets hard to come up with fresh ideas." *Or maybe I just don't have it in me anymore.*

James was rarely so honest. He didn't know what possessed him to be now. He reminded himself that he didn't know Michael, and he shouldn't be blabbing stuff that could end up on the Internet. But looking at the soft light in Michael's eyes made it difficult to believe he would ever do that.

Michael picked up his coffee cup and swirled it while he studied James. "Well, an uninspired J.C. Guise is better than ninety-five percent of all science fiction writers out there, so I don't think you're in any danger of losing your readership. But... it's true that your early books were ridiculously brilliant."

"*Troubadour Turncoat* was born in desperation," James admitted. "I wrote it when I was eighteen. I had pneumonia that year, and I was sick in bed for months. I was so bored I couldn't stand myself, so I started to write."

"Really?" Michael leaned forward with interest.

"It was the only way I could get the fuck out of that room. The things I daydreamed then... It's hard to conjure up that kind of wonder now." He forced a laugh. "Maybe I'm just getting old. It happens."

Wonder. That was it, wasn't it? Wonder and hope. James had lost that sense of itching anticipation, of *wanting life*. He'd wanted it so badly that year, lying in that bed, thinking he might well die before he'd ever really lived. His imagination had soared with dreams. But the years since had taught him that fantasies don't happen and the wondrous doesn't exist and life... life just drags on. Now he couldn't find his way to having that kind of faith and excitement about the future.

"Hmmm." Michael was watching him with narrowed eyes.

"What?" James asked.

"Just making plans," Michael said neutrally. He scooped up another spoonful of oatmeal.

"Ah. Conquering the universe sorts of plans or getting your laundry done tonight sort of plans?"

"That's for me to know and you to find out."

"How mysterious, Mr. Lamont," James commented laconically.

Michael gave him a lazy wink and grinned.

~11~

ON FRIDAY, Michael called James and asked if he was busy Sunday. It wasn't surprising that James wasn't, but he surprised himself by admitting it. Michael asked if he'd be up for a car trip with a two-hour drive each way.

"Where did you have in mind?" James asked. The idea of a drive was seductive. It had been at least a year since he'd gotten out of Seattle. But he was leery about getting into a bad situation with the wheelchair, and he especially didn't want to embarrass himself in front of Michael Lamont.

"Trust me?" Michael asked.

James gave it a moment's thought. "No, not really."

Michael gave an offended gasp. "Well, that's honest. What if I told you that I checked out the place where we're going and it's handicap accessible? I think you'll really, *really* like it."

James was torn between caution and a strong pull to see Michael again. "It's not easy being green," he said, as a way of explaining his hesitation.

"I told you, I've got it covered. Double dog dare ya."

"Bastard. I'm in."

ON SUNDAY, Michael picked James up at 8:00 a.m., and they headed south on I-5.

"It's supposed to be a nice day," Michael said. There was a flush of excitement on his cheek. "Seventy-eight and sunny."

"Yeah, I saw that. In fact, I have weather alerts delivered directly into my skull."

"Do you now?"

"Yes," James said seriously. "So how was your week?"

"Hmm. Do you want the recap with or without the bodily fluids?"

"You're talking about nursing, I hope?"

Michael laughed. "Oh, I wouldn't bore you with *my* bodily fluids. God forbid."

"Then with, please. The day is far too pleasant. I could use a little gore."

"Well, I had to do a morning shift with this older gentleman. Like ninety years old. And I had to change his IV because his vein had collapsed. You with me so far?"

"Fascinating. Pray continue."

So Michael did, explaining all the places he had to try on the man's body to find a viable vein. And James found it satisfyingly gross.

"So tell me about the book you're working on now?" Michael asked, once they had exhausted bodily fluids.

James frowned a bit and looked out the window. "*Star Dance*. It's the third of the Star trilogy."

"Oh, yeah!" Michael's face lit up. "I read the first two. So hit me with some spoilers. What happens when Emeril gets back to his home planet?"

It was a chance to get some feedback from someone who knew the series, and James was more than happy to comply. He explained the ending he had in mind, with Emeril leading a rebellion and becoming sovereign of Abakash.

"It's a bit predictable," he admitted. "But I haven't been able to come up with anything better."

Michael looked thoughtful, but he didn't say anything.

"What?" James prompted.

"Nothing. I'm sure it'll be awesome."

James sighed. "Speak, outrider, or I will be forced to torment you."

"Oh?" Michael looked intrigued. "How would that go exactly?"

"The dreaded tickle torture, outlawed in five galaxies."

Michael gave him a slow, sexy smile. "Oooh, baby. I'm game."

James felt a flush of arousal. He looked out the window, wishing he could hide the color he felt burning his cheeks. "I'm on to your tricks. You're trying to distract me. Tell me what you were thinking."

Michael sighed. "Okay, so this is really random, and I'm not a writer so it probably sucks ass but... I was thinking it would be cool if Emeril was offered the crown of Abakash but he decided instead to give it to Doran and went off to explore the galaxy. My favorite part of *Star Child* was how much Emeril loved traveling, his sense of joy at seeing new worlds. It would be kinda disappointing to think of him stuck in one place with a bunch of paperwork or something. And Doran is perfect for it, all noble and grave. I dunno. I mean, they're your characters."

"That doesn't... entirely reek," James grudgingly admitted. In fact, the more he thought about it, the more the idea grabbed hold. "Yeah. That could be a nice twist right at the end. Would you seriously be okay if I used it?"

"God, I'd be thrilled!" Michael said enthusiastically.

James grunted. "Have you ever thought about writing?"

"Me? Oh, no. I'm a committed consumer. It's just that I've read so much sci-fi. When I was in high school, I read all the time. It was an escape valve, you know? I even read about fifty of those *Star Trek* books. I dream in Klingon."

"You might not want to admit that out loud."

"I think it's best for people to know the worst about each other, don't you?" Michael said, batting his eyelashes. "I still read a lot of sci-fi, but these days I also read, well, romance."

James guffawed. "Really? Like roguish lords and buxom serving wenches, that kind of romance?"

Michael hesitated, biting his lower lip in a move that was far too awkwardly endearing. "Um, more like cowboy foreman falls for runaway gay boy sorts of romances. And a little BDSM."

"Oh-ho! *I* see. Now I've got your number."

Michael looked embarrassed. "No, I don't really... I mean in real life, I don't do that. I read BDSM once in a while, but honestly, I prefer the sweeter romances."

"Sure. I believe you. Bondage Ben."

"Stop it." Michael laughed.

"Cracky McCracken." James flicked an invisible whip.

"I am not! I'm more like Nick Normal."

"Nipple Clamp Ned."

"Vince Vanilla."

James gave him a dubious look and snorted. "I doubt that very much."

Michael shrugged with an evil little smile. "Well, maybe not entirely vanilla."

James swallowed. "So... what do you like about sweet romances?"

Michael thought about it. "I like the idea of two characters who are both caught up in their own lives and with their own problems and seeing how they meet and how they figure out they're meant to be together. I dunno. It sort of fascinates me, I guess. I mean, how do you meet *the one*, and how do you know that you have?"

James made a face. "I don't really think about it."

"You don't?"

James looked at Michael, wondering how he could be so dense. "Not likely, is it?"

But Michael shot him a troubled glance with those big brown eyes. "Why isn't it likely?"

James got a flash of annoyance so he looked out the window at the passing pine trees. They were off the freeway now, and the scenery was lushly wooded. Pretending to be interested in the view was a good excuse to not answer. He knew Michael wasn't being merely obtuse, that he meant it sincerely, but it still hurt.

"So sci-fi... what other authors do you like?" he asked, changing the subject.

IT TURNED out Michael's secret destination was Mt. Rainier. As they wound up the mountain on curvy roads, the views mesmerized James.

Sometimes, the road dropped away steeply, seemingly just a few feet outside his passenger seat window, revealing the tops of pine trees and deep gullies. It was stunning.

"Does this make you nervous?" Michael asked.

James looked at the sheer drop and realized it might make some people anxious. But not him. It reminded him of being in a plane or—a spaceship, that sense of exhilaration and freedom, of slipping the surly bonds of Earth.

"I love it," he said honestly. "I've never been here before."

"Never?"

James shook his head.

"Wow. You need to get out more."

Tell me about it. It did feel good to get away from home and see something new. It felt... invigorating. He could feel some of the cobwebs in his mind blowing away.

They parked at Paradise. It was crowded with cars and visitors. Michael pulled in near a set of restrooms, which, James was relieved to see had a blue handicapped accessible sign on them.

"We should probably hit the restrooms first. They have a paved trail we can take to the lower meadows. I brought stuff for a picnic."

James looked in the backseat where an overstuffed backpack awaited. "You're starting to worry me. Rainier, a picnic.... How am I supposed to compete when it's my turn? I've got pizza and TV. That's what I've got."

James was joking, but as soon as he said it, he wished he could take it back. There was no reason to assume Michael would want to hang out again.

But Michael laughed. "Pizza and TV sound perfect to me. Also Heinlein and underwear."

"What?"

"Never mind. Let's go."

USING THE restroom was something James had worried about ever since Michael invited him for an outing. But it turned out to be fine.

James kept a backpack hooked on the back of his wheelchair, and it contained a number of essential items. One was a plastic urinal with a screw cap. But he would rather die than use it in front of Michael. Fortunately, the restroom had a handicapped stall that he could wheel into and shut the door.

As a man, it was not very easy to pee while sitting on a toilet, and even with the bars in the handicapped stalls, it wasn't all that convenient to get in and out of the chair. He could do it when he absolutely had to, but it was a bit of overkill for peeing. Neither could he stand to pee like any other man. The small urinal he carried was basically a clear plastic jug with a thin neck and cap. It allowed him to pee in his chair. He did that, then poured it into the toilet and flushed it down. Normally, he would rinse the urinal in the sink afterward, but he wasn't going to do that in a public restroom, especially not with Michael anywhere in the vicinity, so he just screwed the lid back on tight and put it in his backpack.

Michael was waiting for him, leaning up against the wall. James felt a flash of disappointment that he had missed Michael using the regular urinals, and perhaps a chance to get a covert glimpse. He thought it and then immediately kicked himself in the ass for thinking it. He made his living from his imagination, but sometimes, it got a little too randy for his own good. He rolled over to the handicap sink and washed his hands.

"Ready to go?" Michael asked.

"Lay on, MacDuff."

A ranger pointed out the accessible trail into the lower meadows. They went up the trail for a quarter mile or so. There was a slight incline, and Michael teased James about taking it easy by using the electric chair, so James leaned back, put one arm over the backrest, and drove with his other thumb like he was cruising in some big-ass old car.

"You're just begging for me to get in your lap, you know," Michael said coyly. Flirting, it was called. Damned if it wasn't.

"The motor is only certified for five pounds more than me," James deadpanned.

Michael snorted.

"So I have to be very careful whilst grocery shopping. Or bowling."

Michael just laughed.

They found a good spot, and James watched as Michael unzipped the ponderously pregnant backpack he carried and took out a blanket, spread it, and then removed a couple of paper-wrapped sandwiches and a few small bags of Sunchips and cans of soda.

"I wanted to bring wine, but I'm honestly such a lightweight. I figured driving down the mountain sloshed was not a good idea."

"I appreciate that. I always hoped that when my time came, I could die in battle." James rolled the chair as close to the blanket as he could and looked at it—and suddenly felt a bit ill. He could crawl out of the chair onto the ground. But it wouldn't be graceful or pretty. He wondered if he could get away with staying in the chair.

"Can I give you a hand?" Michael asked.

"Um...."

"I'm stronger than I look." Michael leaned over the chair and put his hands on the arms. Inches away, he stared into James's eyes.

James's protests, which were about to come out fast and furious, disintegrated on his tongue. Fuck. Michael's baby browns reached right down inside him and flipped the switch on his inner furnace, just like that. *Whoosh.*

"Besides, I *am* a nurse," Michael said. He made a funny face, crossing his eyes and sticking out his tongue, which immediately took the sting out of it. James laughed despite himself.

"Uh... I... suppose?"

James sounded exactly as hesitant as he meant to, but Michael ignored that. In a flash, he ran his hands under James's arms and around his back and pulled James up. For a brief moment, James was on his feet, chest to chest with Michael, feeling the solid warmth of him against his front. He was taller than Michael by several inches, and Michael's gaze seemed to be fixed on his lips. Michael hesitated a few seconds longer than he should have, long enough to make heat flush James's body, but then he turned and lowered James gently to the blanket and released him.

James steadied himself with his hands, his pulse racing. God, that had been way, way, *way* too much—too embarrassing, too feeble, too much contact and… it had felt too good to be pressed against Michael even for a moment. So good he couldn't even be mad about it the way he wanted to be. God, he was such a pathetic virgin.

"So… what's for lunch?" he asked, refusing to look at Michael.

Michael sat cross-legged on the blanket and unwrapped the two brown parcels. "For sandwiches, I've got ham and lettuce or cream cheese and veg. I wasn't sure what you liked."

"Either is fine."

Michael rolled his eyes. "Oh, no. You must choose, padawan."

James pulled a coin from his pocket. "Let's leave it in the hands of the gods. Shall heads be cheese? Cream cheese, that is?"

Michael chuckled. "Naturally. And that leaves tails for meat. That works."

"You're sick."

"You have no idea. Flip it."

James did, caught it, and smacked it on his forearm. "Tails. I'll take the ham, please."

Michael waggled his eyebrows. "I wasn't hoping you'd take my—"

"Don't say it."

"—ham sandwich," Michael finished innocently. "What?"

James rolled his eyes. "That was way harder than it should have been."

"That's what he said."

James took half the veg-and-cream-cheese sandwich and stuffed it into Michael's mouth to shut him up. Michael grinned around the bread and then ate with an air of absolute virtue.

They ate in silence for a bit, and James started to calm down enough to really take in the view. He could not believe how stunningly beautiful the place was, with the white peak of Rainier *right there* against the deep blue sky, the purple and pink wild flowers, green pines, and stunning view over the rolling valley and distant jagged peaks. It was hard to believe it was real. It made him feel happy to be alive in a way he hadn't felt in a very, very long time. And he was here with a beautiful boy, too. Even if this was as good as his life could get, he'd sign the contract with the devil right now.

"Is it a spinal injury?" Michael asked softly, breaking the peaceful quiet. "If you don't want to talk about it, that's fine."

Weirdly enough, James found he didn't mind talking about it. Maybe it was looking at all this majesty, at the heights nature could achieve. It gave him a sense of being just one more tiny instance of life on this earth, imperfect but created nonetheless. It gave him a little bit of distance from which to view himself as a curiosity.

"It was polio."

"Wow. Really." Michael sounded surprised and sad. "I didn't know people our age got polio anymore."

James cleared his throat. "My mother was a free spirit, a hippie. She loved to travel. I was born in Tibet, actually. She specifically went there to have me due to the spiritualism of the place, I guess. She says I was conceived in Spain, or it might have been Majorca. She wasn't real sure. I never knew my father."

"She sounds like quite a character."

"Yup." James fiddled with his soda can. "She traveled with me papoose style when I was a baby. We hung out in Austria for a bit, on a small commune. Then when I was five, she took me to India."

"Oh." The weight in Michael's voice said it all.

"Yup. That's where I got sick."

Michael scooted closer and leaned a forearm on James's shoulder. It was something James maybe would have objected to, normally. But sitting in the sun in this beautiful spot talking, it just felt sort of companionable—and comforting without being pitying. James let him keep it here.

"Both of your legs were paralyzed by the polio virus?"

James nodded. "Polio is weird, you know? Some people who get it don't end up with anything worse than flu symptoms. Others spend their lives in an iron lung. When it infects the spinal cord, the damage can end up in different parts of the body, like a bloody roll of the cosmic die," he finished dryly. "Someone once told me I was lucky, but I'm disinclined to feel fortunate."

"Did you and your mom come back to the States afterward?"

James finished the drink and crushed the can. "Yeah, we did. Uh, maybe now would be a good time to say 'I don't want to talk about it.'"

MICHAEL WANTED to push, to learn more about James's family, to hear about what it was like growing up with his disability. But James had suddenly gone stiff, his voice remote, and Michael knew any more questions would be unwelcome. So he took a couple of breaths to let his curiosity go.

Without really thinking about it, he took James's hand. It was a sort of *I'm sorry if I pushed* and, Michael hoped, *I'm sorry about the polio too, but it doesn't matter to me*. Whatever message James chose to read into it, he didn't pull his hand away. But he did turn his head aside, as if he didn't want Michael to see his face.

There was something so vulnerable about James in that moment. His guard was down, and Michael saw it, saw the bottomless well of loneliness that James hid behind his mercurial mask. Michael's heart responded immediately, swelling with compassion and practically leaping out of his chest onto James's lap. The man was so fucking intelligent and so... good at the core, the living heart of him that beat in his writing. Michael could see his shining soul, even if James wore a prickly shell to disguise it. He deserved so much. And Michael wanted to be the one to give it to him, to ease that loneliness, more than he'd ever wanted anything in his life.

Wow.

Michael cleared his throat. "So tell me more about *Troubadour Turncoat*. You said you were sick with pneumonia when you wrote it?"

James sighed, but when he spoke, his voice was deep and steady. "I was living in a care facility at the time. I was sick for about a year and couldn't leave my room. The woman who ran the place, Felicia, she'd sit with me for an hour every morning, and I'd tell her the story I was making up in my head. She's the one who convinced me to start writing it down. She helped me edit it and find an agent, too."

Michael wanted to ask where James's mother had been at the time, but he refrained. "Felicia sounds like a remarkable person."

"She is."

Michael felt the warmth of James's hand in his and wished he never had to let go. Like a total dweeb, he fucking *treasured* the feel of it. James's hand was much larger than Michael's. Where Michael was slightly built, James had a tall, rangy, almost Lincoln-esque quality to his body—lean but with broad shoulders, big head, big hands, big feet... yeah, the thought did nothing to calm Michael's libido. The flashes of vulnerability he saw in James were an interesting contradiction to his inherent strength—because James was strong. In fact, something about his toughness made Michael feel... safe. James felt *dependable*, like he'd been through hell and lived and if shit came down, he knew how to deal.

All Michael had to do was figure out how to get under that shell so that he could be safe in there with James instead of being shut out. Holding hands was a good place to start.

~12~

MICHAEL CAREFULLY stroked flaming red paint onto the nail of Marnie's index finger and considered it critically. "Good color," he decided.

"Red lips and red nails, cock your hip, it never fails." Marnie winked.

Michael laughed. "I've never heard that one."

"That's because I made it up—long ago. But it's true."

"Not sure it would work for me, but I hear ya."

He took her middle finger and applied the brush again.

They were on Marnie's couch. She was wearing a scarlet red V-necked sweater today with black leggings, and she'd insisted on getting her nails done to match. Michael didn't mind. It was an easy enough way to pass the time with her, and it made her feel good about herself.

"So did you ever go after that writer fellow?"

"I did," Michael said, smiling.

"Oh, ho! That's a cat that ate the canary look. Tell Marnie all about it."

"Well… it's not what you think. He said he wasn't gay—well, what he said was 'what makes you think I'm gay?' *He is*," Michael leaned in and whispered the last to Marnie confidently. "But he's scared of getting hurt, so he said he just wants to be friends. That's fine."

"Doesn't sound fine to me," Marnie pouted.

Michael paused and blew on her wet fingernails. "Actually, it's kind of nice. I have a slight tendency to rush into sex."

Marnie blinked at him for a moment, then cackled outrageously. Michael rolled his eyes and waited for her laughter to subside.

"Oh, Michael, you are a cutup!" Marnie chortled.

"Hey now. I'm not *that* easy. Of course, with my surrogacy clients, it's all about sex. What I'm trying to say is, it's nice to just be friends with a man for a change. We have fun."

Marnie made a face. "Tell me you don't play cards. Or maybe throw horseshoes when your arthritis isn't acting up?"

Michael laughed. "Nope, no cards or horseshoes. I took him to Mt. Rainier for a picnic, we've been to the movies once, and I've been to his house once for pizza and TV. The first four episodes of *Babylon 5*. It was a marathon."

Marnie made a "pfft!" sound. "You're far too young and nubile to waste a day staring at the boob tube when you could be schtupping your brains out. The man needs some tender loving care."

"We'll get there." Michael smiled sadly. "At least I hope so. James has... trust issues. And self-image issues."

"Oh? Sounds like one of your surrogacy clients," Marnie said, looking at Michael shrewdly.

Michael frowned. "No, it's not like that at all. James is brilliant, and strong, and very proud. He's just... with the polio, I don't think he's trusted anyone enough to be intimate, or at least, not many people. He needs time to get to know me. Something happened in his past... I'm not sure what it is, but it really screwed with his head."

"Hmm. Have you told him that you're a sex surrogate?"

Michael felt a stab of fear. "No. I'm done with this hand."

He got up and rearranged the pillows so he could sit on the other side of Marnie. He started painting her left index finger.

"You should tell him about the surrogacy," Marnie insisted, never one to be deterred. "It might make him more comfortable about being with you in a sexual way."

Michael gave a bitter chuckle. "It really wouldn't."

"Why not?"

Michael frowned and blew on her nail. "God, I told you how he reacted when he found out I was a nurse. I'm afraid that if I tell him about the surrogacy, he's going to see it as some sort of personal insult.

You know like...." Michael hated to say it. His mouth twisted. "I dunno. Some people think I have a handicap fetish or something."

"Who thinks so?" Marnie said, perking right up.

Michael shrugged. "My friend, Sammie, for one. He's always trying to drag me out clubbing. He's really into looks, and he doesn't understand what I do at all. He thinks it's gotta be a kink."

Marnie pursed her lips. "Well.... Don't take this the wrong way, but *don't* you have a fetish like that?"

"No!" Michael was indignant. "God, no."

"It's okay, you know. Kinky is as kinky does. I have a few embarrassing secrets locked away in my old bag of tricks." She chuckled with a salacious glint in her eye.

"Oh? Do tell?"

"Never you mind. We're talking about *your* fetishes, thank you very much. Mine are old and permanently retired, and there's no one to give a flying fig. You, on the other hand, have your young gentleman to think about. And watch that polish. You're getting sloppy."

Michael sighed. "Sorry. Well, no matter what anyone thinks, I don't have a fetish for stumps or scars or anything like that."

Marnie waited, batting her eyes at him expectantly.

"I just... I really, really like to be needed. Sexually, I mean. By someone who otherwise hasn't had a lot of sex or couldn't or...."

"Ah, it's more of a virgin thing," Marnie said knowingly.

Michael shrugged. "Maybe a little. It's amazing to be someone's first time. But it's more than that. It's about being special. I'm someone who can bring lonely people pleasure, when most other people wouldn't or couldn't. I make them feel better, give them a few minutes of joy, of forgetting their troubles, of feeling alive, feeling touchable, feeling wanted. Just knowing how much they need and want me.... That really makes me... hot." He could feel his cheeks getting warm and knew he was blushing. This wasn't something he talked about, and it was hard to put into words. "I dunno. Some good-looking guy at a gay bar—I'm just another hole to him. It's not about *me*. But when someone really needs *me*, and I'm the only one who can give them pleasure... that's sexy as hell."

Marnie was watching him shrewdly. She looked like a crow eyeing a shiny object in the grass. "Someone hurt you pretty bad when you were young, didn't they, sweet boy?"

Michael felt the ghost of a mostly forgotten pain, but he shook his head. "The usual childhood bullies. No more than any other offbeat kid."

"Uh-huh. You can't fool me. The kind of compassion you have is like a diamond—won under tremendous pressure. Well, whatever fire forged you, you *are* special. You're a jewel."

Michael smiled and gave her a quick hug, careful not to get polish on her. "Thank you, Marnie. You're sweet."

"So you're afraid if you tell James about your surrogacy work, he'll think you like him because you've got a handicap fetish?"

Michael nodded miserably. "He's very proud. He doesn't want to be thought of as a handicapped man. And I *don't* think of him like that. But even if he didn't dump me for that reason, he'd probably decide he didn't want a relationship just because I'm a surrogate. I've never met a guy who could handle it. It's probably for the best that we're just friends."

But though Michael could *say* that, he couldn't *feel* it.

Marnie wasn't fooled. "Oh, honey!" She grabbed at his hand with her right and squeezed it, nail polish brush and all.

"You're going to get nail polish on those pretty leggings," Michael warned her.

"Pfft! I don't care."

"And you'll mess up your manicure."

That she did care about, because she let go. "You're too hard on yourself, Michael. Let me tell you about true love." She snuggled a little closer. "When it's true love, you just can't give each other up, no matter how mad you get at the other person. Don't you know that?"

Michael shook his head.

"I was really in love with a boy named David when I was in my early twenties. He had this ex-girlfriend who was always hounding him. And he was such a nice guy, he wouldn't just tell her to get lost, no matter how much he and I fought about it."

"One time after a big fight, I snuck away while he was at work, and I took a train home to visit my folks. I left him a note. I was determined that was it, a clean break. I was never going to see him again."

"Well, by the time I got to my parent's house, I felt like I was dying. For four days, I ignored his calls all the while bleeding inside. Until I finally realized—I couldn't do it. I'd left plenty of boys and gotten myself over it, but I couldn't leave David. It wasn't a choice, I just... couldn't."

Michael smiled. "I'm not sure I've ever felt like that. I know no one's ever felt like that about me."

"Well, if Mr. Writer is *the one*, then he will understand about the surrogacy. And if he doesn't, and you can both walk away, then it wasn't meant to be."

It did make Michael feel a little better. He liked James so much. The depth of what he felt was almost surreal. He wanted to be the one to give James a full life, inspire his dreams and his writing. And that was maybe a foolish, unrealistic fantasy, but he thought it was not an entirely selfish one.

He just needed time to win James's trust and his heart. "When we know each other better, I'll tell him. Once it's not so fragile."

Marnie didn't look convinced, but she patted his hand. "Oh, my dear, you know I wish you all the love in the world."

~13~

ON THE first day of April, James got an e-mail from SFFA with the subject line "Millennial Awards." Holding his breath, James opened it.

Congratulations. Troubadour Turncoat has been nominated for this year's SFFA Millennial Award.

James whooped and did a happy dance with his fists. *Oh, thank God. Thank you, God.*

He scanned the rest of the e-mail eagerly. *Oh.* With a knot in his stomach, he called Amanda.

"That's fabulous, James! Congratulations!"

"Yes, but...."

"But what?" Amanda sounded leery. "If you tell me you're less than thrilled, I'm going to smack you, then I'm going to take away your crayons."

"I am thrilled," James said mechanically.

"Good."

"There's just one small wrinkle—they sent me a form for seating at the banquet."

"Yes. And?"

James could feel his gut twisting. "And... I don't actually have to go to that, right?"

"James," Amanda said with a tone of conjuring up great forbearance. "I thought you understood—that was the whole point of that book signing we did. Not only do you need to go, you need to send that form back in as soon as possible, making it clear that yes, you will attend. With bells on."

"But people accept awards all the time in absentia. We could record a little thank you speech and—"

"Let me explain this to you very clearly." Amanda's tone was all business. "This is not the Academy Awards and you are not Brad Pitt. They televise this little award show, and whether it's fair or not, it makes for bad TV if the award winner is not there. If you don't say you're going, I can guarantee you your chances of winning will fall from one in five to cold day in hell."

James shut his eyes, gripping his cell phone so hard his fingers hurt. *Fuck.*

"What's the big deal anyway? You already revealed yourself at that book signing."

Yes, but that book signing wasn't televised. And it didn't have me sitting there with every big author and publisher in this business, sitting where they could all stare at me and whisper. Did you see J.C. Guise? He's a worthless cripple.

"James!" Amanda said.

"Yes. I'm here," he croaked.

"Promise me you'll fill out that form and return it today." There was a stern warning in Amanda's voice.

"Absolutely," James lied.

"We need this award."

"Yup, we do." James hung up.

He opened the e-mail and looked at the attached pdf form. "Will you be attending the award ceremony? Will you be bringing a guest? Name of guest? Chicken, fish, or vegetarian entree?"

Humiliation, scorn, or ridicule?

James closed the blank form, all the excitement about being nominated replaced with a terrible bleakness.

~14~

EXCERPT FROM Sentimental Cyanide *by J.C. Guise*

When the box opened, Lamb was in a penthouse decorated entirely in white with a wall of glass that looked out over a huge city.

"Stand up and take off your clothes."

The man who gave the order was approximately fifty years old. He had a very hard face, and he didn't look in Lamb's eyes. Lamb obeyed, and the man examined him everywhere with his eyes and fingers.

"Nice," the man said appreciatively as he ran his hands over Lamb's rear. "They've made some improvements since my last model." The man was talking, but he didn't seem to really be talking to Lamb. It was a little confusing. "On your knees."

Lamb knew what was expected of him, and he did it as well as he possibly could. But after the man ejaculated into Lamb's mouth, he just sighed and said. "Good. Now follow me."

The man led Lamb down a hallway to a door and opened it. It was a small closet.

"You stay in here when you're not needed," the man said.

When Lamb didn't move forward at once, the man took his arm and pushed him inside. Lamb felt a moment of panic. He didn't want to be shut in the closet. He searched his memory bank for some way to make a connection to his new owner.

"Wait! What shall I call you?" he asked. He added a sweet little smile that was supposed to be irresistible.

The man stared at him for a moment. "I don't expect you to talk. But if you have to address me, it's Feign."

He closed the door.

Lamb hated the closet. Hated it. *Time passed with excruciating slowness. He spent hours wondering what he was doing wrong. No matter what flirt routines he tried, Feign never looked in his eyes and never took him out for cuddles or kisses.*

Lamb longed for cuddles and kisses. He longed to sit on the couch and hold hands or be at the table with his other half and drink a cup of tea. His body didn't need food or drink, but he loved the idea of doing something so... human.

Lamb remembered that Feign had said "I don't expect you to talk," but after a few weeks, Lamb decided to try words. He spent hours in the closet planning it out. The next time Feign wanted sex, he pushed Lamb onto his bed and had Lamb fellate him and then get on all fours so he could be fucked.

When Feign was done, he flopped back on the bed. "Go back to the closet, Lamb."

Lamb fought his instinct to obey. He mimicked weakness and lay down next to Feign. He put his hand on Feign's bare chest.

"I love you," Lamb said.

Feign looked at him in bewilderment. "What?"

"I love you. Can I sleep here with you?" Lamb looked up from under his lashes coyly, flirt routine #38.

"What the fuck? Get the fuck back to the closet!" Feign said angrily.

Lamb felt cold dread. "Yes, Feign. I'm sorry."

As he went back to his prison, Feign's two dogs jumped up on the bed and curled up to sleep. Lamb felt a deep aching pain in his stomach and chest that he had never felt before. In the closet, Lamb discovered that he was capable of tears.

"ARE YOU serious? You'll let me have him tonight?" The man with the greasy red hair was looking Lamb up and down with greed.

"Yeah. They're coming to pick him up tomorrow for a recall so I won't have to think about your jizz and shit. Goddamned factory found out some nutso engineer gave him the wrong programming. Crazy

emotional stuff. I wondered why he was always mooning around depressed. It's ridiculous. They're bringing me a new one, so, hey, happy birthday or what-the-fuck ever. Have at it. Just don't damage him. They might charge me for that."

The man ran his hands over Lamb's chest. He wore a pair of loose sleep pants when Feign wasn't using him, but he'd never been given a shirt.

"Any chance they'd sell him to me cheap? He's a beaut."

Feign laughed. "Even cheap, you couldn't afford him. Anyway, they'll probably refurbish him and put him back on the market. Believe me, you don't want him like this. He's a fucking sex toy, and he practically makes me feel guilty for keeping him in the closet."

The man laughed. "No shit. You feel guilty? That I'd like to see." He tugged down Lamb's pants and exposed him. "Wow. Nice."

"Ain't it, though?" Feign grew more interested. "I got the uncut model. What a plump little morsel it is too. 'Course, it's not my thing to bottom, but it's nice to look at. Get hard, Lamb."

It took Lamb a moment to recognize the command. He could usually force an erection with ease, but at the moment, he felt nothing but fear and confusion. He tried to think of something pleasant. He pictured being on his knees while the man above him looked down into his eyes with a smile and petted his hair.

"Oh, yeah!" the red-haired man said. "Phew. Perfect cock."

"Feels real too. My new bot will look just like this one only it won't be all stupid."

"Gee, thanks, Feign. Fuck. That's hot. I really wanna get him home."

"Just have him back here by eight sharp. I'm not sure what time they're gonna come get him. And remember, you owe me for this."

The man led Lamb from Feign's high-rise apartment. They stood on the street in the rain.

"Wait here. I'll get a taxi. Don't move." The man seemed very eager to find transportation. He walked into the street and held up his arm.

Wrong programming.

So you can love me as much as I'm going to love you, *Winston had said.*

Recall. Refurbish.

Lamb didn't want to be a toy. How much of his mind would they have to take away for him to be happy to live in a closet? He was not a broom.

He made sure the man was looking the other way, and then he melted into the crowd.

~15~

THAT WEEKEND, Michael picked James up on Saturday and they went to a street art fair in Bellevue. James had a tendency to suggest takeout and movies at his place when they got together, and Michael had a tendency to want to go somewhere. After several such outings, which James agreed to under duress, he had to admit that it was nice to get out of the house, and Michael always made things easy.

James had expected the street fair to be crowded and difficult to maneuver, but people were respectful of the wheelchair and Michael walked in front of him. They made their way from booth to booth with little trouble, examining the wares and making wisecracks.

Michael laughed at everything James said, which made James try harder to be witty. It was addictive making Michael laugh. It was addictive having Michael look at him as if he was the cleverest person ever, as if he delighted in James's company.

James had never had a friend like Michael Lamont. He was easy to be with. He was so… positive all the time, smiling easily and often. He had a kind of light—gentle and sweet, yet it could turn smoldering in the space between one heartbeat and the next. Being with him was like stepping into a warm cabin after having been lost in the snowy woods. The weird thing was, James hadn't even been aware that he'd been out there in the cold until he felt Michael's heat.

Part of what made him easy to be with, despite his uncomfortable level of attractiveness, was that Michael didn't take himself too seriously. He was particularly fond of taking selfies of the two of them, usually while pulling some ridiculous face. James had a hard time being so unguarded, but Michael coaxed it out of him. He'd e-mailed James one such picture of the two of them taken at the diner. Michael had his arm around James's shoulders, and he was trying to touch his own chin with his tongue while he crossed his eyes. James was making a silly grimace.

James made the photo the background on his cell phone and found himself staring at it frequently.

Who was the grimacing man in the photo, being silly, goofing off with a friend? He did not recognize that man as James Gallway, the acerbic recluse. The tectonic plates in his life were shifting, and he couldn't see where it would end—whether a new paradise lay on the other side or whether the landscape of his life would be buried like Atlantis, under the waves of disaster.

But nothing, not even that worry, could make him wish it would stop.

JAMES HELD a few places at a picnic table while Michael got their fair food—a steak sandwich for James and a shrimp-and-veggie kabob for Michael. He brought their plates over and sat down, looking far too dignified considering the fact that he wore a blue balloon hat smooshed over his dark locks.

"Are you picking up reception on that thing?" James remarked dryly as Michael sat down.

"I thought those were tin hats."

"Tin hats are for picking up signals from space. Balloon hats get signals from the inner core of the Earth," James said seriously.

"Huh. I wondered where all the demonic laughter was coming from," Michael said nonchalantly.

James was going to make a smart remark, but then he looked down at his steak sandwich and was reminded, from out of nowhere, about the Millennial Awards dinner. He hadn't yet sent in his banquet form, and Amanda was harassing him daily about it. Suddenly, he didn't have much of a sense of humor—or an appetite.

"What's up?" Michael asked. James looked up to find those baby browns studying him. "You've had something on your mind all day."

"Haven't," James protested with a challengingly raised eyebrow. He thought he'd hidden it well.

"Have." Michael stole a small piece of James's shaved steak and put it in his mouth. And damn, that was weirdly arousing. "Out with it, Mr. Gallway, or face the tickle torture."

James grumped, but he didn't try to joke his way out of it. He couldn't summon the mood. He sighed. "*Troubadour Turncoat* is up for a Millennial Award."

"Oh my God, James, that's fantastic!" Michael grinned broadly. "Congratulations!"

"Yes. Woo-hoo. Except for the part where I have to attend the awards banquet if I'm to have a prayer of winning."

Michael studied his face. "Don't you want to go?"

James now regretted having been honest. He couldn't look at Michael's pretty, perfectly normal person and admit aloud that he was so ashamed of his legs that he couldn't face the TV cameras or his peers.

So he just shrugged and took a bite of his sandwich. His stomach clenched with nerves, as if unwilling to receive it.

Michael played with his cup. "I could help you shop for an outfit. We could make you look so hot."

James gave him an incredulous look. "Your optimism fascinates me, Mr. Lamont."

"Seriously." Michael narrowed his eyes and looked him up and down. "I'm thinking a really sharp suit, something edgy like dark maroon or midnight blue silk with a thin black tie. We could probably rent one from a tuxedo shop. A tight shirt underneath—you have an amazing torso."

James gave him a doubtful look, even though he felt a little thrill at the compliment. "Hmm. I appreciate the suggestion, but... I remain unconvinced."

Michael tapped his chin thoughtfully and then got a devious glint in his eye. "I've got it."

"I'm all ears."

"What if I go with you as your guest? I'll wear all black— something skin tight. Maybe leather pants and a long-sleeved sweater. Ooh! And a choker collar! You can call me Dieter. And I'll stay by your side all night and call you 'sir'! And you can order me to get your drinks and stuff."

James laughed. "That's brilliant."

"Seriously! And you have to wear big shades, all night long. And… let's see, carry something leather—oh! A small riding crop. It'd be awesome."

James could picture it. A slow smile spread over his face. It did actually, sound like fun. It would give all those big wigs something to gossip about—something besides his legs. It was bold and cheeky and Andy Warhol weird.

After all, if you can't hide, you might as well be all the way the fuck out there.

"You'd really do that?" he asked.

"Are you kidding?" Michael gushed. "I'd be in pig heaven going to an award dinner with all those sci-fi writers! Even better, I'd be with the very best one."

James snorted. "You don't need to kiss my ass. I know you really just want to meet Neil Gaiman."

Michael's mouth dropped open. "Oh, shit! Will he be there?"

"He went last year. Change your mind about playing my sycophant?"

"Uh-uh! I can't wait. We can practice when we get back to yours if you want." Michael's smile and his eyes warmed in an unmistakable invitation. He let his eyes travel down James's body, and then he winked rather lewdly.

James's mouth went dry, and yes, there his body went again, responding as if Michael had wriggled right down inside him and flipped all the switches on his electrical panel. He needed to change the subject.

"Then let's do it." He pulled out his cell phone and brought up his e-mail. He might as well do this before he changed his mind. It would get Amanda off his back at least.

"I have to give them my guest's name—okay if I use your real one?"

"Sure." Michael leaned forward over the table eagerly.

"Michael Lamont," James typed in. "Now the big decision—chicken, fish or vegetarian?"

"Hmmm. How good is the food?"

James shrugged. "It's banquet food so I'd guess somewhere between 'barely edible' and 'mildly tasty'."

"I'll go with vegetarian."

James entered it and his own info and, before he could second-guess himself, sent it off.

"Done." He put his phone on the table. He felt both relieved and frightened that he'd committed himself. But going with Michael made it seem not so bad, even without the theatrics. After all, wheelchair or not, he'd have the hottest guy in the room by his side.

Even if it wasn't a date.

Michael was still leaning forward with his elbows on the table. His face was soft. "I'm proud of you."

"For choosing the fish?" James asked dryly, though he knew exactly what Michael meant.

"For deciding to go," Michael said, not willing to be put off. Then he waggled his eyebrows. "It'll be fun. Let's go shopping for our outfits soon."

"This weekend?" James suggested without thinking. Immediately, he worried that he sounded overeager. "You probably have to work."

"Nope, I'm not on call this weekend. I've got hot plans."

"Great. Have a marvelous time." James thought he sounded as if he didn't care. But he was dismayed to find that he *did* care, a fact confirmed by the renewed twisting in his gut. It was depressing to think about Michael spending the weekend with a lover. More than depressing. It upset him a lot.

Which was ridiculous. Of course, Michael was dating men. He and James were just friends, and Michael would have plenty of opportunity for sex elsewhere—opportunities with healthy, virile, full-bodied men. James picked at his steak.

"I hope so too," Michael said. "See, I have another epic beauty spot in central Washington I'd like to take you to, if you're free. It's a bit of a drive, but I've got a place we can spend Saturday night. We can make a weekend of it."

James scratched at his neck, keeping his face impassive, even while his heart took off like a shuttle launch. He tried to sound doubtful. "Hmm. Not sure about a whole weekend. I should do some writing."

"What you should do is fill up your soul," Michael said firmly. "You'll write better on Monday."

"Traveling overnight with me—it's complicated."

"Hey, I haven't dropped the ball yet, have I?" Michael sounded matter-of-fact about it, like it was no big deal, but it still touched a tender spot in James's heart.

Why *did* Michael make the effort? Surely, he had other friends to do things with who were much easier companions. But even as he wondered, James felt a lump of happiness in his throat at the thought that Michael wanted to be with him enough to bother.

So he did what any acerbic recluse would do. He glowered.

Michael tilted his head curiously. "Is that a yes? No? 'The magic eight-ball says answer will be clear tomorrow'?"

"Fine. Yes."

"Yes, you bastard," Michael prompted.

"Yes, you *bast*ard," James growled theatrically.

Michael smiled. "That's my boy."

~16~

"ELLENSBURG?" JAMES said doubtfully as Michael activated the turn signal for the exit.

Michael laughed. "Don't worry. This isn't the scenic vista I promised. I just need to stop to pick up a key from my mom."

James felt a pang of dread. "We're staying with your parents?"

Why hadn't he gotten more details from Michael before he'd agreed to this trip? He really didn't want to face the scrutiny of Michael's mom and dad. What would they think? Would they think they were a couple?

Michael shot him a look. "Not *parents*. My dad's been absentee since I was a baby. But my mom is pretty great."

James didn't know what to say to that. He didn't have long to ponder, because their destination wasn't far off the freeway.

James had never been to central Washington and was surprised how different it was from Seattle and Portland. Once over the Snoqualmie Mountains, the land flattened out to open, empty plains between distant mountains. From the freeway, Ellensburg was all cow town convenience stores, chain restaurants, and strip malls, until Michael turned left onto a side street and pulled up outside a nursing home. It was a low, brick complex that looked like it had been built in the seventies. The sign promised, rather redundantly, *Caring Senior Care*.

James was confused. Was Michael's mother in a nursing home? Maybe they were getting a key to a relative's house?

"Come inside with me?" Michael asked after parking.

"It's a pain to hassle with the chair if you're just grabbing a key."

Michael licked his lips, a small frown between his brows. "I... spent a lot of time here when I was young. I'd like you to see it. It won't take long. Okay?"

James wasn't sure what to make of the request, but the place was obviously wheelchair friendly. The front door was level with the sidewalk and the curb from the parking area was cut. Plus, he could use a restroom after the drive and there would likely be accessible ones inside. He nodded. Michael got his chair out of the backseat, and James opened the passenger door and got into it.

"Into the fray," James said when he was seated. "Or the gray, as it were."

Michael laughed. "Yes, indeed. Plenty of gray hair in here."

Beyond the front door was a large common room with comfortable-looking couches, tables, and a TV. There was also a nursing station off to one side. There were half a dozen residents in the room—some watching TV, a few playing cards. They were all well into their senior years. Before James could ask Michael if his mother was living there, an ancient-looking man playing cards spotted them.

"Michael!" he said in a weak but excited voice. He left the card game and came rolling over in his own chair, a big smile on his face.

"Wilson!" Michael bent down to give the old man a warm hug. Wilson patted his back with a gnarled hand.

"You look good," Michael said, straightening up. "You never change."

"I just shrink a little bit every year," the old man chuckled and winked at James. "Wanna know my secret?"

"Absolutely," Michael said.

Wilson leaned in to whisper. "Egg whites and tangerines. Fifty percent of my diet."

"I'll remember that." Michael looked impressed.

Wilson looked Michael up and down. "Gee whiz, you look good! All grown up."

"Wilson, this is my friend James. James, Wilson. I've known him since I was in high school."

"How are ya?" Wilson said gruffly, leaning forward and reaching out a hand. James leaned forward and shook it. Wilson's skin was papery and dry.

"Nice to meet you, sir," James said with a genuine smile.

"Any friend of Michael's has to be a good egg. This kid, he's one of a kind," Wilson nodded toward Michael, a very fond expression on his face.

"Don't go telling stories on me now," Michael warned.

"No, no," Wilson chuckled. "Wouldn't dream of it. Come meet everyone."

Wilson introduced Michael and James to everyone in the common room, telling each person that Michael used to work there and how wonderful he was. Another woman, rosy cheeked and white haired, remembered Michael as well, and Michael gave her a kiss.

Michael eventually pulled him away, and James used a restroom off the main hall. It was, indeed, well-equipped for handicapped, and it gave James one less thing to worry about for a few hours.

When he came out, he asked, "So you worked here? What did you do?"

"I was a nurse's aide here for a couple of years in high school. But even before that, I used to come here every day after school. My mom worked three to eleven, and she hated for me to be home alone, so I hung out here and did my homework, watched TV, played on my Gameboy. I read. A lot."

Ah. Michael's mother worked here. That made sense. Still, James was having a hard time picturing it. Young Michael had spent most of his spare time with geriatrics?

"Didn't you have friends you could hang out with? You didn't play after-school sports?"

Michael shrugged. "I had a few friends. But the school bus would drop me off here, so it was convenient. And sports and I never got along. I wasn't exactly jock material."

Michael said it jokingly, but James frowned. Michael was so... sophisticated and trendy. Hanging out in a nursing home in Ellensburg didn't really fit James's idea of him.

"I want to show you something," Michael said nervously.

"Okay."

Michael led the way to a nearby room. It was a small lending library, no more than eight by ten, with shelves of tattered books and movies. But there was a window seat with a sturdy cushion and a view across an open field.

Michael blushed. "I shouldn't tell you this. It's *so* fanboy."

"I've steeled myself for adoration," James said dryly. "Go on."

"Well… I spent a lot of time reading in that window seat. Mostly science fiction. And I was sixteen when I sat there and read *Troubadour Turncoat.*"

James had a moment where he saw himself, at eighteen, lying in bed writing *Turncoat* and Michael, at sixteen, sitting in that seat reading it. It was a rather awesome thought.

"Before that, I didn't mind coming here to hang out, but I had zero interest in getting involved with the work. But after *Turncoat*… I don't know. It changed my point of view. Acton was such a crazy-ass hero. It was like… he was a powerful warrior in a way, but with medicine, with his mind. I'd never been good at sports. Never was 'macho' like so many of the heroes in the books I read. But Acton Halliway, he was someone I could become." Michael's voice got a little thick, and he frowned. "Sorry. Wow, that's probably way too gushing, isn't it?"

"It's fine," James said. It was way more than fine.

"Anyway, after that I started volunteering here, and then I was hired as an aide. After I graduated, I went to nursing school."

I love that about you. The thought entered James's mind in a sneak attack. It was a strange thought to have. He'd known Michael was a nurse, of course, and that it was a decent profession to have, implied some kind of desire to serve that was admirable, like being a firefighter or a cop. But it had been abstract until this moment, standing with Michael in this nursing home. He saw that being a nurse was more than a paycheck to Michael, that it came from his heart. And James did love that. And he loved that he'd inspired it, even if he really didn't think he could take much credit for it. If not through *Turncoat,* Michael would have found his path some other way. But it was still amazing to have had an influence on someone's life.

He also couldn't help but sense the similarity between this place and where he himself had grown up, Children of God.

"What inspired you to write about a medic anyway?" Michael asked.

"They say to write what you know. Never been around military guys, but I've been around more doctors than you can shake a tongue depressor at."

"Yeah?" Michael studied him. "Was there any one in particular that inspired the character?"

James hesitated. "There was a younger doctor who came to the home regularly, worked with the kids. He was something of a model for Acton."

"Was he—"

"Michael!" A woman entered the room. She was small, no more than five-feet-two and very petite. She wore a uniform—white polyester pants and a crazy colorful printed nurse's smock. With her dark hair and pretty face, James knew at once who she was.

"Hey, Mom!" Michael hugged his mother in a big way, his arms looking surprisingly strong and sheltering wrapped around her slender shoulders. They hugged for a long moment. Their mutual love and affection was obvious.

James felt a strange tension in his body—something deep and pained. He pushed it down, focusing on the facts.

She must have been very young when she had him. She could pass for his older sister. And Michael said he didn't know his father so she was a young, single mother. Like mine.

Only nothing like mine.

"Mom, meet James," Michael said, pulling away.

"Hi, James." Mrs. Lamont wore a weary smile. She came over and offered her hand. He took it, but it didn't seem right to give a manly shake to such a petite woman so he just gently squeezed it.

"Hello. Sorry to impinge on your work day, Mrs. Lamont."

"Oh, honey," she said, still smiling, "this is a huge treat for me. And please, call me Kathy." She turned to look at Michael, but when

James would have let go of her hand, she kept his firmly clasped. "So where are you two headed?"

"Steamboat Rock and Coulee Dam. James has never seen them."

"How fun!" She looked back at James and smiled. "Isn't it funny how kids change? When Michael was young, I'd try to take him out sightseeing or hiking on Sundays, and you should have heard him whine. He always wanted stay at home and read."

"Mom."

"And he couldn't read in the car because it made him carsick, so if he was at a good part in a book, it was like water torture. The glares he used to give me when I dragged his little behind out of the house, I swear you'd think I was driving him to his execution."

"Mom!" Michael said louder. He was giving her a wide-eyed, back-off stare.

Kathy looked guilty. "Er—of course, once we got out where we were going, he always had a good time. Didn't you, babe?" She let go of James's hand to brush back the hair that hung above Michael's eyes. It was obviously an old move. Michael ducked away without rancor.

"No telling stories on me until we've drunk at least a bottle of wine. That's the rule."

Kathy laughed. "I can manage that. I got tonight off so I can cook for you boys."

"You did?" Michael seemed surprised.

"Of course, Michael. You don't come see me very often, so of course, I want to have dinner with you. Janelle's covering for me."

"That's awesome." Michael's eyes flicked to James worriedly, as if asking if that was okay. It wasn't. As nice as Kathy seemed, James really didn't want to have to sit through a family meal, especially not this family. But James didn't give any sign.

"Here's the spare key. I won't be home 'til seven." She pulled a key from her pocket and handed it to Michael.

"Thanks. We'd better head out." Michael kissed her cheek and nodded to James.

"I'm looking forward to grilling you over dinner, James," Kathy said with a wink that was just like Michael's, except hers was conspiratorial rather than stupidly sexy.

James managed a tight smile even as his stomach twisted with dread.

James was quiet when they got back in the car. He stared out the window as Michael got back onto the freeway headed east. Michael kicked himself for taking James inside and bludgeoning the poor guy emotionally.

"I'm sorry. I didn't mean for that to be so, like, Michael's life dump. How embarrassing. First, I do the gushing-about-your-book thing, and then you have to meet my mother."

"Yes, I want a refund on the gas money I haven't yet contributed," James deadpanned. He turned to give Michael an arched brow, and Michael felt a wave of relief. James was joking. That was good, right?

God, he probably should have let James stay in the car, but Michael liked him so much. He had this urge to share everything with James. For God's sake, soon he'd be showing James his fifth grade report card and his dental work. How desperate was he acting? He had to be cooler than that.

"If you'd rather stay at a hotel tonight or have dinner out, that's fine with me," Michael offered, trying to sound casual. "I can call my mom and let her know. She won't mind."

"No, I'm a cheap bastard," James said. "Besides, disappointing your mother would probably ding me major karma points, and I'm saving up for my next incarnation as a porn star."

Michael chucked. "Well, I definitely wouldn't want you to miss out on that. But seriously, this trip is for you and me. I can come back to see her another time."

James looked back out the window. "It's fine."

IT WAS another two-hour drive from Ellensburg to Steamboat Rock State Park, but it was a fine, clear day, and the drive was pretty once they got on WA-17. The landscape there had an Old West flavor. Scrubby brush, reddish brown earth, and unusual rock formations stuck out of the flat ground. The scenery held good memories for Michael— field trips with school or excursions with his mom. And when they drove along the Columbia, it was like a picture postcard. James seemed to be soaking it in, watching out the window with a pleased smile.

To fill the time, they took turns doing voice impressions and quotes from sci-fi films and challenging the other to name the film. James, it turned out, was an impressive mimic.

"Yes! En-Ger-Land!" he gasped in a rough, throaty voice.

Michael laughed. "Thunderbirds! God, that show is so perfectly cheesy. Okay, here's one...." Michael cleared his throat and tried to flatten his voice. "This 'child' is about to wipe out every living thing on Earth. Now, what do you suggest we do? Spank it?'"

James chuckled. "On my God, that's the worst Spock impression I've ever heard."

"Yeah. Voices are not my forte."

"'Please, Captain, not in front of the Klingons'," James said in a voice eerily similar to Leonard Nimoy's.

"Shit! That's amazing," Michael said with a gasp.

"Or possibly pathetic if you think about the hours I spent watching that show. What about this? 'Another one of them new worlds. No beer, no women, no pool parlors, nothin'. Nothin' to do but throw rocks at tin cans, and we gotta bring our own tin cans.'"

"Hmm." Michael was stumped for a moment. "*Forbidden Planet?*" The guess was as much from the context, and James's fifties style voice, as remembering the line itself.

"Gold star for you!" James said, sounding impressed. "Your turn."

"Okay. Let's see. 'You know what they say, human see, human do.'"

"*Planet of the Apes.* You need to try harder, padawan. What about this one: 'I'm scared, Fif. It's that rat circus out there, I'm beginning to enjoy it.'"

Michael felt a little zap of a thrill at the line from *Mad Max.* "Wow, you sound just like Mel Gibson. That made me a little hard."

"Everything makes you a little hard." James sounded cynical, but a red flush appeared on those high cheekbones.

"Not everything," Michael murmured. It came out more seductive than he intended. When James didn't answer, Michael launched into another quote. He tried to affect a robotic voice, "'Dead or alive, you're coming with me!'"

"*Robocop*. God, Peter Weller was hot in that." James seemed to realize what he'd just admitted, because his blush deepened. "Er—we need to up the stakes here. You're too good at this. Let me think of something really hard...."

"I'm thinking of something really hard," Michael laughed.

James rolled his eyes at the ceiling. "Jesus, you have a one track mind. Okay, I've got one. 'A man is defined by his actions, not his memories.'" His voice was breathy and slow.

"Kuato! *Total Recall!*"

"How the hell do you know all these movies? You probably weren't even born when that came out!"

"You're only a few years older than me, oh ancient one. And there's this amazing invention called Netflix."

"Hmm." James looked doubtful. "You know, I had a parasitic twin."

"You did?" Michael asked with surprise.

"No."

Michael took a nickel out of the car's ashtray and threw it at him. "You suck. And it's my turn."

They went on like that until the game devolved into both of them moaning out "Soylent Green is people!" over and over in increasingly cartoonish voices. Fortunately, it was about then that Steamboat Rock came into view.

Steamboat Rock was a stunning natural formation of rock and water. The flat, blue surface of Banks Lake nearly surrounded an island with a high, flat-topped plateau that looked, if you really squinted, a little like a steamboat. It was a weekend, and there were plenty of other visitors at the state park, but it wasn't overcrowded. After using the handicapped-friendly facilities, they looked around. They found a paved trail to a day-use area by the lake where there were picnic tables and a great view of Steamboat Rock.

"You can go hike for a bit if you want. I'm fine here." James tilted his face back to catch the sun.

"No way. I'm good."

James frowned. "I really don't mind."

"Me neither. I wanted to show you the scenery. If I'd wanted to hike, I would have found a place with better accessible trails. So are you starving? I didn't bring food 'cause I figured we'd eat in Coulee Dam. It's just another twenty minutes or so up the road."

James seemed to relax. "I can wait. Let's hang out for a bit. This place is… mildly acceptable." He said the last with a great show of cynical reluctance.

It made Michael smile. "Glad you like it."

He felt absurdly pleased by the small smile that tugged at the corners of James's mouth and the way his eyes roamed over the scenery with an inner light. Michael took his role as a secret muse very seriously, after all. He also hoped to make himself so indispensable to James that he wouldn't, well, be able to dispense with him.

It was his plan, and he was committed to it.

They hung there for an hour. They didn't talk a lot. It was nice after all the chatter in the car to just soak up the sounds of the water and some really loud-ass birds. The sun was warm without being too hot, and the other tourists left them in peace.

After a long silence, James started talking about how he researched landscapes for his books and some of the strange places on Earth he'd based his planets on, which Michael found fascinating. They talked about some of the places sci-fi movies had been shot like the San Rafael Swell and Carlsbad Caverns.

After they'd drunk in their fill of the landscape, and James took pictures with his smartphone, they headed back to the car and continued up WA-17 to Coulee Dam for lunch.

The Grand Coulee Dam had been built over the Columbia River in the mid-to-late 30s. It was an impressive spectacle, and the little town that sat around it was quaint and touristy. They stopped at a viewpoint that overlooked the dam, and then decided to have Mexican for lunch.

Over soft tacos, James asked about Michael's workweek. Michael filled him in on Marnie's most recent antics, including ordering a vibrator called a 'rabbit' for her straight-laced daughter on the Internet. He felt a strong urge to talk about Tommy, too. Michael was really attached to Tommy. Or to tell James about Lem Peterson and the heavy guilt he carried from his upbringing. But of course, he really couldn't talk about his surrogacy clients to anyone, and James didn't even know he was a surrogate. And although Michael recognized that this would be a good time to tell him, he just couldn't make himself do it.

They were having a great weekend, and James was loosening up around him more and more—making more eye contact, even allowing his gaze to linger in a way that Michael recognized as attraction, even if James probably wouldn't admit it. They were starting to build a real friendship. And Michael was so afraid that if James heard about the surrogacy, all of that would be wiped down to ground zero—or at least, any possibility of it ever becoming something more. And he especially didn't want James getting upset when they were hours from home and he couldn't throw Michael out or get away.

So Michael said nothing about his surrogacy work or clients.

James insisted on getting the bill. As they were waiting for the waitress to bring back his card, he said, in a somewhat uncomfortable voice, "Thanks for suggesting this. I really like to travel, but I almost never get a chance to. I guess that's why I like to invent worlds."

Michael forced a smile even though it made him feel sad that James hadn't had the opportunity to get out much. *I wish I could show you the world.* But Michael himself was no globe-trotter. He'd been to Canada and Oregon, and that was it. So for now, central Washington was the tiny sliver of the world he had to give to James.

"I'm really glad you came with me. None of my friends want to do stuff like this."

"Yeah?"

"Yeah. Probably because we'll spend the evening in a little house in Ellensburg. Big excitement." Michael made a funny face.

James smiled and shrugged as if to indicate it was fine, but he didn't say anything.

THE BATHROOM doorway in the house where Michael grew up was too narrow for James's wheelchair.

James had a moment of sheer panic. Then Michael's mother was there, apologizing, sounding genuinely chagrined. She told him she'd suspected it might be the case, so she brought a walker home with her. She ran out to the car to get it.

The walker was the kind with four wheels and a seat, but it was much lighter and smaller than his wheelchair. She put it at the open bathroom door for him. Grateful, James wheeled up to it, set the brake on his chair, and then leveraged himself up, grasping the walker with both hands and lowering himself into its small seat.

It was awkward, but both Michael and his mother hung back and didn't watch, for which he was stupidly grateful. He pulled his backpack off his wheelchair, made it into the bathroom, and shut the door with a sigh of relief. He stared at himself in the mirror, his heart beating way too loud.

James was in fucking Ellensburg. He'd really surprised himself this weekend. He was surprised he'd agreed to come on this trip in the first place, surprised that he hadn't subsequently made up an excuse to get out of it, and surprised he'd agreed to spend the night in Michael's mother's house. Why? Why was he doing this?

Michael.

James knew the answer. He wanted to be around Michael. Somehow, the idea of taking a weekend trip with him sounded so normal, so fun, and James wanted that. He wanted to feel normal, and to show Michael he could be like everyone else, which was, a) untrue and b) way too needy. But really, everything had been fine on the trip so far. He could hardly complain. In fact, he'd *loved* the drive and the state park and seeing that huge Roosevelt-era dam. Yet now that they were back at Michael's house, he suddenly felt uncomfortable and vulnerable. It made him uneasy to be so dependent on other people.

Tomorrow, we're going home. All I have to do is get through dinner with Michael's mother and sleep in the same room as Michael tonight. I can do that. Right?

Michael had briefly shown him the room—his childhood bedroom—and there were two single beds so it wasn't as if they had to sleep *together* together. And if he did something embarrassing in his sleep, like snore or get an erection, Michael would be too polite to mention it.

But James hadn't slept in the same room with anyone since leaving Children of God, and never ever around a super attractive male.

His stomach was tied in knots. Worse, his dick was already half hard. God, he was lamentable.

Nothing's going to happen. Michael wouldn't do anything unless you wanted him to, and you don't want him to. So chill.

He almost believed it. He used his plastic urinal, flushed the contents, and rinsed it. Then, sitting on the walker's seat, he brushed his teeth and washed his hands and face at the sink. The bathroom light was a bit yellow and oddly flattering. He pulled himself up to stand at the sink and studied himself in the mirror. The counter reached his hips, and he looked perfectly normal. With his palms flat on the counter, holding himself up, his arm muscles corded and bunched and he looked built. He was not bad looking on top. He knew this. His hair was thick, and his face wasn't bad.

For a moment, he stared at himself and allowed himself the brief fantasy that he was whole. That he could saunter into Michael's bedroom on two good legs, jump on the bed, pull Michael down to him roughly, kiss him and make love—no, *have sex*. Maybe even raunchy, filthy, headboard-pounding sex.

His cock swelled further.

He took a shaky breath. Okay. That was not helping. He considered masturbating, just to get rid of any potentially embarrassing reaction later. But the thought of doing that in Mrs. Lamont's bathroom, where Michael or his mother might pick up the scent of semen, or wonder why he'd taken so long…. No.

He ran the water in the sink to a nice icy cold and splashed his face with it until he had his body under control.

"SO WHERE did you grow up, James?" Kathy asked politely over lasagna and salad.

James chewed his mouthful very slowly to buy himself a moment. These were the sorts of questions parents asked, and hence why he hadn't wanted to be here.

"Mostly in a children's home in Portland."

Her expression changed, as people's inevitably did, from polite interest to sadness and a sharper perusal, a look James interpreted as "wow, I had no idea you were an orphan, poor thing." Most people would have left it at that, immediately scared off the topic as something distressing. But not Kathy.

"What kind of children's home was it?" she asked with interest.

"My mother's nosy," Michael huffed. "You don't have to answer."

Kathy gave Michael a look, and he looked hard back.

"It was a home for disabled children," James said, picking up his knife to cut his lasagna. "They do good work there."

"What about your parents?" Kathy asked in a neutral voice, as if it were no big deal.

"Mom!" Michael said. "Let the guy eat his dinner."

"I'm just making conversation," she said to Michael, sounding a little put out. "Honestly, James, I'm sorry if I'm being a busybody. You don't have to answer."

"It's all right." James realized he'd cut his lasagna up into a dozen bite-sized pieces like a child. He made himself stop. "I never knew my father. Is there any more bread?"

Kathy passed him the basket, and James took a piece, even though he didn't want it. He felt nauseous.

"How's your work, Michael?" She asked, redirecting her attention and letting James off the hook.

"Good. I think I e-mailed you—I'm getting a lot more hours at Happy At Home now. Almost too many."

"Do you have time to keep up with your other clients?"

James was buttering his piece of bread, but he caught the silence and tail end of a headshake Michael was directing at his mother when he looked up. James wasn't sure what that was about, but he felt as if he was putting a damper on the entire dinner with his reticence and tension. Fuck it. He could do this. He wrote dialogue for a living, after all. And the wine they were drinking helped. He took a deep breath.

"One nice thing about the home was that I grew up with a lot of other kids," he said in an upbeat tone. "There was a boy named Danny who was one of my roommates for years. He had Downs, and he loved to laugh. His favorite thing in the world was blind man's bluff. We'd tie a towel around someone's eyes, spin them a few times in the middle of the common room, and then they had to find the rest of the kids by feel. It was hilarious, because Danny would laugh so hard, you always knew exactly where he was, but the more you pretended you couldn't find him, the harder he laughed...."

He told them about Danny, about his insistence on never wearing matching socks, because then you couldn't have a "favorite," his collection of baseball cards, and his love of Big Bird. He told them about Harvard, a boy with an arm missing due to a birth defect, who'd been abandoned at the home as an infant. Harvard was two years younger than James and had followed him around out of sheer adoration. He told them how he'd gotten Harvard to do his chores until Felicia had cottoned on, and then he'd had to tutor Harvard in reading for an hour every night for a week as punishment. It had been oddly satisfying. James had ended up tutoring Harvard until he started third grade.

It was easy to talk about the other kids in the home, anyone except himself, and his audience seemed to find his stories amusing. Before James knew it, Kathy was clearing the dessert plates, still chuckling. Michael gave him a brilliant smile as she went into the kitchen.

"God, she loves you," Michael whispered. "I may be in danger of losing my status as only child."

James swallowed down a wave of pain and finished off his wine.

JAMES PUT on his pajamas in the bathroom and brushed his teeth again before bed—just because he'd eaten, not because he was hoping anything would happen. He was able to get his wheelchair through the door to Michael's room, and he got into the bed near the window while Michael was taking his turn in the bathroom. James pulled his legs up into the bed quickly, getting under the blankets.

By the time Michael came in, James was settled. Michael stopped inside the doorway and looked at him, *God*, with a soft hunger in his eyes before he seemed to force himself to look away. He was still dressed as he had been all day, and James now realized that Michael had probably skipped a shower because the bathroom was not outfitted so James could have one too. The thought made him feel both guilty and grateful not to be the only one with a day's layer of stink. Michael stripped off his clothes all the way down to well-fitted blue boxer briefs. He didn't look at James as he did so, didn't hurry or linger, just took each article off and laid it on his desk as if it was no big deal. James tried not to look, but he couldn't resist. Michael had been equally uncovered at the pool, but James hadn't known him then.

God, the soft glow of that perfect skin, that tight slim body, and beautifully curved ass! The online porn James drifted toward featured twinks—slender, hairless young men. His favorite was when they were paired with a larger, macho, furrier top.

Michael was prettier, sweeter than any of them. Damn it.

He turned, and James pretended he hadn't been watching. He looked at the ceiling and prayed his semi wasn't visible. He was relieved when Michael got into the other bed and turned off the lamp, plunging the room into almost-darkness. There was still a bit of light coming through the gauzy curtains from some streetlamp outside. James turned his head and saw a dark shape in Michael's bed.

"Good night," Michael said.

"Night," James grunted, not trusting himself to make a quip or otherwise try to be clever.

His heart was back to thumping like a jackhammer. The visual image of Michael standing there in his underwear, *God, that sweet ass*, lingered on the back of his eyelids like an atomic flash. He wanted to touch it. Hell, he wanted to bite it. His cock slowly filled up until he was throbbing against his stomach. *Damn it*! It was going to take him forever to relax and fall asleep.

For a long moment, there was just the faint sound of traffic as James took deep breaths, trying to calm himself.

"James?" came Michael's voice in the dark.

"Still here," James said. "I was going to sneak out when you turned off the light, but I decided against it."

"Good."

He could hear Michael shift around. James turned his head. His eyes had adjusted to the dark somewhat, and he could see the outline of

Michael, lying on his side and facing James, though he couldn't really see his expression.

"I'm really glad that we're friends," Michael said.

James's heart stuttered in his chest. "Friends? I thought you were my sycophant, Dieter."

Michael chuckled. "I wish."

James swallowed—it was audible in the quiet room.

"Seriously, though. I mean... I'm glad I'm getting to know you as a friend right now."

"Good to know."

"But...." Michael's voice was a bit rough. "I hope one day we can be more."

Shit. A slow, hot burn of nervousness and intense longing fired in James's stomach. He gasped and covered it quickly with a cough.

"You okay?" Michael said worriedly. His dark form half sat up.

"Yeah." James's voice sounded deep. He cleared his throat. "I don't think—"

"Would it be okay if I kissed you good night?" Michael broke in.

Damn, the little shit could be pushy. Damn, James wanted him so goddamn bad. He wanted it even though it terrified him.

Where had his immutable defenses gone? His shields had been damaged, it seemed, and he hadn't even been aware that it was happening.

He made himself think about it, hoping the act of using his little gray cells would distract him from the purely physical need raging down below. And he realized that at some point, Michael had stopped being a frighteningly beautiful boy who couldn't possibly want anything to do with James. He'd become a real person. Today, James had seen glimpses of a lonely boy who'd been unpopular growing up and had spent most of his childhood with senior citizens. He saw a guy who grew up in a very modest house in the cow town of Ellensburg in a room with boy band and sci-fi movie posters on the wall. He saw someone who was compassionate, who didn't flinch at hugging a ninety-year-old and kissing them on the cheek, someone who had made a career out of helping people who weren't perfect. A guy like that would know what he was getting into, surely—what James's legs would look like, what it would be like. A guy like that wouldn't gag in disgust. Or laugh. Or leave.

And… it was dark.

"Okay." It was the weirdest thing. The word came out of James's mouth while he was still debating it in his mind, as if his tongue and voice box had staged a coup. He froze, even as Michael, without a moment's hesitation, slipped out of his bed and came over to sit next to James.

James was on his back, and he quickly propped himself up on his elbows, not wanting Michael to kiss him while he was lying flat. It was too loaded and too… passive. Jesus, he was nervous. He broke out in a hot sweat.

Why did I agree? No, don't freak. It's just a good night kiss. It's not a big deal. You've been kissed before.

He started to say something, try to joke the moment off, but Michael didn't give him a chance. He put a soft hand on his jaw as if locating him in the dark and leaned in.

Michael's mouth touched his, closed and pressing sweetly. His lips were warm and so plump and full. It didn't feel anything like the quick, chaste kisses James had gotten at the group home or like the rather sloppy and obligatory kisses from Chris. Those kisses didn't make his body run hot and cold in alternating chemical surges or make the entire universe feel as if it had narrowed down to a singularity at the point where their mouths met.

Michael pressed their mouths together once, for a long, achingly intense moment, withdrew slightly and pressed again. James could sense the tension in Michael's body, feel Michael's soft, ragged breath on his cheek. Michael was aroused. *Michael was aroused too.* And James knew that on the next pass, Michael would open his mouth, try to deepen the kiss. James was so damn hard. If he felt Michael's tongue, that would be it, he wouldn't be able to resist. The last shred of his control was almost out the window, and fuck his embarrassment, fuck everything.

He reached up to grasp Michael's upper arm and pull him down. There was a knock on the door.

Michael snorted a conspiratorial laugh and quickly ran back to his bed. "Come in!" he hollered.

The door cracked open, and Michael's mother was silhouetted against the hall light.

"Hope I didn't wake you. I just wanted to say good night."

"Good night, Mom."

"Good night, Kathy," James said. God, his voice sounded wrecked.

"Good night, James. I'm so glad you came."

She hesitated at the door for a moment, then took a step toward Michael's bed. "Sorry, sweetheart, but I don't get nearly enough chances to do this." She leaned down and kissed him on the cheek with a loud smack.

"Mom!" Michael complained, but he laughed too.

"Love you," Kathy said quietly. She straightened up and glanced over at James. He knew what she was going to do a moment before she did it, but there was no graceful way out, or even time to think one up. In a moment, she was bending over James. She kissed his cheek.

"Good night, James," she said, in a singsongy teasing voice, as if pretending he and Michael were twelve years old.

Michael protested half-heartedly—something like "Stop assaulting my guest!"—but James's brain had frozen at the gesture, and suddenly, the woman standing over him wasn't Kathy Lamont at all.

~17~

Varanas, India, 1992

IT FELT as if James was in the hospital forever. He turned six, and his mother brought him a little cake with a candle on it. The nurses stood around and clapped, and he got some candy and a card signed by all of them.

A week later, he was woken in the middle of the night by his mother, which was strange because she only visited him in the afternoons.

"Shhh. You have to be very quiet, Sweetpea. Promise?"

James nodded. It felt like an adventure was starting, the way it used to be with him and his mother. They had left a few places in the middle of the night. He was excited.

It was mostly dark in the ward, but she got James dressed and carried him out in a blanket. They went down halls he'd never seen before, through an old door, and then they were out in the night air. It felt hot and sticky but so good on James's upturned face.

"Where are we going?" he asked, too happy to be quiet anymore.

"You've been wanting to leave the hospital, so I'm springing you out, Sweetpea." She said it in a funny voice, like a gangster. It made James laugh.

"Yay!" He hugged his mother hard around her neck. He knew he must be heavy, even though he'd gotten very skinny, but his mom carried him for blocks, his legs dangling down and his feet hitting her knees on every bounce. They found a taxi and took it to the airport.

"Where are we going?" James asked. He thought they'd go back to their little room in the hostel.

"We're going to take an airplane to the United States to see Grandma and Grandpa. It's a long trip, so I need you to be very, very good. Can you do that for me?"

James was a little afraid. It had been so long since he'd been out of the hospital, and now his legs didn't work. The nurses wouldn't be there to take his bedpan away and bring him a clean one, or give him food, or rub his arms and legs when they hurt. And he would miss the other children on the ward. But none of that could compare to the idea of being with his mother again, of it being her and him, a team out adventuring.

"Yay! I like going on planes, and I can be good. Tell me more about Grandma and Grandpa. Are we going to live with them?"

His mother had never talked much about Grandma and Grandpa. When James had asked before, seeing all the large families in the countries where they traveled, she told him they lived far away and that maybe he'd see them one day. He was very anxious now and so excited. Would they all be in a house together like other families? Would he have his own room, or would he sleep with his mother? He hoped for his own room, but he was willing to take anything. Grandma and Grandpa would help take care of him, which made James happy, because he knew his mother wasn't always very good at it.

"Do Grandma and Grandpa have other little boys I can play with?"

His mother got a funny look. "Yes, James, there will be other children there. Now hush. Mommy has to focus on getting our tickets."

IT WAS a very, very long trip. James got cranky, tired, and so sore. People stared at him with pitying faces because his legs didn't look right in his pants, and he didn't have a wheelchair so his mom carried him around like a baby. He hated the stares. He put a blanket over his head in the airports to hide, but he had to take it off sometimes to breathe. He tried hard to be good, but he got too tired to care. He slept on his mother's shoulder through a long line at customs to get into the United States. And he cried most of the whole last plane ride because he felt sick and he had to stay buckled in his seat even though he wanted her to hold him. Other people looked at him, and he knew he was being a baby, so he tried to cry quietly.

Finally, the last plane ride was over. His mom said they were in Oregon. It was dark and cold and raining hard. They took a taxi and got out at a big house that looked a little scary.

"Grandma and Grandpa live here?" James asked in wonder.

"No, you'll stay here tonight. I'll take you to see them later."

"But why?" James demanded, getting upset.

"Just for tonight. Be good for Mommy a little bit longer."

A woman greeted them at the door. James fell asleep on a couch while the woman and his mother talked in another room. He was barely aware as his mother carried him up some stairs and got him dressed in his pajamas. He woke up enough to realize they were in a room with three other beds. By the glow of the nightlight, he could see there were children sleeping in them. He sat up, awake.

"Who are those kids?" James asked his mother in a loud stage whisper. She was so pretty in the dim light, with her long brown hair and the red scarf she always wore tied around her forehead. But her face had a strange, pinched look, even though her words sounded bright and happy.

"They're new friends for you. It'll be fun playing with other children, won't it? Go to sleep now, James, and you'll feel a lot better when you wake up." James didn't like the look in her eyes. He frowned.

"Please, Sweetpea?"

"But why can't I sleep in your bed? Why do I have to stay in this room?" he demanded loudly.

"Because this room is where all the good little boys sleep." She hugged him tight, and he clutched at her dress.

"Will you be right here when I wake up?" He didn't want to let her out of his sight. What if something happened? He didn't have his bedpan. What if he needed her to pick him up and carry him to the bathroom? What if the polio came back and he couldn't breathe? He had nightmares about that, about not being able to move his chest, not getting any air.

"Yes, I'll be here," she promised brightly. "Now lie down and go to sleep like a big boy. It feels good to be in a real bed, doesn't it? We had a long trip, and you need some rest."

He *was* sleepy. He could hardly keep his eyes open. And even though he wanted to ask more questions or try to get her to stay with him in the room, he was already sliding under.

The last thing he remembered was his mother laying him back onto his pillow and kissing his forehead.

In the morning when James woke up, his mother wasn't there. Felicia was the lady who ran the home. She said his mother had decided to let him stay there for a while.

"Is she coming back? Is she coming back?" James remembered crying over and over as Felicia held him in her lap.

"I don't know, James," Felicia said, sounding sad. "But I promise you this—you're safe here, and we'll take good care of you."

James had wanted to punch her. He didn't want her to take care of him. He didn't want to be there. He wanted to run, to find the front door and run away, run forever if he had to, to find his mother. But James couldn't run. He could do nothing but wait for his mother to come for him.

Mommy, please don't leave me. I'll be good. I promise.

But she never came back.

Ellensburg, Washington, 2014

"JAMES?" MICHAEL'S voice made James blink, bringing him back to the here and now. Kathy had left, and the door was closed. Michael slipped out of bed and came closer. But James held up his hand.

"I'm really tired. Good night, Michael," he said gruffly.

Michael stopped between their beds the minute James held up his hand. James couldn't read his expression in the dark, and he was glad. He didn't want to see the disappointment or the pity. He turned on his side to face the wall.

"Good night, James," Michael said softly. James heard him slip back into his own bed.

His heart was still pounding, and his stomach felt as if it was filled with curdled milk. He'd come so close to giving in to a weak moment of sexual frustration, to letting Michael touch him. James's chest was tight and hot, and he was so, so glad he hadn't done that. He liked Michael, a lot, but that was precisely why he couldn't do that. Once Michael saw and felt James's legs, his rose-colored glasses would disintegrate and he would see James as he really was—a broken thing, a burden. And that memory of his mother had reminded James of precisely what happened next.

~18~

ON MONDAY morning, Tommy wanted to hear all about Michael's weekend. Michael told him about their trip to Steamboat Rock and Coulee Dam as they played their first round of rummy. He mentioned that James was in a wheelchair, and he told Tommy they were just friends, which was true. Tommy got a bit quiet, though, even as he whomped all over Michael's ass, going out and sticking him with over a hundred points in his hand.

"You okay, champ?" Michael asked as Tommy shuffled the deck for the next round.

"Yeah," Tommy said, though he didn't look up into Michael's eyes. "Hey. Do you think…?"

"What? You can ask me anything."

"Do you think… you could ever love someone like me?"

The question came out of nowhere. Michael felt a catch in his chest, as if someone had put their finger on the trigger of a gun that was aimed at his heart, one he hadn't even known existed. It felt… dangerous. Potentially lethal.

He spoke very, very carefully. "I care about you a lot, Tommy."

"I don't mean… I don't mean you specifically, or me specifically, but in general. Do you think a guy like you could ever love a guy like me?"

Tommy's voice trembled, and he looked down at the deck of cards in his hands, shuffling them over and over. Michael wasn't sure if Tommy was really asking "generally" or not. He suspected otherwise. He mentally reviewed his training for what to do when client got overly attached. You were supposed to let them down kindly but firmly, keep the professional relationship clearly defined. Of course, Tommy had become more than just a client.

God, this was hard.

Michael leaned forward and put his hand on Tommy's. "I think you could meet someone who will love you for who you are, yes. You're a good person, Tommy, and you're fun to be with. I'm your surrogate, so you and I have a different kind of relationship. But you're also my friend, and I care about you as a friend."

Tommy looked down at the cards for a long time, breathing hard. Then he pulled away and started dealing in a subdued fashion. Michael wanted to talk more about it, see if Tommy was really okay. But if Tommy was developing feelings for him, he would need some time to process what Michael had said.

When they finished three games and Michael asked, as he always did, if Tommy wanted to play some more, he said yes for the first time ever. They played a fourth round, Michael lost, and then Tommy stood and stretched.

"I'm beat. Not feeling great today. Maybe we can do a massage next week, Maestro?" Tommy said casually.

Michael felt his face burn. "Sure. Whatever you want, champ. Do you need some aspirin or something? Want me to ask your mom to come up?"

"Nah, just need to sleep it off."

Michael left Tommy and found Mrs. Chelsey downstairs in the kitchen as usual.

"How was he today?" she asked hopefully.

"We played cards, but he didn't want the massage today. He said he was tired and not feeling great," Michael said worriedly. "So I won't charge you for today."

"Nonsense, you came over here. I'll pay for your time." But Mrs. Chelsey looked worried too.

"No, seriously. I won't take anything for today. But there's something else…."

Michael wondered if he should tell Mrs. Chelsey what Tommy had said. On the one hand, it seemed like an invasion of Tommy's privacy. But on the other hand, Mrs. Chelsey paid his fee. She deserved to know if the surrogate she'd hired to help her son was causing difficulties for him.

"Tommy seemed melancholy today. I'm not sure he wants me to continue coming, or that it's best for him if I do."

Mrs. Chelsey looked upset. "Michael, Tommy is getting over a cold. I don't think you should take it personally if he didn't want… that today."

"No, it's not that." Michael sighed. "I'm a little concerned that he might be getting emotional about this, and that he might… get hurt."

"Why? What did he say?"

So much for diplomacy. Mrs. Chelsey clearly wasn't going to let it go, so reluctantly, Michael told her what Tommy had said.

"Maybe I'm making too big a deal of it," Michael said. "But I think you should talk to him, in a roundabout way, and see what you think is best. I'm happy to continue if you think it's good for Tommy, but if not…."

Mrs. Chelsey shivered and crossed her arms. She looked a bit lost. "He looks forward to your visits so much. I can't imagine he would want you to stop coming. But I'll talk to him."

"Okay. I just want to do what's best for him. Let me know how I can help."

Mrs. Chelsey nodded and walked him to the door. As she said good-bye, she looked… resigned. Michael wanted to hug her and tell her everything would be okay, but he wasn't at all sure that was the case. He left feeling uneasy in his soul and determined to talk to Jack about it as soon as he could.

ON WEDNESDAY evening, Michael had a session with Lem Peterson. He was hoping it would go a lot better than his session with Tommy had gone, and he put on his most upbeat personality.

"Hello, Lem!" Michael greeted his client as he came in the door. Lem looked nervous today, though, thankfully, not as nervous as the first time he'd been here.

In the past three weeks, they had progressed from holding hands, to touching each other's face, shoulders, and arms, to kissing lightly with closed mouths—first the hand, then the cheek, then the lips. That had been a very big deal. Jack had been working intensely with Lem and felt he was ready to be pushed a little harder.

"How do you feel about today?" Michael asked when they were seated on the couch.

Lem rubbed his chin. He no longer sweated as much around Michael, or got quite so red, but he looked jittery today. "I'm a little scared. But excited too. I mean, it would be good if I can... can make it through this."

"I promise you will, okay? It's all on me. All you have to do is tell me how you're feeling as we go, just like always."

"I can do that. Where, um...."

"Right here is fine. Just give me a minute, and I'll go change. Okay?" Michael squeezed Lem's arm. It was a mark of their progress that it didn't startle him.

"Yeah."

Michael went into his bedroom and stripped. He'd bathed very thoroughly earlier, and now he put on a thin black silk print robe that he'd gotten at a thrift shop—it was pretty and soft against his skin and he loved it. He wore nothing underneath.

Back in the living room, Lem looked at him as he walked in. He blushed and looked away. "Wow," he breathed.

Michael sat down on the couch. He sat on the opposite end from Lem and waited for Lem to stop breathing quite so hard and look at him.

Michael smiled. "You doin' okay?"

"Yeah," Lem said with only a little tremor in his voice.

"Good. So.... Dr. Halloran wants us to try some nudity today. You guys talked about that, right?"

"He thinks I'm ready."

"What do you think?"

"I... I wanna try it. I told Dr. Halloran if I can handle you naked, then that's a lot, right?" He laughed nervously. "Then maybe it won't seem like a big deal when John comes in for his quarterly taxes fully dressed. Maybe I won't get so tongue-tied. That's in two weeks."

"That sounds like a good plan. Dr. Halloran also wants us to talk about anatomy, to help you get more comfortable looking at the body and talking about it."

Lem blushed. He was sitting forward anxiously, elbows on his knees, twisting his hands. He looked down at them. "He, um, gave me homework. To l-look at myself. With a mirror and all. I never have. Not since I was a kid. I always sort of… tried not to."

"Yeah? How'd that go?"

Lem shrugged. "Weird. And kind of gross."

Michael laughed. "I love how honest you are."

Lem shrugged again, but he smiled, pleased.

"Well, I apologize ahead of time for any grossness."

"No. That's not what I… You could never be gross." Now Lem looked stricken.

"I'm just kidding. Though if you think it's a little gross, it's okay. You can tell me. The human body is a little odd, when you think about it. Let's see, shall we?" Michael untied his robe and pulled it open. He scooted around so his back was against the arm of the couch. He put his legs on the seat cushion and spread his thighs.

Lem was staring at his hands, but obviously he had excellent peripheral vision, because he sort of whimpered.

"Take your time," Michael said quietly. He relaxed back and waited.

After a little while, Lem turned his head and looked at Michael's crotch. He turned back to face forward, face red. He wiped some sweat off his brow and took a shaky breath.

"Can you describe what's going through your mind?" Michael asked gently.

"You're, um, bigger than me. Your thighs are really pale and pretty."

"You sure? You'd better check again."

Lem turned and looked a little longer this time. He turned back around. "You're not circumcised."

"No. My mom is a nurse. She never saw much sense in it."

"Oh."

"Are you circumcised?"

"Yeah."

"That's probably for the best. Most men are. If anything, I think men find it a little intimidating if it's not."

Lem licked his lips nervously, but he didn't say anything. He turned and looked again, though.

"What else?"

"Your, um, your scrotum is smaller and tighter than mine. Less... less hangy and gross."

Michael smiled. "Yeah? Well, I kind of like hangy ones myself, but I'm glad you think so."

Lem swallowed and stared. "You don't have much hair."

"I take most of it off, particularly around my scrotum and down in here." Michael reached down to stroke his perineum, spreading his legs a little farther.

"Okay. Why?"

"I just like it. I like feeling smooth when I touch myself there. And I think some guys like it too. What about you? Do you prefer hairy guys?"

"I... I don't... I never really...." Lem stammered.

Michael just watched him and waited patiently.

"You look good," Lem finally managed, getting redder by the minute. "Clean, I guess. But if someone else that I like, that likes me, I mean, if they were natural, that's okay too. I don't expect...."

"You're right, it's not that important, is it?" Michael agreed honestly.

Lem sighed in relief. "No."

"Would you like to see how the foreskin works?" Michael took himself in hand and rolled back the foreskin. "When I'm limp like this, the foreskin hides the head completely, but when I have an erection, most of it peeks out."

"Oh."

"It's very soft." Michael rolled the end of the foreskin between his fingers. "Would you like to feel it?"

Lem blinked, seemingly mesmerized by what Michael's fingers were doing. "Okay," he said after a bit. He scooted a little closer. Michael released himself and folded his hands calmly on his ribs.

Lem glanced up at them. "You have a n-nice chest."

"Thank you."

"You're welcome."

It was so formal and polite. Michael bit back a smile. Lem wiped some more sweat from his forehead with the back of his sleeve. "I'm sorry I'm nervous. I was doing better last week."

"It's okay. This is kind of a big deal. I think you're doing fantastic." Michael made his voice, his posture, everything about himself relaxed as if to say, *no big deal, just a normal day, ho hum.* He hoped the lack of tension would rub off on Lem. It wasn't working gangbusters, but it was probably helping. He actually reached out to touch Michael's cock.

He tentatively stroked down the foreskin with one finger, petting it. "Soft," he said, drawing his hand back.

"Make sure you get a good feel. You might not see another guy who's uncut like this."

Lem glanced up at him in surprise, as if that hadn't occurred to him. But he reached out and stroked it a little more. "It's really, really soft. Nice."

"Want to check and see how my scrotum feels while you're at it?"

Lem stroked his finger lower, running it over Michael's hairless balls before pulling it back entirely. "Okay," Lem whispered, looking a little shell-shocked.

He shifted uncomfortably, and Michael could tell that Lem had an erection. His hands in his lap were shaking, and there was a pokey tent in his dress pants. Michael wasn't sure how much further he should take this. Jack had wanted him to try a full show and tell, though, and Michael's gut told him Lem was hanging in there.

"Have you ever watched two men having sex, like on a video or online?"

Lem swallowed and nodded. "Dr. Halloran gave me homework. A DVD. It was… better than the stuff they have online. I tried to watch that before, but it seemed so… I couldn't do it. But the DVD had a doctor talking and then two men, and it was more…."

"Loving?" Michael asked.

"Yeah," Lem whispered.

"So in that video, they talk about how the most important thing is finding out what your partner likes and showing your partner what you like. Most men like having their shaft rubbed up and down, but different people might like different pressure, or speed, or more attention to the glans, or less."

Lem nodded. "I like a lot." As if realizing what he'd said, he blushed furiously.

"Yeah? I do too, but only when I'm very hard. Before that, too much attention there feels like too much."

"Oh."

Lem was looking down at his hands again.

"Would you like to see more?"

Lem glanced at him. "Like what?"

"Did you watch the last part of that video, on anal sex?"

Lem nodded, looking a little ashamed to admit it.

"Would you like to see what I look like there?"

Lem hesitated. "That's really dirty," he whispered anxiously.

"It's not dirty, Lem," Michael said solemnly. "It's a natural part of your body like your nose or your ears or your belly button. There's nothing to be afraid of. It can be beautiful to make love to someone there. It feels really nice."

Lem considered it, biting his lips. He nodded again.

Michael shifted a little lower and pulled his legs up to his chest, exposing himself. Lem blew out a big breath and stared. "Wow."

"You okay?"

"That is… this is… really weird."

Michael laughed. "Yeah, it kind of is. But being not-weird is highly overrated, don't you think? And it's educational, right?"

Lem tittered nervously. "Dr. Halloran said I should think of it that way."

"Want to see what it feels like there?"

Lem didn't even answer. He just reached out to stoke his fingertip over Michael's anus. He got a sort of strangled look and stroked it back and forth, back and forth, his fingers shaking. Then the tip of one finger penetrated a little, and Lem shuddered all over and made a strange sound. He pulled back and shifted his body away abruptly.

Michael's heart rate picked up, and he got a flush of heat down his body. He started to plump up, which was really bad timing. He'd thought he might show Lem what he looked like erect, if Lem seemed to be handling things okay. But sometimes, sessions just went sideways, and that was all she wrote.

Michael sat up and tied his robe closed. He shifted to sit closer to Lem and leaned into his arm a little. "You okay?"

Lem didn't answer. His head was turned away, but Michael could tell he was mortified.

"Hey. You did a great job with that. You get a gold star," Michael said warmly.

"I… I came in my pants." Lem's voice was low and embarrassed.

"I know." Michael bumped his shoulder a little harder. "That's kind of hot, really."

"It is?" Lem looked at him in surprise.

Michael smiled. "Totally."

Lem looked confused. "Why? I thought… isn't that called premature, um… you know?"

"Nah, not your first time. You get a couple of free passes 'til you get used to the whole deal. Anyway, it's hot to think that someone was so turned on by touching me that they orgasmed. Wouldn't you feel sexy if that happened to you? If John touched you and thought it was so hot that he came right there?"

Lem got a little humorous light in his eyes. "Yeah. I don't think he'd be touching me there, though. At least not in the office."

Michael laughed. "No, I suppose not. My tax accountant never offered."

Lem laughed out loud. He took a shaky breath. "Well anyway, I'm not attractive like you."

"When you find the right guy, he'll think you are. You did great today. You just looked at a naked man and touched one. That's major progress, isn't it?"

Lem thought about it. He smiled. "I guess it is."

"Totally. So! You can clean up in my bathroom while I make some tea. Sound good?"

~19~

"LOS ANGELES to Denver," James said smugly, turning over his destination card.

"Crap." Lance rolled his eyes. "Between you and Devon, I never win this game."

"And you have to put up with our ugly mugs on top of that," James quipped. "You're either a saint or a masochist."

"He's got five kids, so that goes without saying," Devon snarked, not without affection.

Devon drew a train car. He was close to completing a route from Washington to Boston. It always seemed to work out that way. James and Devon, who was a fierce competitor, always ended up on opposite coasts in Ticket to Ride. And probably in life too, at least metaphorically.

"Your turn," he said to Lance.

It was James's monthly Friday game night with his old writers' group. Five members were left—Devon, Lance, Frank, Allison, and James. They were all science fiction writers, and all but Frank were published. Frank "wrote for himself," and he wrote weird-ass alien bug stuff. Lance had written a series of sci-fi fantasy novels that had not sold well. Allison wrote vampire erotica, and Devon…. Devon had published nearly as much as James. And he never let anyone forget it. When they'd first started meeting, James had been the only one published and a sort of demigod thanks to *Troubadour Turncoat*. Devon lived in a fantasy where he was Anne Baxter to James's Bette Davis, the ingénue showing up the old horse.

James didn't much give a shit.

Though they'd started out as a writer's group, meeting monthly to read and review each other's work, they'd slowly transitioned to playing games. Devon got paranoid about people seeing his ideas, and

James and Lance got tired of Devon's nitpicky critiques. But no one seemed interested in giving up on the group entirely, least of all James, who had few enough friends. And game nights were fun. Usually.

Allison refilled the chip bowl and then sat back down at her chair where she draped herself over Devon. Their PDA always made James uncomfortable. Perhaps it was because he'd known them both before they got together, or maybe it was the way Devon seemed to flaunt it deliberately under James's nose, but it always served to remind him that he was alone, that meeting someone and hooking up was something that happened to other people—whole people.

Devon added three cars to his train on his next turn, nearly catching up to James's lead. But then James had a run of luck and completed Seattle to San Francisco. He won the game.

"Fuck!" Devon turned a disturbing shade of lobster red. He pushed himself back from the table harder than was necessary. "I need another beer."

"I'll get it, hon," said Allison. "Anyone else?"

They all took her up on it. It was still early.

While she was gone, Lance pulled his book bag up from underneath the table. He wore a smile that seemed out of keeping with his just having come in dead last. But then, Lance was a happy soul.

"Hey I picked up the latest issues of *Empire* today. Guess who's in it?"

He took the magazine from his bag and put it on the table, opened it to a marked page. It was about the Millennial Award. The nominees were listed. And there it was—*Troubadour Turncoat* by J.C. Guise.

"I feel so humbled that one of our very own has been honored," Lance said, faking an emotional sniff.

"You dog! Congrats, James," said Frank enthusiastically, finishing off his beer.

James felt a huge swell of pride. He reached for the magazine.

"Lemme see." Devon grabbed it before James could and turned it around on the table so he could see it.

"Nominees—*Troubadour Turncoat* by J.C. Guise, *American Gods* by Neil Gaiman, *Snow Crash* by Neil Stephenson, *The Andromeda Strain* by Michael Crichton, *Doomsday Book* by Connie

Willis, *The Forge of God* by Greg Bear, *Effervescent* by Peter Marlowe. Holy shit!"

James felt his stomach plummet at the list of names. He hadn't known the other nominees until just now.

"Yeah. Good luck with that," Devon snorted. "No way will you beat Gaiman or Stephenson. Though Crichton probably will be the sentimental favorite. And Peter Marlowe, he published *Excelente* last year, a huge hit. That thing was on the bestseller list for months. The Millennial Awards are for classic works, but they always pick someone who's either deceased, like Crichton, or someone who's currently hot." He looked at James with a shrug. "Too bad."

James kept his face cool as if he didn't care, but inside, he was in a stew of anger and bitter disappointment. He was dying to cut Devon's ego down to size with a snappy reply, but he couldn't think of anything, damn it.

No wonder he was a shit writer.

"Hey, now," Lance said defensively. "*Turncoat* has a good shot. People love that book."

"People love all those books," Devon argued snidely. "That's why they're nominated. You seriously think *Troubadour Turncoat* can beat *Snow Crash*? Especially since James has—" Devon cut himself off, but he didn't have to finish the sentence for James to know what he was going to say.

Especially since James has gone downhill ever since, like a slow-moving mudslide.

Allison brought their beers. They all took drinks, an awkward silence around the table. James kept his face blank, but he could feel the heat in his skin rising as he got more and more upset and... humiliated. Fuck. *Fuck.*

He wanted to leave, badly, but he was riding with Lance and he wasn't sure how to ask Lance if they could go without showing Devon he'd won. He was going to be sick.

"Well, it's an incredible honor just to be nominated," Lance said at last. "I mean, look at that list of books. That's fucking amazing. Nothing I ever write will deserve to be in company like that. That's an amazing accomplishment, James."

Lance smiled at James, and he forced a carefree smirk in return. "You set the cockles of my heart all aglow, Lance. Thank you."

But Lance's words felt a little too much like the kind of thing you say to a has-been, a recognition that James had once done something great.

He was proud of *Turncoat,* of course, and he always would be. But it was upsetting to think his best work was done before he was nineteen, that he'd never have that kind of success again. And though he still got trickles of royalties on *Turncoat,* it didn't pay the bills. Nor was it going to help him keep his publisher, not if his sales kept tanking, not if he didn't win the Millennial Award.

What was the old saying? You're only as good as your most recent hit. His publishers had been loyal, but they weren't in the charity business.

Devon didn't say anything to refute Lance's loyal tirade, but he and Allison exchanged a look. James didn't miss the *be nice* warning on Allison's face.

"Sure," Devon said coolly. "Just being nominated is huge. So are we going to play another game or what?"

WHEN LANCE dropped James off at his house, it was after midnight. After he got James's chair out of the back and made sure James was settled into it, he turned to get back in the driver's seat.

"Hey, have a great month. And congrats again on the Millennial Award."

James didn't want to be alone. He thought about trying to talk to Lance, but they really weren't that close. Lance had a wife and five young kids, a job. He had his own life.

"Thanks, Lance. Good night." James rolled up to his door and let himself in. Lance drove off.

Once inside, James was finally able to let down his guard. He sat for a moment in his chair inside the door, with the lights off, trying to catch his breath. It felt like a weight was settling down on top of him, like that old medieval execution method of crushing someone under a huge stone. He knew it was stupid for him to allow Devon to get so far under his skin. But it wasn't just about what Devon had said. It was the list of nominees for the Millennial Award. The truth was, James agreed with Devon—he didn't have a prayer. If there was a dark horse on that list, it was J.C. Guise. And the horrible, breath-stealing disappointment of that made him realize how much hope he'd been pinning on the thing.

But of course, he had. Hadn't he agreed to do a public book signing? Go to an award dinner? He'd pushed himself to do those things because he had this secret hope that winning a Millennial Award would salvage his career, turn the light on the descending darkness of his life, and chase the boogey-men of reality away.

That wasn't going to happen.

He rolled over to the couch and got himself out of the chair. He made himself turn on the lamp on the end table. He sat there, suffused with a numbing blackness.

The truth was, he'd been going downhill for a few years—bouts of depression, having to force himself to write, uninspired, unhappy. Broke. *Lonely.* His discouragement over his reviews and sales had sapped his confidence and made his writing even more stilted, mechanical and forced rather than swept out on a wave of passion. He'd accumulated a ten thousand dollar credit card bill just trying to keep afloat. And he'd been isolating himself too much. That was why he'd stuck with dating Chris, even though nothing about it had felt right, until finally Chris dumped him. James was pathetic, a twenty-nine-year-old virgin with no family and a handful of casual friends. He was tired of living alone, struggling on through life alone. He was tired of seeing other couples like Devon and Allison, while he himself was unloved, untouched.

He had fought so hard to be independent. Maybe, just maybe, he had overshot the mark.

Portland, Oregon, 1992

"JAMES, GET dressed."

Felicia put his clothes within his reach on the bed—a pair of pull-on pants, a T-shirt, socks, and tennis shoes. She started to leave the room.

"I need help!" James said petulantly. How stupid was this woman? He'd been at the home for two weeks, and she always helped him dress.

"James, your arms are perfectly fine, and you can bend your legs up—I saw you do it while you were playing on the floor. If you can reach your feet, you can dress yourself."

One of his three roommates, Danny, stood by his bed watching James intently. James thought about how he would have to roll around on the bed to get his clothes on. He hadn't had to dress himself since he got sick, and he didn't know if he could do it.

He didn't want to try.

Felicia stood waiting. James glared at Danny.

"I can tie my shoes. Want me to tie your shoes?" Danny asked. His face was open and eager.

"James can tie his own shoes. Go on downstairs, Danny. It's time for breakfast," Felicia said patiently.

Danny left.

James pushed his covers aside. He was wearing flannel pajamas, and he pushed them down to his thighs. He was still mad.

"I can't," James said when he'd gotten them down to his knees. It hurt to bend forward any farther—it was tight in his back. He flopped back and waited for Felicia to take over.

But she just looked at him. "Bring your foot up. You can grab the pants at your ankle and pull them off."

"But I can't move my leg!"

"Use your hips, James, and your hands. Pull your leg up toward you with your hands. You were sitting cross-legged on the floor yesterday when you were working on that floor puzzle, remember? Try to sit like that in the bed."

James hadn't been aware of it at the time. But now he tried to pull his worst leg in, pulling at it with his hands. He brought it up to midcalf on the opposite leg, but he was stiff and it hurt.

"I can't!" He flopped down again, now angrier than ever, angry that Felicia had made him try and fail, had made him prove how stupid and weak he was.

"James, you can do it," Felicia said firmly. "You're not trying hard enough."

"No!" James shouted, a denial of everything that was wrong.

"If you want to eat breakfast, get yourself dressed and come downstairs," Felicia said with a trace of steel. Then she left.

She *left him.*

James lay there all morning. He had a bedpan by the bed in case he had to go in the night, and he used it. He had a glass of water too, and he drank it. He was mad, and then he was just stubborn, but he wasn't going to try it again *ever.* That stupid lady was not his mother, and she couldn't tell him what to do. Anyway, his mother would have been happy to help him. Because she lov—

She loved him, she *did.*

I want my mommy.

In the afternoon, Danny and Rick came in to get a game. "Felicia says we can't help you, you have to do it by yourself. I can tie my shoes. Want me to show you how to tie your shoes?" Danny asked. He looked very worried.

"No," James said with an angry pout. Then because Danny looked sad, he added. "No, thank you. I'm okay."

That evening, while the other kids were at dinner, Felicia came into his room. She held a plate with some macaroni and cheese and applesauce. She didn't say anything, but she sat on the bed while he ate it, starving.

"Why are you smiling?" James asked her when he was done.

"You have a very strong will," Felicia said with a sigh. "That will serve you well one day, even if it's a pain in the ass for me right now."

She said *ass*, which surprised James. Mommy's friends said bad words, but James wasn't allowed to, even though he knew a whole lot of them. But he'd never imagined one coming out of Felicia's mouth. She looked so… teacherly.

"Will you get me dressed now, please?" James asked. He used the magic word because he'd been in bed all day and he was sick of it. He wanted to go downstairs and play games.

"No. James, I want to talk to you."

James crossed his arms and pouted.

She touched his leg over the covers. "I need to tell you something. Your legs are going to be like this for the rest of your life, James. Forever."

She sounded very serious, and the words made James's chest hurt like crazy. "No." His throat got hot.

"Yes, James. I'm sorry, but it's the truth."

James couldn't speak because if he tried to he would cry, and he wouldn't cry in front of Felicia. Still, he could feel wetness leaking from his eyes to the pillow. "When I'm as old as Danny?"

"Yes."

"And you?"

Felicia nodded. "Yes. But you're a very, very bright boy. And you have good use of your arms and hands. You can be independent if you work hard." He frowned at her, not knowing what she meant. "I mean that you can live in your own house someday and have a job, maybe even get married and have children of your own, be a daddy. None of that is out of your reach. But you have to choose it. You don't want to live in a group home like this forever and ever, do you?"

It wasn't a question. There was a heavy weight in her voice. James thought she was the meanest person he had ever known, but her meanness was not the kind like when kids poked a stick at a snake or pulled your hair. It was more like the kind that just *was*, like a dead kitten at the side of a road, like the meanness wasn't even her fault.

"But my momma will come for me," James whispered.

Felicia's eyes looked sad. She shook her head. "No, James. I don't think so. I'm sorry."

He didn't, couldn't, say anything. But something in his chest broke. Maybe it was the polio. Maybe his heart was becoming useless, too.

"We have a therapist come a few days a week, and I can have him show you some exercises to make you more limber so it's easier for you to reach your feet. Okay? But you can now, James. I know you can do it if you try. The more you can do things on your own, the less you will need someone to take care of you. And when you don't need someone to take care of you, you can go wherever you want in life. Do you understand that?"

James looked down at his hands clutching the covers and nodded. In truth, it would take him a long time to understand everything she'd said, like about a job and going anywhere he wanted. But what he did understand at that moment was this—his mother wasn't coming back. His legs would never be better, and no one would be there to love him, to take care of him. He had to learn how to take care of himself because no one else wanted to. No one else would.

Felicia got up. "Good night, James."

James cried himself to sleep. They were real tears this time— adult tears. The next morning, it took almost an hour, but he dressed himself.

Seattle, Washington, 2014

JAMES LOOKED in the bathroom mirror. The overhead light was harsh and brutal, and his face was stark, his eyes empty and haunted. He looked like a textbook definition of defeated. He felt edgy and unsettled in his own skin, as if a million ants were crawling around inside him. Desperate. Was this rock bottom? If not, he was close enough to see the light reflecting off it from here. He needed... he needed something, and he needed it bad. Something had to give.

He opened the medicine cabinet door and looked at the bottle of pills on the top shelf.

There's always a way out.

Last year, he'd researched suicide methods. Not because he was all that serious at the time, but his depressive spells had been becoming more frequent and he wanted to know he had an option if things got too bad financially, the old Frank Herbert poison gas tooth. He refused to ever be in a place where he could no longer live independently, whether because of his health or money. He'd gotten a bottle of the recommended drug, Pentobarbital, illegally off the Internet. He knew how much to take and what to chase it with.

Michael.

Michael's face popped into James's mind, making a wave of longing sweep through his body. Michael was the best thing to have happened to James in a long time, a new friend, someone willing to put up with James's limitations and eager for his company. He made James laugh, made him feel... brilliant, happy, full of life. But Michael wanted more. How long would he tolerate being kept at arms' length? Having their progress be a prisoner to James's insecurities? He would find someone else.

James put his hands on the sink and leveraged himself out of his chair, grasped the bottle of pills, looked at the label.

James.

The single word was spoken quietly, beseechingly, in his head. The voice wasn't that of his own conscience, or that of Amanda or Felicia. It was a soft, male voice.

James.

Something had to give.

MICHAEL WAS dragged from sleep by the ominous notes of the *Twilight Zone* music—his cell phone. He kept it on his bedside table just in case there was an emergency with one of his patients. Its sinister song was creepy in the dark night, and he sat up, shaking off his dreams. The caller ID said "James."

"Hello?" Michael answered the phone anxiously. It wasn't like James to call in the middle of the night.

"I'm sorry to wake you," James said, his voice rough.

"Hey, it's okay." Michael sat up fully, swinging his legs out of bed. "What's going on?"

"I shouldn't have bothered you. I just—"

James didn't finish the sentence. The skin on the back of Michael's neck prickled at the tone in his voice. He clutched the phone harder. "Bad night?"

Breathing. "Yeah. Bad night."

"I'm coming over."

"You don't have to." But the plea was there.

"Babe, I'm coming over. I'll be there as soon as I can."

Michael hung up.

HE GOT to James's house around two in the morning. On the drive over, and now, standing at James's door, Michael felt a strong sense of urgency, a need to be with James as soon as possible. Michael trusted his gut. James needed him.

James opened the door. He was in his wheelchair, dressed in soft sweatpants and a laundry-thin T-shirt. He didn't say anything, but the bleak misery and raw need in his eyes shot down inside Michael in a bolt of pure pain.

Michael dropped his duffle bag inside the door, leaned over, and took James's face in his hands. Neither said a word as they studied each other, but Michael knew what James needed. The despair rolled off him in waves—he needed... he needed to be held, he needed to be loved.

"Let me," Michael said quietly.

James closed his eyes for a moment and then nodded, just one little jog of his chin, but it was enough. Michael firmed his hands on James's jaw and kissed him.

Michael had wanted to kiss James for forever—at least it felt that way. That chaste kiss they'd shared in Ellensburg had been incredibly frustrating. He'd wanted so much more—he'd wanted everything. And now... now James was letting Michael kiss him. *James was kissing Michael back.*

Michael was already aroused. But when the desperate need poured forth from James—in the way he took over the kiss, reaching up to hold Michael's neck and plunging his tongue into Michael's mouth, in the way his shaking hand slid around Michael's waist—the passion boiled up, hot and sharp and fast. Michael gasped at the crazed strength of it. With his mouth so thoroughly occupied, the gasp became a whimper. The kiss ramped up even hotter. He devoured James's mouth, and James devoured him back—all tongues and teeth and lips and urgent longing.

All of James's loneliness was there in that kiss—the hand of a drowning man grasping frantically at a rope. It sparked every instinct of love and compassion Michael had.

He pulled away from the kiss so he could slip onto James's lap. He kissed James's throat, hungry for all of him, for every bit of skin. "Let's go to your bedroom," he whispered. "I need you so bad." The fingers of one hand wove through James's thick hair while the other slid around James's solid chest and grasped him firmly. Even in his desire, Michael was conscious about wanting to let James know—*I've got this. Lean on me.*

But James didn't feel weak. He felt strong, deliciously so. His chest was broad, and his hands were large and firm on Michael's back. A bit hesitantly, they slid down to cup the top of Michael's ass, pulling his hip in closer. Michael could feel James's erection, large and hard, in his sweats, and knew the moment James felt his erection—pushing against the forearm in his lap. James made a hungry sound in his throat and gripped him tighter.

God, yes. Like that. Hold me hard.

"I'm... a virgin," James said in a rough voice as Michael kissed his way up James's jaw.

Michael heaved a sigh. He wasn't surprised, but it made him mad—angry that James had missed out on so much. He gave James a searing kiss before pulling away to look into his eyes.

"You deserve to be loved, and I want to love you tonight—so much. Are you okay with that?"

For a long moment, James stared back, not saying anything. The sexual tension was thick as fog between them. James's erection throbbed once against Michael's ass. It was nearly unbearable. He wanted to touch it so badly.

"Yes," James whispered. "I want you. But you deserve better than a phone call in the middle of the night. You deserve to be wooed. We can wait."

Michael was touched by James's sincerity, but there was no way he was going to let this opportunity pass by, not when James so clearly needed him.

"James, you wooed me long ago."

Michael underscored his answer with another long kiss, hot and heady. He kissed James until they were both panting, until he could sense nothing but pleasure and desire in James's trembling—no fear, no second thoughts. When James began tentatively rutting against his hip, Michael pulled away and stood up.

"Let's go to your bedroom," Michael said.

THIS WAS it.

James was exhilarated, nervous, aroused, and terrified. Mostly, he was determined. Very soon, he would no longer be a virgin. Soon he would be in bed with a man, touching and being touched, having sex with another human being. His need for human contact had finally burned brighter than his self-consciousness. And suddenly, he found that he trusted Michael. Even if Michael was disgusted, he would try to hide it, he wouldn't be cruel. Worst case, they could be friends after. Right?

But Michael seemed a million miles away from being disgusted.

They made it into the bedroom. Michael gave him space to maneuver around to the bed while the look of desire in his eyes, and his small touches, made sure James never came down from the lust he'd felt in the living room.

Jesus Christ, those kisses.

No one had ever kissed James like that—hot and wet and hungry. Chris's kisses had made James yearn for something that wasn't there. Michael's kisses burned him up inside, made sensations rush through his body that he'd never experienced before. He was drunk with desire. Nothing existed except Michael's lips and hands and the trembling response of his own body. And Michael wanted him too, that's what was so incredible. He could feel the passion in Michael's kiss, in the skimming glide of those delicate hands, touching him everywhere, in the press of Michael's hardness against him.

It was more than he'd ever dared dream. How had he ever written a passionate scene without having felt *this*? He'd had no fucking clue what it felt like to be set aflame by someone's touch and be burnt down to pure, mindless want.

Michael pulled away long enough for James to swing himself onto the bed. He pulled on Michael's hand, bringing him along. He didn't want to stop kissing Michael, didn't want to have time to think or let his nerves take over. He wanted to drown in the desire and not come up for air. With their lips locked, James pushed himself back on the bed, and Michael climbed over him, laid on top of him softly, his light weight pressing James down as they ravished each other's mouths.

Michael broke the kiss. "I want to touch you." He rose up and tugged at the hem of James's T-shirt.

James let the shirt come off. Michael sat up, straddling James's hips so that he was sitting on James's erection. He rocked on it, very deliberately, as he peeled off his own shirt.

"Oh, God," James groaned. The feeling of Michael rocking on his aching cock and the sight of Michael's chest—so lean, soft, and sweet—almost did him in. He reached up, but Michael scooted backward.

"Let me take care of you," Michael said, with eyelids half-lidded and a flush on his cheeks. He looked like James felt—lost in passion—and James drank in every nuance of his expression like the aphrodisiac that it was. Michael ran his hands over James's chest, pressing his palms against his nipples, making James groan and arch up for more. Then his hands skimmed down and began to pull at James's waistband.

A moment of panic sliced through the haze in James's mind. He grabbed Michael's hand. Michael stopped immediately, looking at him with those big, soft eyes. He didn't fight James's hold.

"I want to touch you so much. Can I pull them down just a bit?" Michael asked, licking his lips.

James felt unsure, the fears reemerging. *If he sees my legs... what if he....* What if that look of desire on Michael's face changed to something else and this was all ruined? James thought he might die if that happened.

He was still holding Michael's hands, frozen with uncertainty, but Michael's thumb found his erection and rubbed it slowly over the sweats. James swallowed a groan.

Michael gave him a wicked smile and scooted back farther so he could lean over and kiss James's cock through his sweatpants. *Kiss. Kiss, kiss.*

Oh, fucking Zeus and Aphrodite and Loki and anyone else you could name. James's hands fell away from Michael's, useless.

Still kissing softly over the cloth, Michael reached up slowly to James's waistband. Big brown eyes full of wickedness looked up at him as Michael mouthed his cock and started to tug down the waistband slowly, god so slowly. James whimpered and canted up his hips.

"Just... not all the way," James gritted out. *Oh, God, please.*

But Michael wasn't rushing anything. He pulled down the elastic waistband of James's sweatpants and briefs just enough to show the tip of his cock.

"Is this okay?" he asked with an arched eyebrow. He stuck out his tongue and flicked it over the slit.

James hissed, canting his hips up again. "*Michael.*"

"Hmm?" Michael tugged the waistband down another inch. "How about now?" He suckled the tip into his mouth.

"Fuck!" James grabbed Michael's hands, needing to hang on to something. He'd fantasized about this a million times, about being in a man's mouth. He could hardly believe it was happening.

Michael dragged the waistband down bit by bit, licking each new millimeter of shaft as it was revealed. Jesus, he was temptation incarnate with those naughty big brown eyes, and his tongue felt.... Christ, it was warm and rough and amazing.

"Oh, shit."

Michael tucked the pants underneath James's balls. "This okay?" he asked, looking up at James seriously, not teasing now.

James nodded, but then, he would have agreed to anything looking down like that, at his own cock, rigidly erect and red, and Michael's pretty face *right there.*

Michael swallowed him down and started to suck.

Oh. It was the most incredible sensation—Michael's warm, wet mouth on him, the vacuum and friction of his drawing sucks. You think you can imagine what a blowjob will feel like, but no, really, you fucking can't. It was the best thing he'd ever felt in his life, and he could easily come like that, and quickly. But James didn't want that, didn't want it to end so soon. And then, as soon as he had that thought, something else pulled at him too. Michael's mouth was heaven, but... no. Something was wrong. James sat up, pushing Michael away.

They looked at each other for a long moment, Michael braced on his hands and knees, James sitting up. Michael studied his face intently.

"Not good?" he said softly.

"I'm... " James said, frustrated with himself.

"It's okay," Michael said, shifting to take his hand. "It doesn't matter *at all* how long you last. It's so hot to be with you, babe. I'm close myself."

James shook his head, trying to put his unease into words. "No, I... don't want to just lie there."

Yes, that was it. Michael was *servicing* him. James didn't like that, didn't like feeling helpless, useless, babied. Why did he have to feel that way *now?* Why couldn't he just accept a blowjob like any man with an inch of sanity would? He looked at Michael in frustration.

Michael studied him for a moment and then gave a shy little smile of understanding.

He got off the bed and pulled off his jeans, underwear, and socks so that he was completely nude. He stood by the side of the bed, stroking himself lightly and letting James look his fill. His cock was larger than James had expected, given Michael's size. It was... unbelievably sexy. He was uncircumcised and very hard. As he touched himself, his cock pointed at James as if begging for his attention, a drop of precum glistening on the exposed tip. Damn, that was.... *God.* It was so much fucking better in real life.

Michael must have seen the desire on his face, because his own expression flashed with lust. "You can touch it, babe," he said, breathing hard. He took a step closer. "Do what you want, what feels right."

James reached out and touched the tip of it. "Can I taste you?" His voice was like sandpaper, and his heart rate doubled as the words left his mouth, but yes, that was what he wanted.

Michael seemed to like the idea too. "God, yes."

James pushed himself up and scooted back against the headboard. "Let me have it," he growled in a voice that was demanding and shaky at the same time. "I'm going to be shit at this, and I don't care."

"Oh, God, I don't either," Michael groaned.

He climbed onto the bed on his knees, moving up close and grasping the headboard in both hands. James scooted down a bit until he was level with Michael's cock. He circled the base with one hand, stuck out his tongue, and licked at the head, looking up at Michael, daring him to come closer.

Michael moaned deep in his throat. "That is so hot," he whispered. He watched, as if wanting to make sure it was okay, as James rubbed the slick head against his lips. It felt right, good, not to be treated like an invalid but to be treated like a man, a sexual man. It didn't matter that James's legs didn't work, or that he didn't have any experience. Michael was surrendering to him, giving him control, and damn if that didn't stir something deep in James that made him feel powerful and potent and so horny he could burst. He leaned forward and sucked the head in.

Michael groaned, low and anguished, making James feel about ten feet tall. Maybe he was shit at this, but it didn't sound like it by Michael's reactions, and it didn't *feel* like it, not when there was the taste of precum on his tongue and a hard cock rocking ever so gently in his mouth. He closed his eyes and took in more, sucking fairly hard. He wasn't sure what the right amount of pressure felt the best, but he remembered how incredibly good it felt when Michael suckled him, and so he did the same. He was rewarded with a whimper of pleasure from Michael and the rocking turned to thrusts, though Michael was careful to keep them shallow.

James sucked in as much as he could, but he couldn't take it all before Michael's cock hit the back of his throat and triggered his gag reflex. So he wrapped a hand around the base and, having measured his limit, felt confident enough to move his mouth up and down, sucking and releasing. It took them a moment, but they found a better rhythm when James put a hand on Michael's hip and guided him. He kept his head still against the headboard while he moved Michael's hips in and out.

James loved the feeling of it, loved the sounds Michael made as he sucked on every withdraw or when he pushed the flat of his tongue against the shaft. He loved the stuttering passion in the cock itself, its demand and unapologetic taking of what it needed, not rough, but not overly gentle either. He loved controlling Michael's movements with his hand, teasing him by forcing him to slow, or making him whimper when he sped up.

"Oh, God, *James*, feels so good. So good. Oh, yeah. Oh, fuck." Michael's words and sighs and moans made James so hard and so turned on. He dared remove the hand wrapped around the base of Michael's cock and shoved it down his sweatpants. He could still control Michael's movements with the hand on his hip, and God, it felt so incredible to touch himself while Michael's cock was hard in his mouth. He was so hypersensitive with arousal and so close.

Michael's fingers stroked his hair, then his cheeks. His thumb went to the corner of James's mouth where it could feel the cock slipping in and out of his lips.

And that felt so dirty, James lost it. He felt the orgasm churning in his balls, and a second later, he exploded. He moaned around Michael's cock. And Michael, still thrusting, growled his approval.

"Oh, fuck, that's so hot. Oh, babe."

He thrust harder for several seconds, and then, while James was still shuddering from his own orgasm, Michael said, "Oh—I'm coming." He tried to pull away. But James reached up with his semen-soaked hand and pulled Michael tight with both hands on his hips. James sucked him hard.

Michael cried out. Cum flooded James's mouth, and it was a little too much and a little too bitter, but the *idea* of it was awesome, and he just swallowed as quickly as he could. He held Michael there, unable to believe he had a warm, living male coming in his mouth, that it was Michael, beautiful Michael.

Finally, it was done, and Michael gently disengaged himself. He fell to the side of James on the bed, limp-limbed and sweaty.

"Come 'ere," he said, trying to tug James down from the headboard. It was extremely lazy and ineffectual tugging, but James went.

He scooted down to lay on his back, carefully making sure his sweatpants were in place, then he couldn't resist rolling onto his side so he could look at Michael. Naked, damp, and sated, Michael was so lovely it took James's breath away. His skin all but glowed. His dark hair was a glorious mess. His eyes were sleepy and content as he gazed back, his lips swollen and red from kissing.

James tried to memorize this image. He wanted to remember it always. It could inspire a thousand stories.

So out of his league. What was Michael Lamont doing in his bed? James had just had the most amazing experience of his life, but... he suddenly felt anxious about what came next. He liked Michael intensely, no matter how much he'd tried to guard himself against it.

"Did you know you were a top?" Michael asked with a little smile.

"I am?"

"Oh, yeah."

James thought about it. He hadn't liked the feeling of being passive. But directing Michael had been as arousing as hell.

"Interesting. I guess I'd better order *Domination for Dummies*. Wouldn't want to leave my natural inclinations unexploited."

"I'd be happy to help you exploit them," Michael said, running a finger up James's chest.

James just looked at him, his breath caught somewhere in his chest. He was afraid to trust this. He could feel the walls inside him rattle, as if reminding him they were there, and that they were there for a damned good reason.

Michael must have seen something on his face, because suddenly, he looked vulnerable as hell. He sat up on one elbow, face stricken. "Do you want me to go?" he asked quietly.

Christ, had so many men really just taken sex from Michael and then thrown him out? It made James want to rip them apart with his bare hands. And it made him want to pull Michael to his chest and reassure him. And suddenly, his own walls were no longer there, or at least no longer important.

"Fuck no, I don't want you to go," James said firmly. He interlaced his fingers with Michael's to emphasize his point.

Michael studied his face, as if he didn't quite believe it. "I really like you."

James shook his head. "Why?"

"Because you're intelligent and funny and brave. You're super cute…."

James rolled his eyes.

"You *are*. And I love your mind—your sense of fantasy and fun and compassion. I think I've had a crush on you ever since I read *Troubadour Turncoat*."

James worried his lip. He was uncomfortable with what Michael was saying. Michael was in love with an illusion. He felt obliged to try to burst that bubble, even though it was self-immolation to do so.

"Michael, I'm permanently handicapped. And my career isn't going well. My book sales are way off. I'm not doing great financially. I don't know what the future holds."

"Hmm." Michael considered that. "You also have a hard time trusting people."

"People leave," James said simply.

Michael's brow scrunched up in pain, and he tucked himself against James's chest. He hesitated. "My mom told me once—relationships end until the one that doesn't. So you can't be sad, really. Because if the wrong ones didn't end, you wouldn't be available when the right one came along."

James thought about it. "I'm sure that makes sense in some alternate reality."

Michael giggled and pinched his side. "It totally makes sense."

James tentatively put his hands on Michael's back. The skin was so soft, and Michael's back so beautifully shaped. It felt incredible to pull him tight and hold him, almost better than the sex. Okay, not really, but it felt damn good.

"You're too beautiful for me," James whispered. "When you first approached me, all I could think was that life didn't work that way. The most beautiful boy in the universe doesn't come knocking on the grisly recluse's door. If I wrote that plot, I'd be laughed off Goodreads."

"Don't they say life is stranger than fiction?" Michael asked sleepily.

"Nothing is stranger than my fiction."

Michael laughed. "That's true. Anyway, you're very sweet, but I'm not that beautiful. Honestly. I'm short, and skinny, and too fem. I have a nervous stomach, and I suck at sports."

"Don't forget the nose."

"What about my nose?" Michael said in mild outrage, looking up to meet James's eyes.

"It's large," James said solemnly. "A monumental proboscis."

Michael huffed and snuggled closer, so close that when he blinked, his eyelids tickled James's chest. "You use your sarcasm to try to keep people out."

That struck a bit close. James swallowed. "You use your sexuality to try to pull people in."

Michael stared up at him. "That's true."

James pushed the hair out of Michael's eyes. "Given the current situation we find ourselves in, apparently you're much more effective at your strategy than I am at mine."

"Also true," Michael said, getting a little gleam in his eyes. Then he yawned, hugely. He covered his mouth, abashed. "Excuse me."

"I'm the one who woke you up in the middle of the night. Want to sleep?"

Michael hesitated, looking uncertain. "Here?"

"I told you I wasn't going to throw you out," James said quietly. "I think maybe we should discuss your taste in men."

Michael smiled. "At the moment, I'm quite happy with my taste in men. I wouldn't mind sleeping, though."

"Mmm." James was thinking that he had to get up, unfortunately, because the inside of his sweatpants was coated in cum, and he didn't want to sleep like that. He worried about how far his chair was from the bed, and how he could do this gracefully. These were all things you didn't have to think about when you lived alone and weren't having sex with someone.

As if reading his mind, Michael pulled away. "Those pants must feel sticky. Let me get something to clean you up." He popped out of bed.

"You don't have to do that," James said, but Michael was already gone.

Fortunately, when he returned with a wet cloth, he only handed it to James and then slipped back into bed, making no further move to be helpful. James pushed the cloth under the waistband of his sweats and wiped himself up. It was still uncomfortably wet, and he wished he could just take it all off. But he couldn't, wouldn't, not with Michael here. With a sigh, he tossed the cloth onto the rug and lay back down. Michael pulled the covers over both of them and wrapped around him again. James pushed Michael's hips back, not wanting him to entangle their legs, not wanting Michael to be able to feel how thin his were. Michael obliged without comment, but he kept his arms wrapped around James. It was not as suffocating as it ought to be. Or at all.

It had been a long time since anyone had held James. Years and years. It felt so sweet it hurt.

Michael fell asleep in minutes, but James lay awake for a good hour, cradling Michael in his arms, stroking his skin softly. He alternately felt hope—hope that this could really be something, that

Michael was something new and marvelous and real—and fear and a bit disgusted with himself for getting in so deep so fast.

He and Michael had had sex. He'd made Michael come, and Michael hadn't for one second seemed disgusted. Of course, James had managed to avoid the big reveal, but still... It was amazing. They had touched and kissed and gotten off together, and... and Michael still wanted him. He was still here.

People leave.

James knew he had to make a decision. He could keep pushing Michael away and save himself from the potential of pain. Or....

Christ. Who was he kidding? He was already in so deep it would hurt if Michael walked right now.

There was no decision to make, really. When, against all odds, the miraculous happened and the spaceship landed for you and the hatch opened, you got on. The end. It didn't even matter if you would wind up as food or taken on a trip to the stars. Some things were worth the risk.

Maybe life *was* stranger than fiction. A few hours ago, he'd been in one of the darkest moments of his life, and now, right now, he was in the happiest, most incandescent stillness. Joy.

Please. God, let me have this, at least for a while.

James kissed Michael's neck and finally fell asleep.

~20~

JAMES DREAMT he was swimming in a viscous, warm fluid that was doing amazing things to his cock. He woke up to see the blankets pulled down and Michael's dark hair working away over his groin. Michael hadn't pulled his sweats down far, only enough to free his cock and, well, damn if James was going to complain about that.

God, he could get used to this.

"Wanna touch you," James mumbled as soon as he was fully conscious.

Michael lithely scrambled around without stopping his mouth action and presented James with the very naked lower half of himself— very naked and very hard. Lords of the seven heavens, but he made James's mouth water. He'd watched a lot of porn over the years, and he'd thought virtual sex was the only kind he was ever going to have. It blew his mind that he had a real, live cock to play with, and such a gorgeous one at that, full and pink, and with that sexy foreskin pulled back just enough to let the glans peek out. With a grateful sigh, James rolled onto his side and eagerly drew Michael in.

Second time having sex and it's sixty-nine. Hell fucking yeah.

The sensation of Michael's hot mouth on him as he himself got to taste and feel Michael was even better than it had been the night before. At some point, he'd convinced himself that sex with another person wouldn't be that much better than masturbation. God, he'd never been so ridiculously wrong in his life.

Several minutes later, minutes filled with groans and heavy, muffled breathing, and more pleasure than ought to be legal without a license of some sort, James felt that Michael was close. He grew impossibly hard and made continual whimpering noses around James's cock. James felt Michael start to go, and he pushed himself in deep and rolled over the edge at the same time. And, *fuck*, that was perfect, coming as Michael pumped into his mouth, like some ouroboros of escalating bliss. At last, they both flopped back, breathing hard. Michael scrambled around again and kissed James's lips and cheeks in brief, silly pecks.

"Breakfast?"

"You offering or ordering?" James grumbled.

"I'm offering to cook if you're offering up the groceries. Do you have eggs?"

"No, I have sperm. What the hell do they teach you in school these days?"

Michael giggled. "Chicken eggs, wise ass. In your refrigerator."

"Oh, I see. Yes, I have chicken eggs."

"Awesome. I make a mean scrambled egg."

Michael hopped out of bed and pulled on his jeans. He absentmindedly pushed James's chair closer to the bed so it was within reach. With a yawn and a stretch, he left the room.

James looked at the chair for a long moment, his heart beating hard. Then he smiled.

JAMES WASN'T quite sure how to act with a boyfriend. Chris had come over regularly, and they'd watched movies and sometimes cooked meals, but Chris had never been very affectionate. Michael was something else. He couldn't seem to keep his hands off James— nudging his arm, placing a hand on the back of his neck and rubbing affectionately, leaning against him on the couch, or giving him a quick kiss, or a not-so-quick one.

It made James feel... giddy. Like Mary Poppins and Dick Van Dyke skipping through a colored wonderland giddy. Michael liked him as much as he liked Michael. He liked James so much he wanted to be touching all the time.

The Saturday morning after James lost his blowjob virginity— twice—they had eggs and toast, then spent time on the couch reading the news on the Internet. They each showered separately and spent more time on the couch comparing their tablet book libraries. James's tended to more classic sci-fi while Michael owned mostly modern sci-fi and m/m romance. Michael didn't mention going home, and James didn't either. They took a nap in the afternoon and did sixty-nine again with Michael teaching him the agony and the ecstasy of edging and James trying out a little bit of toppy aggression with some mild ass slaps, which turned Michael into a moaning puddle of surrender. James fucking *loved* it. It was *the best thing ever.*

Afterward, as sated as he'd ever been, James fell into the sleep of the dead.

Michael woke James up with a nudge. It was dark. "What time is it?" James asked, half sitting up.

"Eight. Hey, I have to go home. I've gotten called in for a shift tomorrow morning, and I don't have any of my work clothes here or my products or anything."

"Okay," James said, looking at him blearily. "You should know that I would never make you appear in public without product in your hair. I'm not that cruel." Michael's fingers were interlaced with his, and it felt so good he didn't want to let go.

Michael smirked. "You think you're joking, but believe me, no one wants that. So… when will I, um, see you again?" Michael looked as reluctant to go as James was to have him leave. All he wanted to do was pull Michael back into bed. It was an intensely physical urge.

Wow, was this what love felt like? Like you were tethered to the other through invisible strings that pumped some ethereal, and completely addictive, joy compound into your veins? So addictive you didn't want to let them go? Or was this merely infatuation?

It probably was infatuation, James decided, but there was no 'mere' about it.

He let go of Michael's hand so he could brush the long bangs away from those big brown eyes. "When do you want to see me again?"

Michael bit his lower lip sheepishly. "Well, I could go pick up my stuff, grab some takeout, and come back here. Or… not. It's okay if you need some alone time."

James gave him a fierce frown. "Eggrolls. And don't forget the mustard."

Michael gave him a blinding smile. "You bastard," he prompted.

"Don't forget the mustard, you *bas*tard," James growled.

"I'M SO in love, Marnie," Michael said with a big, fat sigh.

It was Monday afternoon, and Michael had filled Marnie in on all the deets from that Friday night on, a nonstop Jamesfest that had been broken only when he'd had to go to work.

"Oh, hon, I have a good feeling about this one." Marnie was wearing a hot pink sweater and orange leggings today, with a matching shade of bright orange lipstick. How could anyone who was that bold a dresser be wrong about anything?

"You do?" Michael asked hopefully.

"Absolutely." Marnie squeezed his hand. "Not a doubt in my mind."

"I really, really like him. I mean, I like him more than it makes any sense to, do you know what I mean? Like my heart has already signed the contract and picked up the keys even though my brain is still going 'wait… what?'"

"Makes perfect sense to me. Heart, brain, and cock—they're all independent systems. They may cooperate at times, but clearly, it's your heart calling the shots this time. It may take a little while for your head to catch up, but that's okay. New love is grand. Savor all the crazy, muddled might of it."

The crazy, muddled might of it. Michael liked that. It felt exactly like that.

"I'm just afraid something will go wrong, like maybe he'll decide he wants to go back to just being friends."

"Oh, hon!" Marnie said with a brassy laugh. "You got that boy into bed for the first time in his life, and from what you've said, you had a fine time there—"

"We did." That was putting it mildly. Michael found James so attractive—with his sharp mind, handsome face, and swimmer's torso. He also had a gorgeous cock and a toppy streak that turned Michael on so hard he could barely stand it. It surprised him. He'd never had a boyfriend who was so assertive in bed, and he found he loved giving up control, letting someone else take charge. It made Michael feel lusted after, sexy, adored. And James's large, wide mouth sucked like nobody's business. Marnie would love to hear all of that, point for point, but there were some things that were just too wonderful to share.

"Well then, if you think he's going to walk away now that you've gotten him laid, you're crazy. He's gonna be a heroin cowboy for the foreseeable future, and you're the only horse in town."

"Marnie!" Michael gasped, laughing.

She feigned innocence. "What? You were lovebirding for the past two days, weren't you? And having lots of takeout, and I don't mean Thai."

Michael giggled. "Yeah. I think I've had my protein allotment for the week. Damn, that was fun."

"Uh-huh. You two have a connection, and it's strong enough that neither one of you wants to let the other out of your sight if you don't have to. I've never had a casual thing start that way, and my two big loves did, so there you go."

"Thanks, Marnie." Michael felt reassured. She was right. He'd never felt this strong a connection to anyone. And even though James tried to play it cool, Michael was pretty sure he felt it too. It was just that Michael wanted things with James to work out so badly. He knew in his heart it was right. But it was new and fragile, and that was scary.

He frowned. Okay, very scary. "I still haven't told him about the surrogacy."

"Oh, Michael." Marnie gave him a pitying frown. She shook her head and made sympathetic noises. "Honey, what are you going to do?"

"I don't know. I'm so afraid to tell him now. What if he hates it? What if he gets his feelings hurt? What if he decides I'm a slag and dumps me?"

"Well, what choice do you have? You can't lie to your one true love, Michael," Marnie said this softly, but with utter conviction.

Michael smiled despite his worry. *His one true love.* What a beautiful idea. "No, I know that but... I've been thinking...." He hesitated. It was hard to even say it. "I was thinking maybe I should quit. I can't expect any guy to be okay with it. I never had a special someone that was important enough to me before to consider quitting. But if it came down to choosing between the surrogacy and James...."

Marnie rubbed Michael's arm. "I know how much you love that job, Michael. Maybe you should just talk to James. Maybe he'll understand."

"Maybe," Michael said doubtfully.

But if I quit now, he never needs to know, and I never need to risk losing him.

Looked at that way, it seemed the path of least resistance. Maybe he wouldn't have to tell James, ever. Or maybe he could explain about the surrogacy later, after he'd quit. That wouldn't be so bad, would it? James couldn't be upset about it if he'd already quit.

But then he thought about turning in his resignation at Expanded Horizons, which he loved. He thought about telling Tommy and his mother that he couldn't come back anymore, or stopping his sessions with shy Lem Peterson, who was making such brave progress. And that felt really, enormously crappy.

"Michael, what are you thinking?" Marnie asked suspiciously.

Michael hugged himself, feeling cold. "I don't know what's right anymore."

"Did you see a client this morning?"

Michael smiled a little. "Yeah. It went very well." Tommy had been really upbeat that morning, and they'd had a good session. Seeing him like that had eased Michael's fears about hurting Tommy.

"And how did that feel to you?" Marnie prodded curiously.

Michael shrugged. "I dunno, Marnie. It's like... it's a different part of my heart." Michael rubbed his chest. Sometimes, he could actually *feel* that part of his heart, like a little extra chamber where he kept his love for his patients. "It doesn't feel like I'm doing something with another guy—it's just not the same. What I do for my clients is about... my work. Healing. Giving. Some of the men I work with are so... broken, you know? And I just want to help them."

"And that's not how it is with your writer in the wheelchair?" Marnie sounded skeptical.

"No," Michael said firmly. "James is... strong and so fucking brilliant. And he's beautiful and.... he has all of me—the part that I give away and the part that I keep just for myself. When I'm with him, it's about *me,* I mean, about living my life, being complete, having what *I* want and need, having a love of my very own. He fits me. Damn, I can't even explain it to you. How would I ever explain it to James?"

"Well, sweetums, you're gonna have to try," Marnie said wisely.

But the thought terrified Michael. He *would* leave surrogacy for James, if it came down to it. But it would be foolish to do that before he was sure that he and James were going to last. It was still so new. What if he quit his job and then James withdrew again? That wouldn't be fair to Jack and Trudy, or to his clients. No, he would wait, at least until he knew they were going to be a real relationship. Then he would quit.

It didn't make him happy, but the alternatives were worse.

Michael sighed. "Come on, Miss Thing. It's time for your meds."

~21~

JAMES GAZED down into Michael's eyes from his position leaning over him in bed. There were little bits of amber in there, James decided, but only when the morning light hit them from the window just like this.

James loved to stare at Michael. Neither his eyes nor his hands could get enough. Fortunately, Michael didn't seem weirded out by it. He just stared back.

They'd been hot and heavy for two weeks now, and so far, the desire to be together as much as possible hadn't faded for either of them. Some days, especially when Michael was at work, the thought would just strike James from out of the blue—*Michael is my boyfriend. He wants me, and I want him.* And it seemed so unreal, like a marvelous dream he would surely wake from. He tried to hang on to his reticence and his dignity, a little bit, but it was a losing game.

"See any motes in there?" Michael asked.

James smiled. "No motes, but I got a glimpse of a logo. It says 'made in Taiwan.'"

Michael huffed. "Are you implying that I'm a living doll? Or that I'm cheap?"

James smirked. He was about to answer when there was a knock on the front door. James rolled off Michael and frowned.

Michael sat up. "You expecting someone?"

"No."

"Postman? UPS? Candygram?" Michael twirled a bit of James's hair.

"Might be something from my publisher." James was expecting a box of some German editions, but usually, the postman just left packages at the door.

"I'll get it." Michael hopped up and dragged on a pair of flannel PJ bottoms. Damn, his ass was so cute. He went to answer the door.

James heard him open the door and then... voices. It took him a minute to realize that one of the voices was female. Concerned, James sat up and reached for the shirt draped over the nightstand. He still wore his sweatpants to bed with Michael—always—so at least he didn't have far to go to get dressed.

He pulled down his shirt and looked up to find Michael entering the room. He closed the door quietly and came to squat down by James's side.

"Who is it?" James said, frightened by the concerned look on Michael's face.

"James, it's your mother."

James wouldn't have gone out into the living room, but Michael convinced him he had to face it. After all, the woman had come to his house. She knew where he lived. He might be able to avoid it today, but he wouldn't be able to avoid it forever.

He felt like running as fast and far as he could. Irony.

He felt like puking.

Michael handed James a shirt from his closet—a nice black button-down—and chewed his lip. "There's a story here. What is it? Your mom asked if you lived here. I take it you haven't seen her in a long time?"

James shook his head. He wasn't able to speak, not with what was waiting for him in the next room. He just wanted to get it over with. Michael seemed to understand.

"You going to be okay?" he asked, rubbing James's shoulder.

He wasn't. He was about as okay as a bleeding man who'd just been thrown into a lion's den. He fussed at his hair anxiously. "How do I...," he managed to croak out. He didn't give a shit really, but he wanted his mother to see that he was not the helpless baggage she'd left in that home for broken toys.

"Let me," Michael said softly. James let Michael finger comb his hair and even put some clear balm on his lips.

"You look handsome as the devil, m'lord," Michael said.

"You and your romances," James said roughly. "Fuck it. Let's go."

His mother was standing in the living room. Seeing her face again took James's breath away, and not in a good way—in a can't-get-air, may-die kind of way.

How many times had he dreamt about her? He'd been only six the last time he'd seen her, but she'd left him a photo, a photo he'd almost destroyed a dozen times but, mindful that he might one day regret it, had instead buried in a hat box at the very top of his closet. He hadn't looked at it in years.

And still, he would have known her anywhere.

Her hair was still long and brown, though it was thinner now and streaked with gray. She had a strong Roman nose and square jaw that looked a lot like the ones he saw in the mirror every day. She was tall for a woman, maybe five eight, and carried a bit of bulk. Her body was shapeless under a long Indian-patterned skirt and thick sweater.

He stopped his chair across the room from her, frozen in the spot where he'd entered from the hall. He felt Michael slip around him and put a hand on his shoulder. But he couldn't look at him, couldn't move.

Emotions bubbled up like from some subterranean pit... hurt, annoyance, confusion, and rage. *So much rage.*

And then she burst into tears.

They were great, wracking sobs that nearly doubled her over. Michael rushed to her side and maneuvered her into a chair. She let him, all the while trying to get control of herself. James was glad when Michael didn't offer her much comfort, didn't hug her, for example. Instead, he moved the tissue box over to her and came back to stand by James. Michael gave him a worried look.

Maybe both of them were seeing something on James's face that was freaking them the fuck out. James was so incredibly angry, but now annoyance was gaining ground. How dare she walk in here and try to make *him* feel guilty with those crocodile tears, make this about *her.*

"I'm s-s-s-sorry," she gasped out, before collapsing into sobs again.

Michael motioned his head toward the couch, silently asking James if he wanted to move there. James hadn't planned on conversing with his mother. He'd planned on throwing her out as quickly as possible. But her emotional cyclone took the steam out of that idea. Still, he didn't want to leave the wheelchair. It was his ticket to a quick exit, if nothing else. He shook his head, but he rolled forward a bit so he was closer to the sofa and chair. Michael grabbed a dining room chair and brought it over so he could sit close to James. He offered his hand while James's mother tried to get it together. James took it, squeezing hard.

It occurred to him that his mother didn't know he was gay and here he was holding hands with his boyfriend. And then he remembered he didn't give a righteous goddamn what his mother thought.

Finally, his mother quieted. James spoke tightly. "I didn't agree to see you. You have no right to come here."

"I know you must hate me, James. But… I had to see you." Her voice was ragged.

"You gave up any rights to see me when I was six fucking years old."

He heard his mother swallow a fresh sob. "I—I know. I know. But… I've been tormented about this for years. I thought if I could just see you and explain—"

"I don't give a shit if you were 'tormented'!" The rage was back. James glared at his mother. "And I don't want to talk to you or see your stupid face. Just get the fuck out!"

Michael squeezed his hand, hard, but James couldn't look at him. All his attention was fixed on the woman who'd betrayed him, the one person in the world who should have loved him no matter what. And didn't.

Her face fell into a deep sorrow. Her tears were gone. She dropped her eyes and looked down at her lap, not moving to leave, and not trying to say anything more. And James found he didn't have enough anger to repeat himself, to be that cruel twice.

"Want to tell me what happened?" Michael asked James quietly.

James knew Michael was asking in the hope that he might be able to help. And James found the words pushing to be set free from his throat, as if a faucet had been turned on somewhere inside him. He had to let it out, or he'd drown. He spoke loudly.

"My mother snuck me out of a hospital in India when I was six, no doubt to avoid the hospital bills. And then she dragged me across the world back to the States. The whole way she told me we were going to see my grandparents. Keep the kid quiet, ya know? Keep him from crying too loudly on the plane. The night we arrived, she took me to a home for disabled children in Portland and left me there. Fucking abandoned me. I never saw her again until just now."

James's voice shook. But there was no way in hell he was going to cry.

"Oh my God, oh babe," Michael tugged his hand out of James's grip and put it around his shoulders, hugging close to James's side—no mean feat given that, even seated, the wheelchair arm was in the way and James was several inches taller than Michael.

James was staring at his mother. She raised her eyes to meet his.

"I couldn't take care of you," she said in a tone that begged him to understand. "I was young and stupid and completely broke. I couldn't pay the hospital bills. I couldn't pay for your care, or even for a place to keep you dry. And I—"

"You don't leave your child." Michael said it quietly, but there was utter steel in it that was unmistakable. James squeezed Michael's thigh.

"You didn't have to just dump me somewhere like a sack of garbage and never visit again, *ever*. Do you have any idea how long I waited for you to come back? What that did to me, knowing that even my own mother didn't want me?"

She leaned forward then, placing her forearms on her skirt-covered knees. Her face was so pained it was difficult to look at her, but her tears had run out. "James, after I left you, I… I was so low that I got into trouble, bad trouble. A guy paid my way to Hong Kong, and I got into drugs there. It was the only way I could… forget. And then I had to do things to get the drugs—I transported some opium and was caught. I spent five years in jail."

James just stared at her, not sure if he should feel sorry for her or be ashamed that this was his mother. But she didn't look like a drug addict or an ex-con. She looked like an aged version of the hippie he'd once adored, nothing more, and nothing less.

She swallowed and blew her nose with the tissues Michael had given her.

"You didn't love me, or you never could have left me," James said, with flat conviction. "That is unforgivable."

"Oh, James! Of course, I loved you! But I felt so *guilty*." Her face was furrowed with anguish. "I felt so damned guilty for dragging a baby around with me, for not getting you vaccinated because I was on this natural health kick, for taking you to India in the first place. Do you have any idea how I felt knowing that I had damaged you *for life*? That my beautiful baby boy would be crippled forever because of my i-idiotic lack of responsibility?" The tears started up again. She struggled to speak. "I told myself you'd be better off without me, that I wasn't fit to be a mother. I researched, and the Children of God was the most acclaimed home I could find. I knew Felicia was a better person than me—that she would be able to help you. And I... I think I was punishing myself, hurting myself because you had gotten hurt."

There were so many things James wanted to say, but his mouth could only twist bitterly.

"And then I got so screwed up in Hong Kong. I was a mess for years. And when I finally got my life back together, I thought it was too late. I thought you would probably not even remember me, and certainly never forgive me if you did. But don't ever believe that I didn't love you. I loved you, I *love* you, more than anything in this world."

She spoke passionately, convincingly. But then, James reminded himself that she always had been a good liar.

He felt numb. The rage had left him, along with everything else. He felt hollowed out inside. He said nothing.

His mother fumbled with her purse. "I'm living in Olympia. I moved there years ago. I... I wanted to be close to you. I work as a school librarian now, and I'm married. I never had any more kids." She pulled out a small white card. "This is my address and phone number. My e-mail is on here too. I hope... I hope one day you'll want to talk to me. Maybe get coffee. I can drive up anytime."

She sounded so hopeful. James said nothing, but Michael went over to take the offering. His mother looked at Michael and gave him a small smile. "I'm glad he has someone."

Michael nodded and glanced at James. He walked her to the door. She hesitated.

"If you decide you never want to contact me, I just… want you to know that I'm proud of you. And I'm sorry."

She opened the door and left.

"I don't want to talk about it," James said, when an expectant silence had gone on for at least five minutes after his mother had left.

"Okay." Michael was still sitting in the chair next to James's wheelchair. And then, after a minute, "It must have taken her a long time to work up the courage to come see you."

"Fuck that! You have no idea what that did to me, her abandoning me. How worthless I felt—*for years*."

"I know, babe," Michael said soothingly. "Can I tell you something?"

James looked at him, mouth tight.

"Whatever you want to do, I'm on your side. I will *always* be on your side," Michael said with absolute sincerity.

James frowned at him, trying to comprehend all the ramifications of that. Had anyone always been on his side? What a concept.

James huffed. "You and what rebel army?" he said archly.

Michael smiled. "There's my sarcastic little trooper. So what would make you feel better? A backrub? Foot massage? Pizza and beer?"

"Are those my choices? No blowjob? Handcuffs? Red lace panties?"

"That could be arranged," Michael said with a heated look that usually would have gotten James instantly hard.

But the emptiness inside him was too all-consuming. He took a shaky breath and thought about it. "*Outer Limits* and cuddling on the couch?"

"You got it. And James?" Michael took his face in both hands and kissed his lips. He brought their foreheads together with a *thunk*.

"Now I get it. I understand why it's hard for you to trust people. But I swear, I will never, ever, *ever* just walk out on you like that. If I ever leave you, it will be after long and tedious weeks of conversation about our relationship, and if we both agree it's for the best, and... I really hope that never happens."

James did believe Michael. Mostly. But hearing it made him suddenly feel a whole lot lighter.

Children of God was the most acclaimed home I could find.

It had never occurred to James. He always thought his mother had just dumped him somewhere random. But, of course, the home *was* excellent and Felicia had helped him a great deal. His mother had researched, and then she'd flown him around the world to take him there, to take him to a good place. That wasn't an excuse for what she'd done, but... it showed more care and forethought than James had believed.

I loved you. I always loved you.

He didn't care what his mother had thought or felt. *He didn't.* Yet the words were like psychological molasses, slowly creeping down into his brain. And maybe it was just a little easier to believe that Michael could love him.

He knew for a fact that he could love Michael Lamont.

~22~

EXCERPT FROM Sentimental Cyanide *by J.C. Guise*

The bundle of rags in the chair straightened up, a great shaggy head raised, and Lamb saw a face. It wasn't like any face he'd ever seen. It was as strong as the winds of Eran, as sorrowful as a dying star, ugly and beautiful in equal measure. The scars on his cheeks repulsed and fascinated. But it was the eyes... the eyes were pure light, and they reached inside Lamb and lit up places he didn't know existed.

"A stowaway, Rebben. Found him in the hold."

"Do the guards know he's here?" Rebben asked. His voice was deep but breathy, as if he had difficulty breathing.

Lamb's system included a chip that stored over one thousand different languages. They were speaking Mongalon. Lamb did a quick search of his species database. Mongalon was spoken on the planet Z-Base 10, a fairly primitive warrior clan society. Lamb's database supplied a red flashing message—WARNING: Z-Base 10 is medically quarantined from all interplanetary traffic.

"I'm sorry," Rebben said in a heavy voice. "You picked a terrible ship to stow aboard. This is a medical prison galley. My people are being taken to Oriven to die. We're the last of our kind. I'm afraid you've been exposed to the Virillium virus we carry. You have my deepest regrets."

Lamb searched his database. Virillium virus: a slow-acting viral infection that transmutes cell DNA causing deformity, illness, and eventual death. Although mercurial infusions can cure the virus, the cost of treatment is prohibitive. Infectious rate: 80%. Mortality rate: 95%. Average length of life after infection: 15 years.

"I have no DNA," Lamb said. "I cannot become infected."

The men holding Lamb let him go abruptly, taking a step back in fear.

But Rebben's eyes lit up with curiosity. He looked Lamb over from head to toe with interest and wonder. "Yes, I see. Come closer."

"He could be a weapon," one of Rebben's men protested.

But Rebben waved him off. "What more can they take from me? Step forward."

Lamb stepped very close, fascinated by Rebben's eyes, at the way they seemed to really see him. Lamb stared into them and smiled.

"What is your name? And what are you?" Rebben asked gently.

Lamb hesitated. He didn't want to admit what he was because then they would all treat him differently. Maybe they would put him in a closet. Maybe they would use him until he was all used up.

So he lied. "You can call me Lamb. I'm a domestic bot. But I can feel. I can think and love. I am not a toy. I am not a broom."

Rebben's expression changed slightly—disappointment, perhaps, or sadness. He studied Lamb for a long time. He studied Lamb's face and glanced down at his body. When he looked back up, Lamb could tell Rebben did not believe him, that Rebben saw he'd been built for pleasure, not housework. Lamb silently pleaded with those eyes—for something, he did not even know what.

Rebben stroked the scar on his cheek thoughtfully. "Are you willing to work? Help with food preparation, cleaning, caring for the sick? We've a long journey ahead and few healthy hands."

"Yes, anything!"

"Then... you have my protection. I was once mighty, but I have been taught humility," he laughed bitterly. "I am Rebben, king of the dying and the dead, the shackled lion. Who am I to judge the marvels and mistakes of the universe?"

"Thank you," Lamb whispered, though he wasn't sure if Rebben considered him a marvel or a mistake.

"No one touches him," Rebben told the guards firmly. "He is to be treated with respect."

One of the men protested, eying Lamb hungrily. "But he's a machine! The men would—"

"No one touches him!" Rebben barked. "Your crimes were pardoned when we left our world. The past is one burden we do not carry with us. Lamb will be what he wants to be here. We've little enough to offer anyone, but that much, I will give him."

The man glanced at Lamb with confusion, but he nodded obediently. "Yes, Rebben. But if the guards see him, they'll use him quick enough. Probably take him to sell."

"Keep him in the quarantine area. The guards won't go in there."

Lamb felt dizzy with gratitude and something that might be joy. He fell to his knees in front of Rebben and took the king's hand. It was square, strong with veins and resilient with life, even though a few of his fingers had been clubbed and twisted by Virillium. How much of the body under the heavy robes had been maimed? Lamb could not tell, but he had an urge to see, and comfort, all of him.

"Thank you," Lamb whispered again.

Rebben looked abashed at the display of sentiment, but he did not withdraw or rebuke. Hesitantly, he reached out and rubbed Lamb's cheek with his thumb. "Your beauty will lift my people's hearts. Go now. And think you on how you might find your way off Oriven once we get there. It's no place for you."

Where you are is my place, *Lamb thought, as the last of his heart turned its face toward the light.*

~23~

MICHAEL WAS daydreaming in the Expanded Horizon's weekly meeting when his name caught his attention.

"—need Michael," Jack was saying.

Michael sat up straighter. Jack was looking at him expectantly.

"Er… what?"

"Late night?" Jack asked with a mildly annoyed smile.

"Sorry." Michael had been thinking about James, of course. He grimaced sheepishly. "Could you repeat—"

"I said I have two new patients that I'd like your help with. The first is Miles Darvin." Jack waved at the projection on the wall where the bio sheet for the patient was displayed. The headshot showed a fragile-boned young man. "I've had two sessions with him so far. He gets performance anxiety that leads to difficulty maintaining an erection. Unfortunately, Miles had a rather abusive lover in the past who belittled his endowment. He needs to regain his confidence."

Michael nodded, chewing his lip as he studied the picture. Poor guy.

Jack changed the screen to a new patient bio. "And the second is Rupert Jones. He has problems with premature ejaculation. I think he'd really benefit from working with Michael on techniques to delay orgasm."

"Sure," Michael said enthusiastically—and then he caught himself and remembered what it was he had to do. His heart sank.

Jack was watching him closely. "Everything okay, Michael?"

"Yeah, Jack. There is, uh, something I want to discuss with you later."

Jack nodded reluctantly and went on. "I also have another new gay patient scheduled for later this month. Seems our reputation is spreading out there with the gay community."

Trudy smiled. "It's about time. You deserve it, Jack."

Jack smiled at Michael. "We have a good team."

Michael forced a smile back and looked down at his notepad. He scribbled down the names of the new patients and next to them he scribbled *fuck me*.

Of course, his surrogacy work would be picking up *right now*. Of course, it would be the worst possible timing.

AFTER THE meeting, he and Jack made coffee in the staff kitchen and took it to Jack's office. Michael didn't perch on the desk as usual. He needed some space. He plopped into the patient chair.

Jack frowned at him and sighed. "I'm not going to like this, am I?"

Michael put his coffee on the desk and leaned forward, elbows on his knees. He rubbed his face with his hands and peered up at Jack through his bangs.

"Well?" Jack insisted, his mouth firm.

"I met someone."

Jack nodded as if he wasn't surprised, his jaw tight. "He doesn't want you doing surrogacy?"

"He doesn't know," Michael admitted. He put his face in his hands. "God, Jack. I'm a fucking mess."

Michael heard Jack move around the desk, felt a firm hand on his shoulder. "Are you planning to tell him?"

Michael stood up, shaking off Jack's hand. He started pacing. "I thought I'd… I thought I'd just quit. And then he wouldn't ever have to know. I know it stinks, Jack, but I'm *in love* with him."

Jack sat on his desk and crossed his arms. His face was serious. "Michael… you have a gift. You're very good at what you do."

"Not helping," Michael mumbled, his stomach in a knot. God, he really didn't want to do this. When he thought of Tommy, and Lem, or even the new patients Jack had talked about in the meeting today, his first instinct was to raise his hand—*Choose me. I can help.*

But it wasn't right to keep this from James. And the idea of telling him was terrifying. He felt as if he was being torn in two, like the proverbial baby sentenced by King Solomon.

"Maybe if I talked to him," Jack offered. "Tried to help him understand surrogacy from a professional point of view."

Michael shook his head, more uncertainty than a '*no*,' and bit at a nail. He didn't stop pacing.

"Michael, look at me for minute," Jack ordered. The tone Jack used—you did not disobey that tone.

Michael managed to halt his anxious feet and look Jack in the eye.

Jack hesitated. "As a therapist, there's a lot I can do. But sometimes, words aren't enough. I meant what I said in the meeting. We're a good team, Michael. I'm sorry if I haven't told you how much I appreciate working with someone of your caliber to improve the lives of my patients. You're… a gentle soul."

Michael sort of melted, but it was a bittersweet rush. Very bittersweet. He got a bit choked up. "Thank you, Jack. I really like working with you too." And he did. Jack was right—they were a good team. He appreciated having Jack's guidance on his sessions, knowing Jack was backing him up with the best therapy possible.

But.

He shrugged. "I love him, Jack. I won't hurt him. And I definitely won't lose him."

"Okay," Jack said in a resigned voice. "But my advice, *seriously*, is to talk to him. Try to explain. Don't give this up before you're certain it's a problem."

Michael didn't answer; he just bit his nail worriedly.

"So… is this your official notice, then?" Jack asked, sounding unhappy about it. "If it is, you should tell Trudy yourself, and we'll have to start looking for a replacement right away."

"No!" Michael felt a sense of panic at the words, though of course, that had been his intention. It had been his intention for several weeks now. But now that it was here, the line in the sand, it was so, so difficult to step across it, to give up his work with Expanded Horizons for good.

His palms were sweating.

"Talk to him," Jack urged quietly.

Michael nodded. "Yeah. Okay. Can you give me a few weeks?"

"I can hold off on the new patients for a bit. Can you still handle Tommy and Lem Peterson?"

Michael nodded. "Yes, Jack. Of course."

Jack put a hand on Michael's shoulder. "Sorry I haven't said it yet, but I'm thrilled that you've found someone. He's a lucky man."

"Thanks, Jack," Michael said, and then he gave Jack a hug because, well *shit*.

Jack hugged him back, patting his back awkwardly. "You're still dangerous, Michael Lamont," Jack muttered in his ear.

Michael grinned. "Yeah."

~24~

"YOUR NEW book comes out, when? Next week?" Devon asked, picking up a card from the deck.

James looked at him suspiciously. "Yes."

"Hey, congrats!" Lance said. "What's this one called?"

"*Tears From The Dragon's Eye*," Michael said proudly, looking up from his cards. "James let me read it. I loved it."

Michael had come to James's monthly writer's-group-turned-game-night for the first time. It was clear no one was quite sure what to make of him, but James thought it was amusing to let them speculate. Of course, James had a hard time keeping his eyes off Michael in the sexy burgundy sweater he was wearing, so it really wouldn't take a genius to figure it out.

Devon discarded. He was currently beating them all in Pinochle. He snorted sarcastically. "Yeah. Too bad real reviewers aren't so easy to impress. Saw a two-star and a three-star on Goodreads on the ARC yesterday. That's never a good sign, is it?"

His voice—fuck, Devon had the ability to be so goddamn *insulting* just with the tone of his voice. Was he purposefully trying to make James look bad in front of Michael? Or was he just being an oblivious ass?

Knowing Devon, he had every malicious intent in mind. James opened his mouth to retort but was distracted when Michael shifted in his chair and winced. James gave Michael a worried look.

"Ow. Sorry. Ignore me," Michael said.

Devon looked at Michael blankly. "Lance, go, man."

Lance picked up a card from the deck.

Michael sat forward gingerly on the edge of his chair. "No, it's just…. James is really hung. I mean, *God*! Aren't you, babe?" Michael leaned over and kissed James on the cheek and then, when James turned his head to look at him in surprise, planted one on his lips.

Mmmm. James kissed him back. With tongue.

"Worth every inch, though," Michael breathed seductively as he pulled away with a last little lick. He gave James a lewd wink and picked up his hand, ignoring the circle of slack jaws around the table—and James's sudden erection. "So… whose turn is it?"

BACK AT James's house, James handed Michael a glass of lemon-lime sparking water along with a warning look.

"What?" Michael said innocently.

"*You,*" James said with a low growl that was part amusement, part reprimand.

"I liked your friends." Michael put his glass on the coffee table and flopped down on the sofa. "Even if I did lose every *single* game."

"You're the worst game player in the history of forever. I mean, if you'd been in the cave when the Neanderthals invented the first game of tic-tac-toe, you would have lost," James said seriously. "You should call Guinness. Bet you could nab a title." He leveraged himself from his wheelchair onto the couch.

"I know, right? I guess that means I'm lucky in love." Michael batted his eyes at James flirtatiously and took a sip from his glass. "Anyway, it was nice to meet some of your friends."

"Nice, huh? You told them I had a big dick," James said with a sigh of resignation. He leaned his head back on the couch.

"Well, you do! And that Devon guy was pissing me off! I bet he's, like, four inches. Did you see his face when I said that?" Michael giggled. "He looked like a lobster."

Michael was a little tipsy, James decided, even though he'd only had two beers at Devon's place. And it was, fuck it, damn adorable. It was very hard for James to pretend he was annoyed when, honestly, he'd about burst a seam on his stupid ego when Michael shoved their sex life in Devon's face.

"It was epic. Except for the minor detail that we're not even *having* anal sex," James reminded Michael in a dry voice.

"They don't know that. Besides, we should be."

James turned his head so he could grace Michael with an arched eyebrow. *Oh, really?*

"Only…. you're so big!" Michael cooed with huge scared eyes.

James laughed. "Shut up."

"I don't k-know if I can *take* it!" Michael flopped over into James's lap like a fainting damsel.

"I'll make you take it," James growled.

And just like that, he was hard. Fuck, what Michael did to him. And yes, he'd been thinking about it, but the idea of actually fucking Michael, as in *tonight*, had just jumped his libido into hyperspace.

"Come 'ere," he ordered, and then to help matters along, he grabbed the back of Michael's neck and brought him up for a kiss.

Michael responded with a moan that said he was just as turned on as James was. They kissed for a long moment, the tide rising between them, but when James cupped Michael's groin in one large hand, he pulled away.

"Wait. I… wanted to try something tonight. Do you trust me?"

James studied Michael skeptically. "That depends. What does this relate to exactly?"

Michael arched an eyebrow. "Sex," he said in a lascivious tone, accompanied by a deliberately slow tour of his lips with the tip of his tongue.

James swallowed. "I could possibly be persuaded to trust you," he said with a straight face. "What did you have in mind?"

Michael got a serious look. "I think we're both ready for more, babe… I want to explore and kiss every inch of you."

A bolt of fear offset James's arousal, but he didn't flinch. "Why?"

"Because I don't want anything between us. Because I want to show you that I want all of you, just as you are." Michael dropped a kiss just under James's ear—one of his most sensitive spots. "Besides, there are some choice bits of you I can't really get too with your sweatpants in the way." He scooted to the side and put his head into

James's lap, nosing into James's scrotum by way of demonstration. "Like right here."

James laughed. "Hey now, that tickles!" Which was true. Michael's breath and his nuzzling chin tickled the hell out of his upper inner thighs, which weren't used to getting much attention. But he was panting.

"Twenty minutes of free exploration, carte blanche," Michael bargained, sitting up. "And in return, you'll get the same."

James thought about it. He knew he didn't have to comply. He could continue to push Michael back on the issue. But eventually... he did want to be able to be naked with Michael. And the truth was, they'd been intimate for six weeks now and James did trust him. He was still afraid. It was not something he really wanted Michael to see. But he knew Michael well enough to know he wouldn't run screaming.

Besides, it was hard to say no when Michael was making it very clear what the rewards would be.

"Thirty." James gasped as Michael drew his finger up his denim-clad erection. "You—*ah*—get twenty minutes. I get thirty and I can do *anything*."

"Oh-ho," Michael laughed. "It's like that is it? Very well, Mr. Gallway. But I think I need a safe word. How about 'clusterfuck'?"

"Is that a safeword or an order?"

Michael gave James a chance to get undressed alone in his bedroom. By the time he was naked, his nerves had taken over and his erection had deflated like a slow-leaking balloon. It was slightly chilly, or possibly, he was hyperventilating and about to pass out. He shivered as he used his hands to swing his bare legs up under the cold covers. Part of him wondered what the hell he was thinking letting anyone, much less a gorgeous, whole man he was crazy about, see his unattractive appendages. But James understood it was an issue he had to get past. It was a test of sorts—for both of them. It felt heavy with the chance for disaster.

Michael came in.

"Hey, babe." He looked at James with those big brown eyes. He undressed quickly, dismissively, his gaze never leaving James's face. Michael was only semihard himself, but he was lovely and lean and delicate as a nymph as he stepped to the bed and slipped under the covers.

James shivered as Michael's legs tangled with his. It was difficult, but he didn't pull away.

"It feels so good to have all of your skin," Michael said. He rolled on top of James and propped himself up with his hands on either side of James's head. "Is this okay?"

"Yeah."

Although James didn't like to be in the bottom position, he accepted his current surrender as an act of courage. Besides, he'd get to turn the tables, and he planned to make the most of it. And it did feel nice to have Michael naked on top of him without the heavy cloth of his sweatpants between them. He could feel Michael's cock in exhilarating detail as it expanded against his groin, a heady witness to the way he turned Michael on. It made his own cock grow heavy as Michael gazed down at him, those big brown eyes dark with sin, full lips parted. Was there any more beautiful sight in the world?

James tilted up his chin, silently demanding a kiss. Michael smiled. "You just can't help topping from the bottom, can you?" he purred as he leaned in. James would have had a smart reply but his mouth was occupied with a much more pressing concern—Michael's wicked tongue.

He palmed Michael's pert little ass with both hands—still amazed at how it fit his large palms perfectly—and gave in. Michael kissed him and just barely rocked against him until they were both rock hard and precum was slicked between them. God, the man could kiss. With more determined thrusts, James could come like this.

He broke away to look at the clock. "Fifteen minutes."

"My timer did not start yet!"

"You're on top. You're on the clock."

Michael hissed and pushed himself up. "Fine. Then I'd better get started, hadn't I?"

With a look part daggers and part promise, he began to lick and nibble at James's neck. "Do you know your Adam's apple was one of the first things I noticed about you? It's very masculine and just a bit geeky. I love it." He scraped his teeth against it.

James swallowed, causing it to bob up and down. "You're very strange," he said, his voice deep.

Michael kissed lower and dipped his tongue into the hollow at the base of James's throat. "You have a long neck. Not too thick and not too thin. It's perfect."

"Thank God," James quipped, but he started to shiver as Michael shifted his thighs to the outside of James's hips and sat up a little so he could pepper James's shoulders with kisses. The position, quite deliberately no doubt, dangled the soft sac of Michael's balls over the head of James's dick in the most decadent and filthy manner. He groaned.

"And your shoulders. Definitely one of my favorite James Gallway body parts. They're so broad and *manly*." James rolled his eyes as Michael licked and nibbled his way across the right shoulder, sucking hard enough to leave a little mark. He reached around and pulled James's hands away from their favorite place on Earth, Michael's ass.

"Hey, now," James warned.

"I'm on top, remember?" Michael pinned them up by James's head so his elbows and shoulders were flexed, bunching up his muscles. "Look at that," Michael whispered. "You have such gorgeous muscle tone from the swimming." Michael sucked on James's bicep.

"Hmmm," James agreed doubtfully, but he couldn't stop himself from flexing a little.

"That day I saw you at the pool, and that drop of water slid down your chest, you made me so hard." Michael mimicked the path with his tongue.

James was already extremely turned on, but a spike of hot lust speared through him at those words. He pushed his hips up, and Michael held firm so that he pushed against Michael's perineum. The friction was exquisite.

"God I want you," James gritted out.

"Soon," Michael whispered. He flicked a nipple with his tongue. "I love these. Dark brown, big, and just a tiny bit pouty. They make me so hot." He sucked on it, sending fingers of pleasure down through James's stomach to his balls.

James pressed his lips tight to stop a moan. Michael made sure the other nipple got equal attention.

"Your skin is so lovely here," Michael licked at his sternum. "You have a beautiful chest. And here...." He nuzzled down farther, tickling James's stomach with his nose and bangs. "No pooch but enough padding to be succulent, and your treasure trail—God, it drives me mad." His tongue traced paths on James's stomach, completely ignoring the head of his dick. Michael pushed it out of the way gently with his cheek as he traced the line of fuzz that ran from James's navel to his groin.

James couldn't stop a small groan or his hips from trying to bring his cock closer to Michael's mouth. But Michael only gave it a chaste kiss—or as chaste as a kiss can be when delivered by a sexpot to the head of someone's dick. "This, of course, is my all-time favorite, all of this luscious beast. But you already know that, and I'll come back to it later." He gave James's balls light pecks. "And these. These bad boys—big and low just the way I like them. They're definitely getting some attention in a minute."

"Remember, payback's a bitch," James threatened as Michael very deliberately bypassed all the best parts. And then his mind was diverted because Michael was slipping lower and taking the blankets down with him, and suddenly, there was nowhere to hide.

James took in a sharp breath and forced himself not to sit up and grab for the blankets. Michael had released his arms somewhere around the nipple play, and he grasped Michael's shoulders now in a last bid to keep him from going much lower. But Michael brought his hands up to interlace his fingers with James's. He held them tightly as he squirmed down the bed.

James shut his eyes and held his breath. He felt a sudden wave of panic. Michael's hair and then lips brushed his inner thighs. James let out a tense sigh and gripped Michael's fingers even tighter. *Please.*

"Don't you know that you are beautiful to me?" Michael said. "You are beautiful, and you are lovable, every inch of you."

James's clenched his jaw tight, unable to speak as Michael licked at his inner thighs, taking broad strokes up to his balls and licking them lightly before returning a bit lower every time. James had to admit, as positive reward therapy went, it was goddamn effective. His hands started loosening their grip on Michael's, and his mind was taken up in the pleasure rather than thinking about what Michael was seeing.

Michael pulled one hand loose and massaged James's legs as he kissed. "Can you feel this?" Michael asked, slipping his fingers up James's calf to his knee.

"Yeah," James said, his voice thick. "I still have my sensory receptors. I have a few numb spots, though."

Michael shifted down and kissed James's knee. "That's fantastic. I'm so glad you can feel me."

"You don't have to do that," James said tightly. "You don't have to pretend they're not hideous."

Michael caressed James's legs with both hands. "I'm not pretending. There's nothing ugly about you. I want you to understand that, James. I like all of you. I *want* all of you. You don't need to hide anything from me."

James felt a crushing pain in his chest at those words, spoken so simply and sincerely as if they were true, as if they were obvious. It felt as if he might crack in half. He let his hands fall to his side, and he looked up at the ceiling, swallowing hard and blinking back heat as he felt Michael kiss his calves and then his feet, massaging them and giving them sweet, open-mouth kisses. He clutched the blankets.

"Oh, God," James whispered.

"You have pretty feet, actually," Michael said, sounding a little surprised. "They're very soft."

James couldn't look as Michael lifted a foot, licked up his insole, and then sucked a toe into his mouth. He flung an arm over his eyes and swallowed back a sob, his body shaking.

Michael stilled and then kissed his feet a little more, both of them, before kissing his way delicately back up James's leg. James could feel Michael's lips along his knee and inside his thigh before he settled back on top. "Hey. You all right?" he asked gently.

"Yeah." But James wasn't all right. He struggled to hold in the emotions that wanted to pour out of him like muddy storm water behind an overwhelmed dam. It swirled inside him, burning and stinging—self-loathing, bitterness, anger, abandonment, loss, fear, resentment—all things he had locked away so tightly. Michael lay carefully to one side and pulled James into his arms, and James lost the battle, great sobs wracking him.

Michael murmured soothing words like *it's okay* and *I'm sorry* and *I have you* and *let it out*, all the while rubbing James's back with sure hands and running a hand down his hips and thigh too, as far down as he could reach, then back up, rubbing everything firmly and lovingly. A strange sensation struck James then—his legs were *actually part of him*. Until that moment, he hadn't realized how much he had disassociated from them, detached himself from those hated things, but he had.

His sobs gradually stilled, and he was left with a huge empty space where so much had been bottled up and freed. It felt okay, though. It felt pretty good actually. He took a deep breath into Michael's neck.

"That was too much, huh? I'm sorry." Michael sounded worried.

"No. I just…. No one's ever…." He squeezed Michael tight. James felt overheated and sweaty from the tears and the emotion, as if he had a fever, yet the press of Michael's skin against him was exquisite in every way, and he didn't want to pull back. A thread of renewed desire wove through the lifting darkness in his heart. He pressed Michael closer.

Michael ran his fingers through James's hair. "I know it's too early but… I…."

James stiffened, his heart tripping over itself.

"I really like you," Michael whispered. "I think it's possible I could… maybe fall in love with you."

James couldn't stop a laugh as desire sparked brighter along with something vaguely like joy. "What? That's the most half-assed declaration I've ever heard. I'll have to write that down."

Michael giggled. "Shut up. I'm trying not to scare you away."

"Baby, it would take a hockey mask and a chainsaw." James tried to sound as if he was joking, but he wasn't much. He rolled on top of Michael, pressing him down. "And now… It's. My. Turn," he said ominously.

"Yeah?" Michael gave him a sexy and relieved smile. "But I didn't really make it to the good parts yet."

"Oh, you'll get the good parts—exactly. Where. I want. To put them."

Michael got a heated look and ground up into him. Michael's cock was hard again, and James was too. "God, I love it when you take charge."

James felt a little thrill at that, and the last of his embarrassment melted away. He felt... really, really amazing. And horny. And oh, yes, he was going to dole out some payback of the very best kind. He started by teasing Michael's mouth with his tongue—tracing the tip of it along Michael's lips, sucking gently to the left or right, but never letting Michael pull him into a full-on kiss until he reached up to tug James's head down and forced one.

James allowed the kiss for a moment, then pulled away with a grunt. "Looks like it's time for the restraints."

He managed not to feel too smug when he heard Michael gasp.

MICHAEL HAD uncaged a beast. He'd known that he had to push to get James past the barrier of feeling so self-conscious about his legs. But he didn't realize how deep the pain of that went or how much it would affect James when he loved on him there.

He'd actually been surprised and pleased that James had any feeling in his legs, and with the legs and feet themselves. His legs were stick thin, the muscles atrophied from the damage inflicted by the polio, but the skin was pale and soft as a baby's, especially on his feet, which were not subjected to the normal wear and tear most peoples were. Perhaps all the swimming in the chlorinated water had softened them too. They were downy and fragile-looking, and Michael was happy to show them attention.

When James lost it, he'd worried he'd screwed up big time. But the storm that had gone on inside him had blown over, and now he was filled with a dark intensity that was dangerous and, well, *thrilling*.

James secured Michael's second wrist to the slatted headboard with a blue and gold striped tie, one of a pair he'd grabbed from the nightstand drawer.

"You've been planning this," Michael said, feeling a little breathless.

James gave him a wicked smile that could have melted the paint off walls.

"Shit," Michael whispered. He swallowed a slightly hysterical giggle.

James reached over to the drawer again and pulled out a black sleep mask. "I may not have a lot of experience, but I have a good Internet connection and a *very* active imagination."

"Oh, fuck me," Michael murmured, with great anticipation, "But… do we have to do the mask? I want to see you."

James hesitated. "Are you clusterfucking?"

"No."

"Then we're on my clock, so take it like a good boy."

He slipped the mask over Michael's head. Michael thought James was kidding—maybe. But the *good boy* was firm and without a trace of irony, and it made a shiver of delight run up Michael's spine. Shit, James was so freaking hot when he was being toppy.

Now blinded, Michael felt the blankets being entirely pushed away, and then James began exploring him. Of course, James had touched him many times since their first time together. But this was different—James was more confident, more demanding. With the last barrier between them gone—and probably the mask and restraints didn't hurt—James was much more mobile, scooting around Michael to get exactly where he wanted to be.

Which seemed to be deep between Michael's legs.

"Oh my God," Michael gasped softly as James licked and sucked at his perineum.

"Oh my *God*!" Michael said loudly as James licked over his hole with lewd intent.

"Buckle up, baby," James growled. He hooked a hand behind each of Michael's knees and pushed them up toward his ears.

And *oh, fuck, yes*!

Michael had a very sensitive rim, and it wasn't something he often got to indulge. It had been years since he'd had a real boyfriend, it was not something he'd ever do with a surrogacy client, and he never took the time to tease himself when he masturbated. So it was sensitive as anything and, oh *hallelujah,* it was heaven the way James licked and teased. The man had a mouth made for sin, there was not the slightest fucking doubt about that. Michael was in wet, wonderful, tickling, squirming heaven for long, gasping minutes. And then it was torture. James wasn't touching his cock, and Michael couldn't touch himself with his hands bound. The more James licked and sucked, grazed with his teeth, the more turned on Michael got until he thought he might split like an overstuffed sausage.

"James, please, babe," he pleaded. "I'm so hard. I need you."

And then somehow, James had lube, because he rubbed a slick finger over Michael's hole and pushed it slowly, slowly inside.

"Oh!" Michael planted his feet on the bed and lifted his hips as high as he could, chasing the sensation, chasing more.

"Good little boys don't lie," James said in a filthy tone from somewhere in the vicinity of Michael's thighs. "You need to make good on that complaint of being sore."

"*Yes,*" Michael groaned, as James probed with a second finger. "I want that. I want you to make love to me, be inside me. Please."

James licked the sensitive flesh around his two fingers as they pumped slowly in and out. Michael thought he might seriously pass out, his head was so light from the sustained intensity of his desire.

"You want me to do what?" James reprimanded, removing his fingers and tongue completely.

Michael lay there for a moment, breathing hard, trying to get his brain unscrambled enough to figure out what it was James wanted.

"Fuck me," Michael said in a rush. "Please, James, I want you to fuck me."

"You bastard," James prompted.

Michael gave a hysterical little laugh. "Fuck me, you *bast*ard. And I mean it, damn it! Right now!"

He felt James shifting over him until his rock-hard cock was against Michael's and James's breath was in his face. Michael lifted up his head, seeking those wide lips.

"Do you want me to wear a condom?" James asked quietly.

Michael's breath caught in his throat. First, at the somehow shocking intimacy of it—James *was really going to fuck him at last.* And then at the power of the idea. *Bare.* That was what he wanted, God more than anything, even though it went against all his training. He'd never fucked or been fucked bareback in his life. He stammered.

"I-I know you haven't been with anyone else, and I haven't been with anyone like that for months. I've been tested since then, and I'm clean. But, if you don't... maybe you should...."

"Quiet," James said firmly. "Nothing between us."

His tone brooked no argument, and Michael didn't have it in him to insist, even if he should. And really, it felt right. He'd always dreamed of having an exclusive boyfriend someday, someone he trusted enough to be bare with, and, God, he wanted it to be James.

Michael relinquished control, melting back into the bed. He started to tremble as he felt James shift and rub lube on his cock. By the time he'd poised the blunt head at Michael's entrance, Michael was shaking like a leaf. He felt like a virgin all over again. And he was, in a way. He'd never done this with someone he felt so connected to, someone who had so much of his heart.

"Wait. I want to see you," Michael whispered. "Please."

James hesitated, then released himself and pushed up the sleep mask. Michael blinked and stared up into those chestnut-colored eyes, so serious and determined, so strong.

"I love you," Michael said on an exhaled breath as James pushed against him.

There was a moment of pressure and then the head was inside. They both stilled, breathing hard, James staring down intently.

"I know," he said.

A laugh-cry escaped Michael, and he pulled on his bound hands. "Bastard."

James quirked a brief smile, but then he settled down more firmly on Michael, his broad chest and hips pinning him down hard as his eyes burned. Michael had no choice but to pull his knees up higher. James sank a little deeper, staring at Michael all the while, intent and fierce in his concentration.

"I know that I love you too, Michael Lamont."

Michael swallowed a hot ball of joy that threatened to choke him. "James."

James finished his entry with a hard thrust, making Michael cry out.

"God, it feels... we need to do this a lot more often," James said, his teeth clenched.

"I agree. Now give it to me, babe."

James withdrew slowly and slammed back in hard. He'd used lots of lube, but it was still a little raw and a lot hot. There was a pinch of pain. It had been so long since Michael had bottomed, but the feeling of fullness, the sensation of James's cock inside him, was more than worth it.

"Like that?" James asked. It sounded like a threat.

"Yes. More." Michael tried to spread his thighs even farther.

"Research indicates there's something...." James withdrew and pushed back in, aiming himself up toward Michael's navel.

"Oh god oh god oh god," Michael chanted as a jolt of sensation spiked from his prostate to the tip of his cock. "Right there. Touch me. Please."

But James didn't. He propped himself up on his hands and started to pump steadily, hitting Michael's prostate every time. He watched Michael's face, his jaw clenched.

Michael couldn't speak anymore. He grasped the silk ties with both hands and pulled as hard as he could and just hung on. There was the sensation, so all-consuming, of James's large cock filling him so decisively and brushing against his prostate over and over. And there was the look on James's face as he fucked someone for the first time— amazement, lust, love, and a sheer determination that was pure James— to make it last, to make it good, to take Michael completely.

And suddenly, Michael was right there.

"I'm going to come," he gasped. "Touch me."

This time, James did. He shifted onto his left hand and wrapped his right around Michael's cock. One squeeze, and he was coming. It felt as if his heart was pouring out of him in thick, racking spurts. And then James pounded into him hard and held. His face tensed with pleasure. Michael could feel his cock pulse deep inside and the warm wash of his cum. Michael shut his eyes to savor the sensation. His man was inside him, *his*.

James reached up and untied Michael's wrists, pulled out, wetly, and collapsed.

Neither of them said anything, but when Michael rolled onto his side and wrapped his arms and legs around James, he didn't pull away. He moved his arm under Michael and pulled him in, holding him so tightly, he almost couldn't breathe. His hand caressed Michael's back. James didn't say a word, but Michael had never felt so treasured, nor had James ever felt so strong and confident in his arms.

He'd meant to talk to James tonight about the surrogacy. That had been the plan—get James to let him touch his legs and maybe use that as a lead-in to discuss surrogacy afterward. But now that they'd had this amazing moment, it just... it wasn't the right time. This moment was too perfect. It was too important to James, too important to them, a key step on their path to falling in love. He couldn't ruin it.

So Michael just snuggled farther into James and closed his eyes.

~25~

THE NIGHT of the awards dinner, James was a nervous wreck. He'd written and rewritten an acceptance speech even while telling himself not to expect to win. He and Michael had their "master and sycophant" outfits, and, yes, that did make it better, but still. Being in the spotlight was terrifying. What if he won? What if there were obstacles and he wasn't able to get up to the podium?

Amanda hadn't been able to tell him much about the setup at the banquet. But she assured him that the people in charge were well aware of the fact that he was in a wheelchair.

Pretty words, my friend, pretty words. He never had much faith in other people's ability or desire to deal with his issues.

He told himself it would be all right. Michael would be with him, and he'd get through it. It would be fine.

He bathed and fussed for a long time over his new haircut, flossed his teeth, and checked his skin, which was thankfully clear. In the bedroom, he pulled out the tux Michael had rented and brought over the night before. It was a dark blue silk blend suit, actually, and Michael had picked out a black shirt and black tie to go with it. It did look damn good. Michael was going to wear a skin-tight black sweater and black leather pants. He'd looked fantastic in the pants when he'd modeled them for James. He found them on eBay—an easy grab since he was a size that was too small for anyone else on the planet. And God, weren't they hot as sin on him? They hugged his lean thighs and ass like nobody's business and gave him a bad boy vibe that was irresistible. And Michael was going to wear gauges in his ears and biker boots too.

The only thing about tonight that James was looking forward to was having Michael by his side. The fact that it wasn't even just pretend, but that Michael really was his boyfriend and would be there for moral support, made it so much better.

He was falling for Michael, hard. Hell, he'd already fallen. He knew he should be cautious. It had only been two months. But he had hopes. He had very high hopes. For the first time in a long time, he felt good about himself. He loved his life.

Or he would, after this damned awards dinner was over.

It's an honor just to be nominated.

He started getting dressed.

MICHAEL WAS running late. The entire day had been one disaster after another.

It started when he woke up with a cold—a serious red-noser. That was the last thing he needed for tonight, but he figured Sudafed and aspirin would see him through. His car had started making a weird sound this morning, and the "Service Engine" light was on, something he had no time to deal with. He'd had a shift at Marnie's, and she was not feeling well and was a real handful. Then the nurse who came on after him had been an hour late due to some family emergency. Michael had been afraid for a while that she wouldn't show at all. He'd called his supervisor twice, making sure she understood he couldn't cover the shift, he had a very important engagement that night. It hadn't endeared him to said supervisor, but he didn't care. Now he was due to be at James's in exactly ten minutes and he'd just gotten out of the shower.

He'd planned to go all out tonight, but he'd have to make do with a quick hair dry and some product.

He was just wriggling into the black leather pants, *wriggle* being the operative word, when his cell phone buzzed. He grabbed it and saw the name. A shot of worry hit his gut.

"Hello?"

There was sobbing on the other end.

"Mrs. Chelsey? What's wrong?"

JAMES WAS trying very hard not to sweat in his tight black shirt and suit jacket, but it was a losing battle. He considered making his way back into the bathroom to apply yet another coat of antiperspirant, but his underarms already had so much aluminum on them he'd probably set off the metal detector.

Amanda stood fidgeting near the door. She checked her watch. "We really need to go."

"He'll be here," James said coldly.

Despite his bravado, he was getting upset. They'd agreed to meet at James's house at six thirty, and Amanda was going to drive them. The plan was that she'd drop off James and Michael in front of the convention center and then go park. But it was six forty-five, and Michael was not there.

James took out his phone and checked it. It was dead.

"Fuck! I'm out of batteries. Oh, the irony," he grumbled, thinking about a sci-fi writer up for a major award having a dead twenty-first century mobile device because he'd forgotten to, like, plug it in.

"We need to go. Michael knows where it is, right? Maybe he can meet us there."

"Wait." James's tone brooked no argument. Why had he forgotten to charge his cellphone that morning? He'd been obsessing over tonight for days, and he forgot a simple, basic preparation. He wheeled over to the outlet near the dining room table where he always charged. He plugged it in and waited, more than impatient, for the phone to get enough juice to boot.

Where the hell was Michael?

When the phone finally kicked on, there were several voice mails, but he didn't need to listen to them. The text on the screen was clear enough.

At the hospital with a friend. Will try to meet u there later. Sorry.

James felt a cold horror spread from his stomach through his chest and his limbs. Michael was standing him up.

We're going to see your grandparents.

I'll be here when you wake up.

I love all of you.

Fucking promises. Fucking lies.

He looked up at Amanda. He wanted to vomit.

"Oh, James," she said pityingly, and that was the worst thing of all.

"Let's just fucking go." James left the phone charging on the table. If he picked it up again, he'd probably smash it against the wall.

THE AWARDS dinner was the worst night of James's adult life. Amanda sat on his left and to his right was an empty place with Michael's name on a place card. It was humiliating—a glaring signpost to everyone that James's date hadn't shown up—had stood him up for a major awards dinner. James was angry, embarrassed, and hurt. He tried to be polite and socialize. There were a lot of authors there whose names and faces he recognized, but whom he'd never met.

People were nice. They introduced themselves. They said glowing things about *Troubadour Turncoat*. But there were the subversive glances at his chair, his legs. There were the constant pitying smiles. J.C. Guise, the cripple.

"I had no idea," one woman had said with a you-poor-thing tsk, whoever the fuck she was. And once they'd introduced themselves, the other authors mingled with people they knew, people who had been out and about in the scene for ages. James was left to make small talk with Amanda so that he didn't look like the wallflower he obviously was.

He shouldn't have taken any of it to heart. Maybe if things had been different, he wouldn't have. But it was like walking onto a battlefield already shot in the heart. His confidence and spirit had been blasted by Michael's abandonment, so every little thing stung worse than it had any right to. Michael's absence at the table, with that empty place setting, was a slap in the face. And all night long, a part of him kept checking the door, imagining Michael slipping into the chair beside him. And of course, he'd left his phone at home in a fit of pique so he couldn't even check for messages.

The food tasted like cardboard. And when the awards portion started, the only good thing about it was the dimmed lights so James didn't feel he had to guard his expression every moment. They gave out spaceship trophies for all sorts of things—best character, best debut author, best sci-fi thriller, best space epic, etc., etc., all of which were for titles that had come out in the previous year. James had released two novels that year, which should have qualified for a half-dozen categories, but they were not nominated. He watched other authors, his competitors on the book charts, look humbled or arrogant in turn and give lumbering speeches. His spirits sank and his self-pity climbed.

And then it was time for the big award of the night, the Millennial Award. Michael still was not there.

Amanda put her hand on James's arm as they read off the nominees. And despite all of his praying he wouldn't be called up there, at the last moment, he couldn't help but want it desperately—to have his work matter, to *be someone.*

And he couldn't help but feel crushed when the winner's name was called.

Troubadour Turncoat did not win.

AMANDA DROPPED James off with a lot of platitudes, and James acted as if he'd never expected to win and there was nothing wrong. When he was finally alone in his little house, the first thing he did was check his phone. There were four voice mails from Michael and several texts. The last one said he wouldn't be able to make it and to call him.

James was debating whether or not to call when the phone buzzed. It was Michael. James was mad, very mad. But he answered it.

"Hello," he said tersely.

"James, I'm *so* sorry. I know how worried you were about the dinner. How did it go?"

"Fine."

"Yeah? Did you win?"

"No."

Michael was quiet for a moment as James's flat responses sank in. "I'm really so, so sorry. Was it okay, though? Amanda was with you, right?"

James didn't answer. Michael spoke in a rush. "One of my surrogacy clients tried to commit suicide. He's still in ICU. I felt like I *had* to be with him and his mother. I hope you're not too mad."

James tried to parse what was just said. "Surrogacy clients? What do you mean?"

There was a heavy, tense silence on the other end of the phone.

"What do you mean by 'surrogacy client'?" James asked again, his stomach knotting up.

"I meant... a patient. His name is Tommy. He's only twenty-one."

"You never told me about him." James was feeling more anxious by the minute. Michael had told him all about Marnie, and a few of his other regular patients, all of whom were elderly. But he had never once talked about some young guy named Tommy. Why would a twenty-one-year-old need in-home nursing anyway? Something wasn't right.

"James...." Michael's voice was desperate, but nothing more was forthcoming.

"Look, I have to go. I need to say good-bye to Amanda," James lied.

"Okay. I'll be at the hospital a while longer. Call me. Please?" Michael hung up, sounding shaken.

James stared at the phone for several minutes.

Surrogacy? What the fuck was that about? Obviously, Michael wasn't carrying some infertile couple's baby. James had never heard nurses referred to like that. And there'd been something guilty in Michael's tone, as if he'd been caught out. Something was wrong, something awful.

James booted up his laptop. He sat looking at the screen for a long moment. Did he want to know? A sick feeling in his stomach told him the answer was *no.* But he couldn't just leave it. He intended to google different types of surrogacy, but once the search window was up, he decided to try a direct approach. He typed in *Michael Lamont Seattle surrogate.*

The webpage that came up was for a group called IPSA that certified sex surrogates. Michael's name and photo and a brief bio were listed under the state of Washington. The website claimed surrogates helped individuals overcome social and sexual problems—through intimate therapy.

Michael had sex with his patients. He was a sex surrogate.

Hot bile burned in James's throat, and he barely had time to grab a nearby wastebasket before he was losing the wine and salmon he'd consumed at the awards dinner. He sat there, sweating, black threatening the edges of his vision, and the smell of vomit ripe in the air. When he could finally move, he rolled into the kitchen and put the entire waste can in a big trash bag and set it outside the back door. Then he rinsed his mouth and washed his hands at the kitchen sink before going back into the other room and picking up the phone.

He typed out a text message: *I found a website about your sex surrogacy. You lied. Please don't contact me ever again.*

He pressed SEND, unplugged the phone, and powered it down. His hands were shaking as he took two valium at the bathroom sink. He took off his award dinner clothes, put on pajamas, and went to bed.

All he wanted was to hitch a ride with Morpheus and escape his broken heart.

~26~

MICHAEL KNEW he'd blown it the minute the words "surrogacy client" left his lips. But he was so strung out from the horrible day, and from Tommy, and from hearing the cold tone in James's voice. He'd just opened his mouth without thinking.

God, he should have told James *weeks* ago. But he just hadn't been able to do it. He kept telling himself that when they were more stable, when they'd been together longer, when James trusted him more, when Michael was sure they were for keeps, he'd find a way to break it to James and offer to quit if that's what James wanted.

Too late? Please God, don't let it be too late.

He went back into Tommy's room with heavy footsteps and more than one reason for the dread chilling his bones.

The other reason was lying in the bed in ICU. Tommy had taken a bottle of prescription sleeping pills he'd gotten out of his mother's bathroom cabinet. He'd not regained consciousness since his mother found him early that evening. Several of his organs, including his liver and kidneys, were failing. The doctors weren't sure he would recover.

Do you think a guy like you could ever love a guy like me?

Was it Michael's fault? Should he, could he, have handled that conversation better? He'd been back to see Tommy twice since that day, and things had seemed pretty normal, but were they? Had Tommy been hiding his heartbreak? Michael had discussed it with Jack, and Jack had advised him to tread carefully, see how Tommy progressed. But Jack wasn't there; Michael was. Maybe he hadn't taken it seriously enough.

Was Tommy's suicide attempt a result of unrequited love? Or, even if not, had Michael's gentle rebuff left Tommy even more depressed than before? Should he have been more concerned with

Tommy's mood the past few weeks? Had he been too over-the-moon with his own life to be paying the best attention to his client?

Whatever self-doubts he had, Mrs. Chelsey didn't seem to share them. She was a wreck, alternatively sobbing and angry. But for some reason, she latched onto Michael as soon as he'd arrived at the hospital, and she seemed to need his presence specifically, despite the fact that several of her friends had come and gone. It was Michael's hand she clung to, Michael she was leaning on emotionally.

There was no way Michael could leave Tommy and his mother, not like this. He just had to hope that he could make it up to James later.

Please, God, let it be okay.

Michael sat back down next to Mrs. Chelsey, and she immediately took his hand.

"Everything all right?" Mrs. Chelsey asked.

Michael nodded and forced a smile. "I'm okay. Just worried about Tommy."

Mrs. Chelsey nodded. "You don't have to stay, you know." She so completely didn't mean it.

"Yeah, I do. I'm staying."

She squeezed his hand. "Thank you. This has been a long time coming. I think he would have done it sooner if not for your visits."

Michael didn't answer. He was thankful for her faith in him, but he wasn't sure it was justified.

He'd nearly dozed off when his cell phone beeped. He wasn't really supposed to have it in ICU, and he gave Mrs. Chelsey a sheepish look before he glanced at it.

He read the text from James, and his life disintegrated in an instant. It felt as though a nuclear bomb had been set off in the desert of his heart.

I found a website about your sex surrogacy. You lied. Please don't contact me ever again.

He put the phone back in his pocket very slowly, his fingers completely numb. He stared at the floor.

"Michael? What is it?"

Don't contact me ever again.

It was the last, devastating straw in a really, really awful day, and he just couldn't help himself. Pain choked his airway and burned his eyes.

There was nothing worse than being rejected for who you really were. Michael was a surrogate. Yes, he liked to help people like Tommy. Yes, he used sex to do it. Was that really so wrong? Did he deserve to be punished by never having anything of his own?

Don't contact me ever again.

And he realized that deep down inside, he had nursed the hope that James would understand, because of his disability, because of his upbringing in the children's home, because of his innate compassion and intelligence and liberal nature.

You lied.

"Michael? My God, what is it?" Mrs. Chelsey tried to get a look at his face, which was probably purple because he could not breathe. The sobs finally began to escape his throat, and they were so loud and so horrible he clasped his hand over his mouth and ran from the room.

~27~

JAMES SAT at his computer staring at the screen. He had to finish the last ten thousand words of this novel, and he simply couldn't do it. His characters had run out of steam twenty thousand words ago, and were now stillborn in his head. Everything about the ending he'd planned felt fetid and trite.

God. How could he find the motivation to write when even forcing air to move in and out of his lungs was a Herculean challenge?

He felt lifeless, barren, destroyed. It had been five days since the disastrous night of the awards dinner. Michael had left him a number of voice mails and texts that James did not listen to or look at—he couldn't. It hurt too much. He'd expected Michael to show up at his door, but he hadn't. Like that day at the pool, when James had insulted Michael and stormed out, Michael respected his space. James felt a weird mix of relief and disappointment about that. But what good would it do if Michael did come? After all, there was nothing to explain. Michael had *lied*. He flat-out lied about what he did for a living, from day one. He'd hidden something that anyone in a romantic relationship with him would find extremely relevant. Michael had no doubt cheated, too, by having sex with other men, with his clients, the whole time he'd been seeing James, and he'd never mentioned a word.

True, they'd never explicitly said they were exclusive, but it was understood. It was as plain as the light on a sunny day. And if Michael thought it was okay they weren't exclusive, then why did he hide what he was doing?

James wished to God it wasn't so black and white. He wished there was an easy explanation. But there really was no way to sugarcoat it. Michael had lied, and he'd cheated.

Since that terrible night, James had researched sex surrogates. He couldn't help the part of his brain that had to try to understand exactly what Michael had done, *was doing*. He bought a biography written by a female surrogate for his kindle and rented a documentary. He found websites and a forum.

As he read about the sorts of clients sex surrogates worked with—people with physical problems like erectile dysfunction or frigidity, or mental blocks like extreme shyness or fear of intimacy, he found he could easily see Michael in that role. Sex came so naturally to Michael, and he was an innate empath. It even explained why Michael had been able to overlook James's legs and be sexual with him. But that only made it worse somehow, that James was in the category of "freak" that Michael was trained to deal with. He wasn't special after all. Michael didn't see him as a whole man. He was just another gimp body through the revolving door for Michael Lamont, magnanimous slut. The thought was so vile he wished he could open his skull and scrub it from his brain.

And yet.... James could not forget what it felt like to hold Michael, the passion in his kiss, the fun they'd had together even when they were just friends, the way Michael had, so convincingly, said "I love you." And James.... James had been so fucking in love. *Was* in love.

Had it all been lies on Michael's part? It was tearing him apart. It felt as if the polio had returned to seize his heart. It *ached*, withering inside him like his dying legs.

HE WAS still staring at the computer screen when there was a knock on the front door. His first thought was that it was Michael.

He debated not answering for about half a second before he was heading for the door in his chair. He felt his anger surge again, but this time, oh this time, he'd have a target he could aim it at. And maybe, just maybe, *God please*, Michael would have something to say that would make it all less horrible.

He opened the door to find a woman on his doorstep. She was middle-aged, thin and exhausted looking.

"James Gallway?" she asked.

"Yes?"

"I'd like to speak with you. May I please come in?" There was a tense edge to her voice, as if she was angry with him. Hell, he didn't even know this woman.

"What is this regarding?"

"I'm a friend of Michael Lamont's. I'd really like to speak to you."

James stared at her for another moment, then he rolled back and let her in the door.

"Can I get you something? I have coffee, soda, or water." James wasn't sure if he wanted to delay her, placate her, or get her to stay longer, but any of that sounded good about now. He was suddenly sweating.

"No, thank you."

She sat down on a chair and clasped her hands in her lap. "I'm not sure where to begin. I know this is none of my business, but I felt compelled to do something."

"Maybe you can start by telling me who the fuck you are," James suggested coolly.

She sat up straighter and gave him a dirty look. "My name is Cindy Chelsey. My son, Tommy, is a client of Michael's. He tried to commit suicide last Friday night. I called Michael, and he came over to the hospital to help. I guess that got him in a lot of hot water with you." Her voice shook a little—with tiredness, anger, or maybe both.

"I'm... sorry about your son," James said, not knowing how else to respond.

"Michael is like a son to me, too. He's hurting very badly right now. And that is just not fair." She took a tissue from her pocket and wiped at her nose, but she didn't cry. She looked too tired to cry. She seemed to be gathering herself to go on, but James spoke.

"I don't understand," James said, a bit tersely. "Michael is your son's *sex* surrogate?"

"Yes."

"And that makes you... what? Like his mother-in-law? I'm not getting the situation here."

She shot him daggers. "My son, Tommy, and Michael are not in a romantic relationship. I hired Michael because my son is badly disfigured. He has difficulty making friends his own age, much less finding anyone who.... He was depressed. He was withdrawing from life. I thought having intimacy with someone would help. And it did. It's helped a great deal for the past six months."

Her voice trembled as she talked, the emotion spilling out. "Unfortunately, lately Tommy took another turn for the worse. It's not Michael's fault, he's been a good friend to Tommy, but he feels guilty. And then he got that text from you. I've... I've never seen anyone grieve like that over anything less than death." She looked down at her lap. "Except maybe Tommy's father and me the night of the fire."

James felt sick at her words. Obviously, the woman had been through a great deal. But there was a rising darkness was in him too—the anger he felt was all too familiar, but the bitter jealousy was new.

"I can appreciate the fact that you like Michael. But I don't see what that has to do with Michael and me. He's been having sex with your son for six months? And god knows how many other clients—and he never told me. He said he was a nurse."

"He is a nurse!" Mrs. Chelsey looked up sharply. "He works for an in-home nursing care company. From what he's said, I don't think he has that many surrogacy clients."

"Obviously, he has at least one, doesn't he?" James shot back bitterly.

Mrs. Chelsey clenched her jaw, but she took a deep breath. "Tommy deserved what happiness I could give him. And Michael made him happy. He talked to Tommy, played cards with him, told him jokes. They traded books. And yes, he gave Tommy a massage with a happy ending. Maybe you can understand what it's like when no one wants to touch you, when you feel isolated from everyone your own age, ugly, unlovable. Michael relieved that pain for Tommy." She took a photo out of her pocket. Her hands were shaking. It was a color photo that had been printed on a home printer. She stood up and brought it to James, held it out to him.

"This is my son."

James took it. In the photo, a figure lay in a hospital bed. Michael was in a chair next to the bed, and he was leaned over, his head on the bed, asleep. He held the boy's hand in his. The boy, Tommy, was asleep or unconscious. James swallowed a gasp of pity at the boy's melted, scar-twisted features and bald head.

"Are you seriously jealous of my Tommy?" Mrs. Chelsey asked. "Because that's ridiculous. Michael doesn't love Tommy; he loves you. He's absolutely devastated by the way you dropped him. If you're angry about him missing that dinner with you, blame me. I called him to the hospital Friday night, and I asked him to stay. And if you're angry about my son, then get over it! Tommy is no threat to you."

"He lied to me," James said tightly, unable to stop looking at the photo, at Michael's sweet face. He looked pale and miserable, even in his sleep.

"Yes, he told me." She sighed. "That was wrong, but he is well aware of that."

James looked up at her sharply but said nothing.

Mrs. Chelsey wrapped her arms around herself. She looked a little lost. "I just came here to tell you one thing. Michael Lamont is the sweetest, kindest, most loving young man I have ever met. He has a rare gift of being able to look past the surface to the person inside. And if you let him go, you are making a terrible, *terrible* mistake." She stood up straighter. "Now. That's all I have to say. I'll see myself out."

She went to the door.

"Wait. Your son, Tommy, how is he?"

Mrs. Chelsey swallowed, her eyes growing sad again. "He's still in ICU. It's not... not good. But thank you for asking."

"Thank you for coming," James said haltingly.

Mrs. Chelsey nodded and left.

~28~

ON SATURDAY, Michael arrived home only minutes before his scheduled appointment with Lem Peterson. He'd been at the hospital all morning, and he might have cancelled with Lem, only he couldn't stand to let his clients down. Besides, his heart might be breaking but life went on.

Life went on.

He showered quickly and was trying to boot his laptop to remind himself of Jack's outline for this session when the doorbell rang.

"Fuck!" He gave up on his computer. He should have left the hospital sooner, left time to prepare. But he was pretty sure the goal for this session was to touch Lem, a full body massage if possible, with or without and sexual contact, depending on how Lem handled it.

But when Michael pulled open the door, there were two people there—Lem and another man. The stranger was shorter and rounder than Lem, bald and with a sweet face. Put a beard on him and he could have been Lem's brother.

"Hey," Michael said, forcing a smile.

"Hi, Michael. Um, this is John."

"Hello." John held out his hand.

"Hi, John. So lovely to meet you." Michael shook it.

"Is this okay?" Lem asked nervously. "I didn't get a chance to ask Dr. Halloran. But John thought maybe.... He wanted, um...."

John placed a patient hand on Lem's arm. "May we come in?" he asked Michael politely.

"Of course." Michael stood aside so they could enter. He had no idea what was going on.

Lem and John sat on the couch, so Michael took the chair. "So... what's new, Lem? Is this, um, your accounting client, John?"

"Yeah." Lem's eyes were sparkling. "We went on a date last weekend."

"It was a very nice date," John said. He took Lem's hand and smiled at him.

"That's amazing, Lem!" Michael enthused sincerely. "That's fantastic."

"Yeah so, um, I kind of told John about my mom and all of that. And about Dr. Halloran and you."

"He's said nothing but wonderful things about you and Expanded Horizons," John told Michael earnestly.

"So, um, I mean, if this isn't okay, John said he'd wait in the car, but...."

John squeezed Lem's hand and spoke confidently. "I know you've been working with Lem to help him get past his issues with body shyness and, well, sexuality. I thought, if you don't mind, I would really like to hear any suggestions you have on how I might be able to help in Lem's therapy. I want to make sure I don't impede his progress or push too much. And if there are simple things he and I could try that would be... less stressful for him, that would be very helpful."

"If that's okay," Lem put in quickly.

Michael blinked hard as his heart swelled and ached. "I think that's the sweetest thing I've ever heard," he said quietly.

John and Lem looked at each other and grinned.

"I'd be more than happy to talk to you about some of the ideas Dr. Halloran and I had for Lem's therapy. Maybe you and Lem would like to try those things together."

Lem looked down at his lap and blushed. But he was smiling.

"Thank you. I would really like that," said John.

Michael talked to John and Lem for an hour. They were both very engaged in Lem's therapy approach and goals, and Michael liked John a lot, a whole lot. They were... perfect for each other.

Michael managed to keep it together until they left, with warm thanks from John, and a bottle of Michael's massage oil stashed in John's pocket. But as soon as he shut the door, Michael went into his bedroom, tossed off his clothes, and buried himself under the covers.

He was thrilled for Lem, he really was. And it was super rewarding to think that he'd helped Lem get over his issues enough to get together with John. But....

Why was it so easy for everyone to find love but him? Why was he always the bridesmaid and never the bride?

Really, Michael had been dumped before. It shouldn't be anything new. But it was. It was the worst pain he'd ever felt. He'd wanted James so, so much, and it had seemed so cosmically right. He was perfect for James and James for him. What hurt so bad was that, not only had he screwed this up for himself by not being honest, but he'd screwed it up for James. And James had such a hard time trusting, such a hard time letting someone in. Michael couldn't bear the idea that he'd only proven to James that people let him down. Every text and voice mail he'd sent had been ignored. He wanted to go to over there and try to explain, but Michael knew he deserved James's anger. He just couldn't face seeing the loss of trust, the pain, on James's face.

His tears struck the pillow in time to an endless refrain—*I'm sorry. I'm so sorry.* Exhausted after a week of hospital duty, Michael fell asleep before his tears stopped falling.

~29~

THE SAME day Mrs. Chelsey visited, Michael's mother, Kathy, called James. She was not angry or rude. She was sad and worried. She spent an hour talking about Michael—his sweet nature, his fears and insecurities, his tendency to avoid things he knew would hurt others, how much he loved James. In the end, James listened, said little, thanked her for calling, and hung up.

The next morning, when he answered yet another knock on the front door, he found a little old lady there, her blond hair teased several inches high, her lips smeared with carmine red, and a purple polka-dot fur coat plumped over her tiny, hunched frame.

"Marnie," James said flatly, without introduction.

"You bet your sweet ass!" Marnie snapped. She started to push her walker inside, insistent despite her frail frame and the steadying hand of... her daughter? Said daughter gave James an apologetic look.

Marnie had some tea and stayed until she had said her piece. And boy howdy, Michael hadn't exaggerated about her one little bit. James's ears were flaming and possibly damaged for life by the time she left.

That afternoon, Dr. Jack Halloran showed up.

James *really* had to do something about getting himself out of those online white pages.

Halloran gave him a stern lecture on the value of sex therapy and surrogacy and told him in detail about the two clients Michael was treating currently and why. He told James how good Michael was at his job, how professional he was, how compassionate, how much Halloran admired him.

"Michael knows he was wrong for not telling you about the surrogacy sooner, but he was afraid you would react badly."

"Uh-huh," James said. It was at least the third time he'd heard that.

"Whatever you want to make of that is up to you, but Michael is a good man and he deserves a second chance," Halloran insisted with all the subtlety of a drill sergeant. He wasn't exactly threatening, but James could swear there was a baseball bat somewhere in his future should he prove to be stubborn.

Marnie had been even more blunt. "Michael is a mess because of you! That boy loves you to pieces, and if you throw that away, you're a stupid idiot!"

Yes. Well.

After Dr. Halloran left, James locked the front door and put the security chain on. He drew the front curtains. He was not going to open the door anymore—period, not if the Pope himself came to intercede on Michael's behalf, holy writ in hand. At this point, it wouldn't surprise James in the least.

He drove into his bedroom and got into bed. He stared up at the ceiling.

He wanted to still be pissed off. He wanted to hold on to his anger. Michael had stood him up, abandoned him on the most important night of his life, and made a very public fool of him.

But he'd had a good reason.

Michael had had sexual contact with other people while they were dating.

But far less than he'd imagined, and it wasn't that threatening the way Dr. Halloran had described it.

Michael had lied. He'd crushed James's heart.

But....

Shit. People fucking loved Michael Lamont, didn't they? If James was ever in trouble, who would fight for him like that? No one.

Wrong. Michael would.

It was too much. James wanted to take a nap. He tried for two hours, but it was just not on. His brain was caught in gear. And... he was hungry for the first time in days. Finally, he got up and made himself a cup of tea and a bowl of cereal. Mrs. Chelsey had left the photograph of Michael and Tommy in the hospital. James sat at the kitchen table with it propped up against a canister while he stared at it and ate.

There was something growing inside him—something huge. Momentous, like an enormous airship appearing over the horizon. He could feel the deep shadow and the heavy pulse of it even if he didn't yet know what it was. It happened with him that way sometimes. A seed of an idea penetrated his psyche and grew until it burst, like Athena, full grown from his head, spear in hand and ready to kick ass. It had been years since he'd felt anything quite as strong as this, though. He stared at the photo and let whatever it was develop, gaining definition and form.

He thought about Michael. He thought about the Michael he knew—pretty, almost fragile-looking, flirty, pushy, insecure, thoughtful, determined, vulnerable, generous, and loving. And he thought about the one he didn't know, the one in the photograph who had more than befriended a scarred boy. There was a new Michael in his imagination too, one brought to life by the words Mrs. Chelsey had spoken, a being so empathetic he would give anything to help others feel better—even himself.

It took about a half an hour before James realized that what was growing in his chest was not a decision about what to do about Michael. It was a story. A big story. And he could figure out what it all meant later, but right then, it was so hot and dense and powerful he had to goddamn well excise the thing by writing it.

He grabbed his laptop, set it up on the kitchen table, and began.

JAMES WROTE sixty-five thousand words in ten days. He slept maybe four hours a night before he'd awaken when it was still dark and the story was there, dialogue was happening, and he had to get up and get to his keyboard before he lost it. He ate microwaved canned soup at his computer. He got so desperate for real food by day six that he called Amanda. She showed up with a bag of takeout Chinese, took one look at him, and fixed him a plate. She insisted on seeing what he'd done so far. Too distracted to even argue, James saved a draft and e-mailed it to her. She sat there and read on her tablet while he typed furiously.

"It's wonderful, James. It's… heart-wrenching," she said, after several hours. Her face had a strange sort of beatific glow. Perhaps it was an agent's sugarplum visions of profits to come. But no, that wasn't fair. She looked *happy* for James.

"It's good," he agreed. He knew it was. God, how long had it been since he'd written something this inspired?

"How much longer?"

"Dunno. Few days. A week. It's all in my head, just have to get it out."

"Damn. This is… this is really exciting. I'm going to start talking to people."

James thought she was crazy. "But it's not edited. It's not even finished."

She gave him a tremulous smile. "James, it's really, *really* good. Trust me."

That reminded him of a piece of dialogue, and he started typing again. He didn't hear her leave.

ON DAY ten, at eight in the evening, James finished the novel. He sat skimming over the manuscript, reading bits and pieces, and chewing on the fingers of one hand. He was exhausted, physically and mentally, as if he'd just pushed a boulder up a mountain or maybe given birth to a twelve-pound baby. He couldn't even think about where this story might go, or what it might mean for his career, he could only be grateful that it was done. It was done, and it was out of him now, and it would have a life of its own, for good or ill. Whether or not anyone ever read it, it was beautiful and he was goddamn proud of it.

He was also incredibly, humbly grateful. Like an alchemist, he had taken something dark and painful and he'd transmuted it into gold. In doing so, he'd created a new reality within himself, a new understanding and a bridge—a bridge to Michael.

He checked his phone. He'd turned it off for most of the intense writing session, other than calling Amanda that one time. He hadn't wanted to be taken out of his own head. But now he looked for messages. There was nothing new from Michael, not since that original flurry of texts and voice mails that James had ignored after the awards dinner.

He didn't want to listen to those now. They were messages from a time and place that no longer existed. But he was suddenly worried about how Michael was doing. Calling him felt like too little too late, and, God, he didn't want it to be too late. So he scrolled to the start of his manuscript and wrote the dedication. He worked that one sentence over more times than he had any other in the book. Then he e-mailed the manuscript to Michael and Amanda.

And went to bed.

~30~

MICHAEL CAME home from his nursing shift at Marnie's exhausted. It was midnight because he'd stopped by the hospital on his way home. Tommy had regained consciousness a few days ago, and he was doing much better. But he was asleep for the night, and Mrs. Chelsey insisted Michael go home and rest.

He preferred being at the hospital to being at home where there was nothing to do but think about James. Being with Tommy helped give Michael's heart a more immediate, more selfless heartache than the torn hole in his chest that had James's name written on it. It was like when Michael was little. He'd been terrified of shots, so whenever he had to get one, he'd dig his fingernails into his palm. Distracting himself from the pain he couldn't control with pain he could control was effective. In this case, there seemed to be nothing he could do about James, no way to make it better, but at least Michael could do something about Tommy, even if that something was just to sit and hold his hand.

Michael stared at the interior of his fridge without interest. His stomach was a mess. He'd lost a good ten pounds in the past two weeks.

He got a glass of water and a mug of chicken noodle soup and changed into comfort clothes—flannel PJ bottoms and a soft, overly large sweatshirt. He turned on the twinkle lights in his living room, the lights he used when he had clients visit, and settled down on the sofa. He opened e-mail on his phone.

There was a new e-mail from James.

Michael's thumb paused midpush, and his heart stuttered to a halt. He almost opened it, but he wanted, *needed*, to see it on a screen bigger than his phone. And also, he needed a moment to stop hyperventilating. He grabbed his laptop and sweated through the boot-up, his foot bouncing like mad.

James wouldn't write to him just to brush him off again, right? Maybe he wanted to talk?

Michael opened the e-mail.

I'm sorry I overreacted. It was wrong of you not to tell me about the surrogacy, but not so wrong that we shouldn't be speaking to each other. Mrs. Chelsey came to see me and told me about your work with Tommy. You have many minions. I've tried to understand. Attached is a story I've been working on. I hope you like it.

I miss you, you bastard.

James

A sob of relief escaped Michael's throat. *Not so wrong that we shouldn't be speaking to each other.* And, even better, *I miss you.* Oh, thank God! Maybe James would forgive him. Maybe they could actually get past this.

Mrs. Chelsey had gone to see James? Really? And what did he mean by "you have many minions"?

There was a Word doc attached to the e-mail. The title was *Sentimental Cyanide.* It wasn't a title Michael had heard James mention before. He opened it. On page two was a dedication.

To Michael, the real life Lamb, who must have been given special programming because he loves more generously than any other human being I know.

Michael stopped breathing, his eyes growing hot. Was that *him*? He, Michael? Michael Lamont, Michael? Did James know a different Michael? But if this story was brand new, it had to be him, right?

Forgetting the fact that he was tired and had planned to go to bed, he turned the page and began to read.

~31~

EXCERPT FROM Sentimental Cyanide *by J.C. Guise*

They were attacking another ship. Lamb could feel the faint shudder, like a distant sonic boom, as weapons hit their shields. He knew what they'd been chasing—a renegade medical prison ship. He'd heard the Chief Strategist say it when he'd called the commander to the MAST.

Apparently, they had caught up with it.

Lamb left the commander's bed, went to the terminal, and touched the screen. "External view, enemy ship," he said quietly. The screen flicked to life. Yes, there it was. A prison ship. Its left hull was blackened and smoking from a hit, and it wobbled slightly against the backdrop of a billion stars. She was damaged, and her shields were failing.

"Serial number of enemy vessel," Lamb ordered.

"YHS333u21," The computer said.

"Occupants?"

"One thousand three hundred and one living entities aboard. Sixty-eight inert life forms."

Lamb felt a surge of an emotion he identified as... triumph. Rebben had done it. He'd taken over the prison ship and killed the guards. The last remnants of his species were aboard. All ill, but still fighting.

Oh, Rebben, the mighty! My love.

Another explosion hit the prison ship close to the first, where the shields had failed. Flame and death blew outward. No time.

"Connect me with the enemy ship's commander," Lamb said.

"Not possible. Communication is blocked by our shields."

"Keep trying."

Lamb went to the wall where there was a locked panel. He coughed up the small key he had hidden in his throat, a key he'd copied from the one the commander wore around his neck while the man slept. He'd followed instructions he'd found in his database—made a wax mold, melted down a silver buckle, and filed the tiny prongs carefully. He'd never had the chance to test it—opening the panel would alert the MAST immediately. He would have to act fast.

The key stuck. It wouldn't turn. Lamb jiggled it carefully. There.

Inside the panel was the commander's emergency com with controls so powerful they could destroy the ship. Lamb hesitated. The commander had not been a cruel master, not like Feign, Lamb's first. He did not put Lamb in a closet, though he did keep him confined to the commander's quarters. He let Lamb sleep in his bed.

But he did not look into Lamb's eyes as he took him. He did not look into Lamb's eyes at all. There were no whispered dreams, no words of adoration.

"You give me such joy and comfort," *Rebben had whispered, holding Lamb tight.* "You make my heart soar to the sky. You make me greedy for life."

The commander had bought Lamb's body, but he could not buy Lamb's soul. That had already been freely given.

Another shudder rocked the ship. Lamb touched the keys to bring down the shields. He entered the commander's passcode.

"Shields down," the computer said. "Connecting."

Lamb ran over to the screen. The prison ship was still there. Then the view of it was replaced by Rebben's face.

"Lamb!"

"I brought down the shields. Fire everything. Fire now!" Lamb ordered.

Rebben hesitated, his eyes drinking in Lamb's face, his protest unspoken.

"Hurry! Fire now!" Lamb shouted. "Oh, please! Please!"

"Control diverted to MAST. Shields powering—"

"FIRE!" Rebben screamed.

Lamb touched Rebben's face on the screen and smiled.

~32~

WHEN MICHAEL finished the manuscript, he was surprised to find himself on his own sofa, he'd been so lost in the story. He put his laptop down and covered his face, breathing hard into his hands.

He couldn't untangle the mare's nest of feelings overwhelming him, they were so big, so amazingly huge.

Still trembling, and in no way able to talk, he picked up his phone and sent James a text message.

I read it. Can I see you?

The reply came immediately. *Come over.*

Michael jumped up and spent five minutes in the bathroom trying to get his mind refocused on the here and now and to get his breathing under control while hurrying as fast as he possibly could because…. *James.*

By the time he came out, there was another text.

Bring stuff. In case you want to stay.

With an inarticulate groan that was part happiness, part heartfelt agreement, Michael packed a bag.

MICHAEL WAS coming over. It was not yet 6:00 a.m., so if Michael really had read the whole book, he must have stayed up all night. James had gone to bed, but he'd taken his cell phone with him in case Michael called. As soon as he saw the text, he was up and anxious.

Michael was coming over.

James showered as quickly as he could. He got dressed in jeans and a decent button-down shirt. He sat in the living room near the front door waiting. He was terrified and elated. What did Michael think of the book? What if he hated it? James had put Lamb through some pretty brutal things, and he hadn't minced words. Lamb was abused, and James hadn't whitewashed Lamb's own complicity in that. But still, his heart shone through.

What if Michael didn't want it published? What if it hurt his feelings? James loved Lamb, just as he loved Michael.

Ultimately, of course, the book didn't matter. Because James was about to see Michael again, and the only thing that really mattered was that Michael forgave him, that they were all right. He'd been distracted through his long writing session, but now he didn't think he'd survive another five minutes without seeing Michael, holding him.

He rubbed his sweaty palms on his pants and stared at the door, his ears perked for the sounds of a car outside. It took forever, but he finally heard it—a car pulling up in front of his house. It sounded like Michael's car. There was a tentative knock on the door.

James wheeled the chair forward a few inches and opened it.

The most beautiful boy in the universe stood on his doorstep, his dark hair mussed and his brown eyes slightly reddened and glistening. Dark smudges under his eyes spoke of sleepless nights. He had his hands stuffed in the pockets of his big brown jacket, but James could see he'd lost weight. Even his skinny jeans were a little loose on him now.

It hurt James to see the evidence of Michael's pain. "I'm sorry," he croaked out.

Michael's brow crumpled like a car hood meeting a tree. He stepped forward and threw himself into James's lap, putting his arms around his neck and burying his face in James's shoulder.

"I should have told you about it. I'm so, so sorry. It was completely and horribly wrong of me. But I was so scared you'd hate me. I was scared I'd lose you. But it still was wrong and—"

That was about all the words Michael could choke out. James made shushing noises and held him tight. The front door was wide open as James sat there, holding a fragile Michael on his lap. He looked out onto the quiet, dark street and felt so happy, he thought he might explode into a million stars.

Michael was in his arms. He was home.

"Never again," James said, stroking Michael's hair. "We'll never keep anything from each other again, and we'll never be apart."

"No," Michael agreed, nodding into his neck. "Never."

There was so much more James wanted to say. But he had already spilled all his words into the computer, and if Michael had read them, he knew how James felt. So he just held Michael, squeezing him over and over, rubbing his back, kissing his hair. For the first time, he felt as if he could fully accept Michael's love for him. He didn't know if it was because he understood Michael well enough now to know the size of his heart, or whether almost losing him had finally banished the last of his own self-doubts, but he felt Michael's love down to his bones, warm and so exquisite he wanted to dance for joy.

At last, Michael got restless. He pulled up to look at James and wiped at his red eyes.

"James, the book is brilliant. I can't even believe it."

"Really?"

"Babe, it's the best thing you've ever written. It's better than *Turncoat*. It's fantastic."

James nodded, his chest tight with happiness. "Good. So you don't mind? That it's about you? More or less?"

Michael gave him an incredulous look. "I... I'm so fucking honored. And I'm so fucking touched. I mean... fuck."

"That good, huh?" James smirked.

"You blew my mind," Michael said with absolutely sincerity. "You're so amazingly talented."

"I know," James said with a smirk. He brushed Michael's hair out of his eyes. "You're not bad yourself, as muses go."

"Listen," Michael said, getting solemn. "I don't know if you heard the messages I left on your phone or not, but I meant what I said. I'll quit doing surrogacy. Nothing is more important to me than you are. I don't want to do anything that upsets you."

James thought about it. It was tempting. Part of him wanted to hold Michael close and not share, ever. But he knew telling Michael to quit would be the coward's way out.

"I think we should talk about it. Maybe we can set some boundaries. I'd like to know who you're working with and exactly what you're doing and why. But I don't want you to quit. I know you help people, and I'd be an ass to take that away just because I'm insecure. I trust that you love me. And I'm stronger than that."

Michael's face crumpled again, in a good way, and he hugged James tight. "Oh, God, I do love you. We can do boundaries. Boundaries are good."

"Okay."

James was starting to feel the heaviness building in his groin, just from having Michael warm and sweet on his lap. When Michael began to kiss his neck, he groaned.

"Fuck, yeah, makeup sex." He looked over Michael's shoulder at the open door and saw a woman with a dog walk past on the other side of the street. "Babe...."

"Yeah?" The word was muffled around kisses.

"Want to maybe shut the door?"

Michael looked up and laughed at the wide-open doorway. He jumped off James's lap and closed it, then turned with a mischievous, dead sexy look in his eyes. "There are oodles and oodles of sexual payment due for that story of yours."

James grinned and began wheeling backward toward the hall. "Mmm. What would be an appropriate tribute? A lick a word? The book is sixty-five thousand words long."

Michael raised an eyebrow, stalking James. "Sure. Just give me a week."

James laughed. "It'll take longer than that. If you want to leave my skin intact."

"I'm not going anywhere. Am I?" Michael asked hopefully.

"No, Mr. Lamont. You are my prisoner for life."

Michael smiled. "Good."

EPILOGUE

June, 2015

"AND THE winner of the best science fiction novel of the year is.... *Sentimental Cyanide* by J.C. Guise."

James released Michael's hand, which he'd been clutching for dear life, and met him in a hug.

"I knew it," Michael whispered in his ear. "You're my hero."

James pulled away and gave Michael a kiss before he floated his way, on a wave of applause, to the stage. It was the third time that night he'd had to go up to the podium. *Sentimental Cyanide* had also won for best artificial life form and best sci-fi novel with a romance subplot.

He was on top of the world tonight and so, so grateful.

A beautiful girl handed him the spaceship trophy, and he found himself, once again, in front of the lowered mic in his wheelchair.

"Thank you." He hesitated, trying to swallow down his emotions.

The room stilled. James licked his lips, his mouth dry. Somehow, he managed to find his droll voice. "I've already thanked my wonderful agent and editor and publisher, and the people who support me so stupendously earlier tonight. I guess there's not much else to say except that, having not been at the top of my game, or my life, for a number of years, this is all the more meaningful to me."

Every person in the room was looking at James. And it was hot under the TV lights.

"A science fiction writer without dreams is a rather pathetic creature. I lost my dreams for a while. But fortunately for me, the universe is full of marvels and wonders—and one of the most marvelous things in it is my partner, Michael. Stand up, babe."

Michael, seated a few tables from the stage, looked abashed, but Amanda prodded him with a smile. From their table at back of the room, James could hear Michael's mom, Kathy, and his mom, Lynn, cheering Michael's name. Michael stood, looking all sorts of delectable in those black leather pants.

James looked into Michael's eyes. "*Sentimental Cyanide* would not exist without you. Thank you for reminding me that love is the most powerful force in the universe."

Michael got a little starry-eyed. He blew James a big kiss.

James waited until the "aws!" died down, and then he deadpanned. "Excluding, of course, antimatter and the Iln machine."

Everyone laughed.

"I'm thankful every day for the work I'm able to do and for the people who never stopped believing in me. As a writer, you put your work out there, and you never know how it will return to you. *Troubadour Turncoat* brought me my heart, and *Cyanide* gave me a second chance. I'm a lucky man. Good night."

AFTER THE awards show, they all went out to celebrate. They got a table at James's favorite restaurant, Wild Ginger. Amanda came, as did Felicia, and Michael's mom, Kathy. And then there was James's mom, Lynn, and his step-dad, Ryan. Lynn was so thrilled to be included it was almost embarrassing. But James had met her for coffee over the summer, and they'd slowly been building up a cautious relationship ever since. Michael liked Lynn, and he thought it was healing for James to forgive her, but he didn't push. James could be stubborn. It was best that he took things at his own speed.

As for Felicia, Michael adored her to pieces. He and James had driven down to visit her at Children of God a few times, and they'd immediately formed a bond. For now, Michael was just ecstatic to have all of his favorite people together, especially to celebrate his love's well-deserved success.

"So how's work going, Michael?" his mom asked, giving him a quick squeeze.

"Good. Things have been busy. I have three surrogacy clients right now, and I'm doing thirty hours a week with Happy At Home."

Michael had lost his favorite patient, Marnie, last year. It had hit him hard. But she'd had a good life and a good death. She was ready to go.

She'd been buried in flaming hot pink.

Tommy, too, had moved on, though fortunately less drastically. He'd joined a burn victim support group and made some new friends. He'd decided he didn't need the massages anymore. He told Michael solemnly he wanted to "save himself" for someone special. Michael still went over there to play cards once in a while and to visit with Mrs. Chelsey.

"Do you have any interesting cases right now?" his mom asked, fully in nursing mode.

"With Happy At Home, I did a week of hospice recently with a really sweet old man. His family loved him so much."

His mom smiled sadly and pushed the bangs out of Michael's eyes. "I'm sure that was hard, honey."

"Yes but… it was beautiful to see someone with that many people who love him there at the end." Michael exchanged a look with James, a look that said they were glad to have each other.

Michael's mom smiled. "It's so great of you to support Michael's work, James. I'm proud of you for that."

"So am I," Felicia said, with a tone that said she'd expect no less.

James quirked an eyebrow. "Oh, it's fascinating. The only ones I really dislike are the E.D. patients. I don't understand why they get to wake Michael up at three a.m. if they get an erection, but I have to wait until seven."

Poor Ryan choked on his cup of coffee.

"James!" Michael laughed. "You are such a liar! First of all, I've never actually had an E.D. patient call me in the middle of the night. And secondly, you can wake me up anytime and you know it."

James smirked. "I know. But it does get such interesting reactions from people. Sorry, Ryan."

Ryan coughed into his napkin. "S'all right. I'm good." He gave Michael a weak smile to prove it.

Actually, Lynn and Ryan had been great about their relationship. And James…. James was amazingly open about Michael's surrogacy work. He'd attended staff parties at Expanded Horizons, and they'd even gone to Jack and Tony's a few times for dinner. Michael discussed patients with him in the abstract, even though James never knew their names or specific details about them to protect the patients' privacy. They had an agreement that if there was ever something James was uncomfortable with, Michael would work with Dr. Halloran to find an alternative. But so far, that hadn't happened. Maybe because the two of them were so connected and so in love—and so smoking hot in the bedroom—there was no room to feel threatened.

It was more than Michael had ever expected—to be able to have love and have his work too.

"So is Cyanide 2 going to be done by the end of the month, as promised?" Amanda asked James.

Michael couldn't believe his ears. "What?"

James glared at Amanda. "Why, yes it is. However, it was *going* to be a surprise."

Amanda looked horrified. "Oh God, James, I didn't know."

But Michael was so excited he couldn't even stay in his seat. He jumped up. "The book you've been working on, the one you haven't let me see, is *Cyanide 2?*"

"Surprise!" James said flatly.

"Oh my God, babe! But how is that possible? Lamb dies at the end of *Cyanide*."

"Did you *see* him die?"

"Well, no… but Rebben fired on the ship and…."

James quirked an eyebrow.

"Tell me how he did it!" Michael demanded.

"Noooo."

"Oh come on! What's the fun of sleeping with my favorite author if I don't get to read stuff early?"

"Excuse me?"

"Come on!"

"No."

Michael heaved a sigh and slumped back in his chair. He wasn't going to pout. Even though he really wanted to.

"It was going to be a surprise. And your birthday is coming up in a few weeks…," James said leadingly.

"Really?"

"… so you'll be a year older, and therefore mature enough to wait until the book comes out next year."

Lynn laughed. "James!"

But Michael wasn't fooled. "It is a birthday present, isn't it," he said softly. He couldn't resist getting up and going around the table to James's wheelchair. He sat in the lap of his true love and gave him a passionate kiss.

"You look so hot in that suit," Michael whispered in James's ear. "I think when we get home you can have the *other* big trophy of the evening."

James chuckled. "Tell me it's not shaped like a spaceship, because that would hurt."

Kathy had out her camera. "Okay, you two. Pose, please! I want a picture of my award-winning boys."

"Wait!" Lynn said. "Me too." She got a camera out of her purse. Amanda and Felicia both scrambled for theirs.

Michael and James turned to look at the wall of cameras and the women who held them. Michael had his arm around James's neck. He pooched his lips way out and crossed his eyes. James stuck out his tongue.

And their mothers took the picture.

ELI EASTON has been at various times and under different names a minister's daughter, a computer programmer, a game designer, the author of paranormal mysteries, a fanfiction writer, an organic farmer, and a profound sleeper. She is now happily embarking on yet another incarnation, this time as an m/m romance author.

As an avid reader of such, she is tickled pink when an author manages to combine literary merit, vast stores of humor, melting hotness, and eye-dabbing sweetness into one story. She promises to strive to achieve most of that most of the time. She currently lives on a farm in Pennsylvania with her husband, three bulldogs, three cows, and six chickens. All of them (except for the husband) are female, hence explaining the naked men that have taken up residence in her latest fiction writing.

Her website is http://www.elieaston.com.
Twitter is @EliEaston.
You can e-mail her at eli@elieaston.com.

Sex in Seattle Series from ELI EASTON

eli easton

the TROUBLE
WITH
TONY

http://www.dreamspinnerpress.com

Sex in Seattle Series from ELI EASTON

eli easton

the
Enlightenment
OF
DANIEL

Also from ELI EASTON

Read more from ELI EASTON in

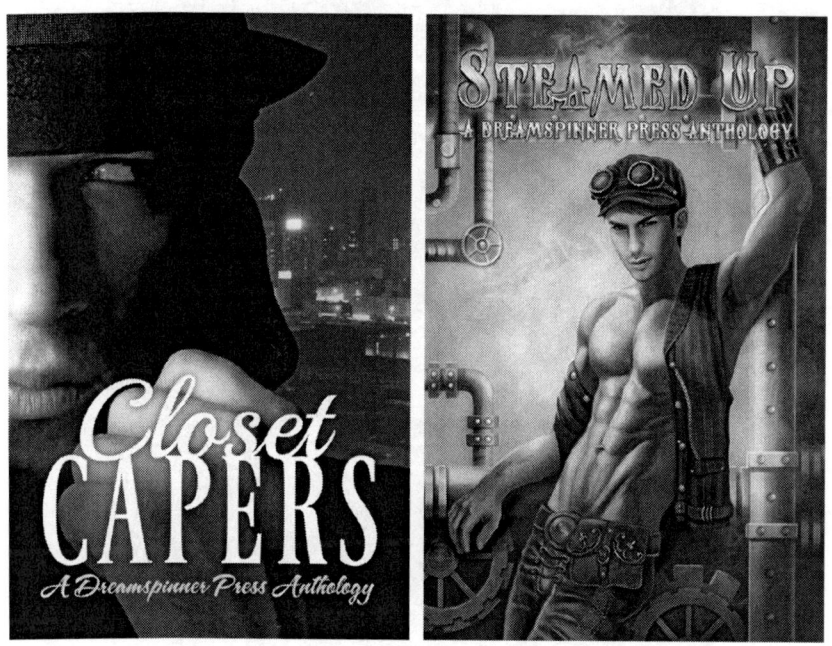

http://www.dreamspinnerpress.com